Ann... ...ng
auth... NEWCASTLE LIBRARIES ...rn
novels, is one of science fiction's most popular
authors. She lives in a house of her own design,
Dragonhold-Underhill, in County Wicklow,
Ireland. Visit the author's website at
www.annemccaffrey.net

Elizabeth Ann Scarborough, winner of the
Nebula Award for her novel *The Healer's War*,
is the author of numerous fantasy novels. She
has co-authored eight other novels with Anne
McCaffrey. She lives on the Olympic Peninsula
in Washington State.

www.**rbooks**.co.uk/annemccaffrey

Anne McCaffrey's books can be read individually or as series. However, for greatest enjoyment the following sequences are recommended:

DELUGE

Book Three of

THE TWINS OF PETAYBEE

Anne McCaffrey
Elizabeth Ann Scarborough

CORGI BOOKS

TRANSWORLD PUBLISHERS
61–63 Uxbridge Road, London W5 5SA
A Random House Group Company
www.rbooks.co.uk

DELUGE
A CORGI BOOK: 9780552154420

First published in Great Britain
in 2008 by Bantam Press
a division of Transworld Publishers
Corgi edition published 2009

A CIP catalogue record for this book
is available from the British Library.

Addresses for Random House Group Ltd companies outside the
UK can be found at: www.randomhouse.co.uk
The Random House Group Ltd Reg. No. 954009

The Random House Group Limited supports The Forest
Stewardship Council (FSC), the leading international forest
certification organisation. All our titles that are printed on
Greenpeace approved FSC certified paper carry the FSC logo.
Our paper procurement policy can be found at
www.rbooks.co.uk/environment

Typeset in 11/13pt Plantin by
Falcon Oast Graphic Art Ltd.
Printed in the UK by CPI Cox & Wyman, Reading, RG1 8EX.

2 4 6 8 10 9 7 5 3 1

ACKNOWLEDGMENTS

Besides Adrienne and Zuzu, we would like to thank
our friends and research assistants, Lea Day and
Richard Reaser, as well as the Poole family for
sharing their insight into Hawaiian culture.

And, of course, Anne McCaffrey owes the Irish
aspects of Petaybee to her adopted homeland of
Eire and her friends there, as Elizabeth Ann
Scarborough owes the Arctic aspects of the planet
to her former hometown of Fairbanks, Alaska, and
her many wonderful friends there.

1

The sentient world Petaybee, its northern continent blanketed in snow, appeared deceptively serene. Cold enough to freeze a sneeze in midair, but peaceful beneath its dark sky, it seemed an easy target for the troops whose arrival disturbed that peace.

Although they knew that the people in the village of Kilcoole were hostile and armed, the Company Corps soldiers did not worry unduly about resistance. Their landing was unannounced and they believed unexpected, so their superiors were confident that the soldiers could simply storm into house after house, waking the villagers and hauling them from their beds while they were still befuddled by sleep.

Instead, the soldiers were the ones who were befuddled as they slammed open unlocked door after unlocked door to find vacant unheated rooms with ice frosting the inside walls. Wild animals darted down the street or across it but no domestic beasts or human beings remained in the village.

The sergeant in charge of the ground mission regarded the village suspiciously. 'Fan out and search but be damned careful,' he ordered. 'These people are hunters. They won't be far and they'll be watching us.' He returned to his flitter, kept running and warm by the driver, and called the captain on the com. They'd hoped the blade of the Petaybean winter would still be a few weeks away but it seemed they were out of luck. Much of their equipment would be useless now with the extreme cold. 'They're gone, sir.'

'I doubt that, Sergeant,' the officer replied. 'They must have been warned. Now we'll have to pursue them outside the village on their own turf. I'll consult High Command. Meanwhile, search the houses and see what intelligence you can gather. The governor's mansion is a log cabin at the end of the street nearest the river. Seize records of any kind, books, computers, storage chips – anything. If they make grocery lists in this godforsaken hole, I want those too. Governor Shongili has a laboratory west of the village, according to our sources. Search that in the same manner.'

'Yes, sir.'

'Then you can make a bonfire out of the place.'

'With respect, sir, if we do that we lose the chance to catch them when they try to return home.'

'It's minus ninety degrees Fahrenheit, Sergeant. If they can't return home, they'll have to show themselves to seek other shelter. Once the village is leveled, we'll search the surrounding villages and see if they're hiding there.'

'Yes, sir,' the sergeant said.

But as they fanned out to search the houses, snow began falling. It wasn't supposed to be possible for snow to fall at such extreme temperatures, but this weird world was a law unto itself, or so the residents seemed to believe.

As if it wasn't cold enough already, a killing wind began to drive the falling snow into the soldiers' thermal-masked faces, into the open doorways, scraping huge drifts from the piles on the ground and flinging them against the houses. The sky grew white too, and within moments the sergeant couldn't see his own mitten when he put it in front of his face.

'Take cover,' he yelled, and maybe his troops did, but his voice was blown away on the wind.

* * *

Less than three miles away but nearly a half mile underground, the occupants of Kilcoole were awakening.

Clodagh, the community's shanachie – storyteller, wise woman, and native healer – was wide-awake, sitting with her back and hands flat against the cave's sides, her buttocks and feet flat against the floor. Self-appointed disciples of the planet and would-be students of Clodagh's – Brothers Shale and Granite, and Sister Igneous Rock – watched her, trying to feel what she was feeling.

Yanaba Maddock-Shongili, co-governor of Petaybee and former colonel in the Company Corps, opened one eye and looked up at Clodagh. She'd been up half the previous night plotting with Marmion de Revers Algemeine's employees: Captain Johnny Green, the skipper of Marmie's ship the *Piaf;* Petula Chan, Marmie's security chief; and Raj Norman, a well-armed associate of uncertain status. Also included in their group was helicopter pilot Rick O'Shay, a former officer in the Corps, like Yana, but a native Petaybean as well.

When she finally turned in, the twins and Sean were all sleeping near her. Now none of them were there.

'Where?' she asked Clodagh and the rock flock, as Petaybee's worshipful admirers

14

had been dubbed by the other inhabitants.

Sean's sister Sinead and her partner Aisling had just entered the communion cave from the outer chamber.

'They're here,' Sinead announced tensely, but Yana knew she was not referring to her family. The Company Corps, once more under hostile leadership, had landed with the intention of arresting her and her family and most of the villagers as well. Although it was now widely known that a Petaybean adapted by the planet to its extreme climate could not long survive offworld, the authorities responsible for Marmion's arrest – abduction really – intended to take the rest of the Petaybeans to Gwinnet Incarceration Colony to join their friend.

'When?' Yana asked.

'A few minutes ago.'

'Is that where Sean went?'

'No, he's gone to round up your kids. Aisling said they decided to go for an early morning swim to the coast.'

Yana swore an unmotherly oath beneath her breath. Her children's selkie seal side was a great trial to her and, with increasing frequency, a source of not just worry, but of anxiety that bordered on terror for their safety. She had thought the planet was giving her a gift when it healed the cause of her infertility and allowed her to have the twins when she was well into her forties. Obviously she had offended it in some way for it to have afflicted her with such an unruly lot of semiwild animals for progeny. Their father, much as she loved him, was often no better. And now they had all broken cover and were out there in harm's way in places where she could not hope to follow.

Clodagh said, 'Sean will be fine, Yana. Coaxtl and Nanook went with him to guard him if he comes to shore.'

'And the kids?' Yana hated to ask.

'Gone,' Clodagh said. 'Sean didn't reach them in time.'

'Gone? You mean . . . ?'

'I mean gone. The children have left the planet.'

The deep sea otters' city-ship ascended into the sky from the depths of the Petaybean sea. Though the vessel's departure for space seemed more controlled than the previous ones, which had displaced the waters to catastrophic effect, its upward spin still created a vortex in the seabed from which it rose. Salt drops fell from the invisible force field that formed its hull, showering down on the furry round faces of the sea otters and the sleek brown

heads of the river otters watching it rise.

In seal form, Murel and Ronan watched first the otters, then the sea, and finally Petaybee grow smaller as the city-vessel left Petaybee's space.

The twins watched from the dome in the sursurvu, through which Kushtaka had once monitored the sea life around her city. Kushtaka was the leader of the occupants of the city-ship, a colony of an ancient race of non-human shape shifters best known to their fellow sea creatures as deep sea otters. The view from the sursurvu – a network of surveillance devices deployed by the aliens in the vicinity of their ship – was more impressive than that from the viewscreen of the regular spaceships in which the twins had previously traveled. From the chamber's dome they could watch the faint lightening of the sky as they climbed higher into it. Somewhere below them in the black sea, icebergs still churned round and round in the whirlpool created by the wake of the city-vessel's spin.

They saw Petaybee as they had never seen it before in those few brief moments before they left the atmosphere and entered space. The volcano's red-hot lava was visible even from very high up, and more surprising, they saw several other bulging domes thrusting out of the water to the south and east to form a ridge beyond the original volcanic cone. Their entire northern continent was pure white, but the southern one had not yet had its first snow.

Once they were in space, it was much like being inside the city underwater, except that the vastness was far greater, deeper, and seemingly uninhabited. Being aboard the city-vessel was also a lot like being in another sort of spaceship, except for the all-encompassing view afforded by the transparency of the shield.

A bit unsettling, that, Ronan remarked in his thoughts to his sister, his eyes widening as he tried to twist his thick furry neck to take in the scenery.

Sky, the twins' otter friend, ran from one side of the domed sursurvu chamber to the other until he finally flopped down between his friends' flippers and said in a rather sad voice, *Otters who are not me and not deep sea are gone now.*

Murel nuzzled him with her nose. *You could have stayed behind, Sky.*

Sky otters go where river seals go, he told her.

As Petaybee seemed to shrink with distance, Murel and Ronan continued to watch, while Sky curled up for a nap. The twins' thoughts spun as the vessel had when rising. They were not yet eleven years old and this was their third journey into space on behalf of their family and their world. This one promised to make the other two trips seem like – well, child's play. Explanations about why they had to be the ones to go were unnecessary this time. Even the river and sea otters, who normally cared only about swimming, sliding, and catching fish, had sensed the urgency of their need and sent messengers to the chilly waters of Perfect Fjord to summon the creatures they considered to be large otterly cousins.

Kushtaka's species had lived on Petaybee when it flourished the first time, before the Company Corps' terraforming that had made the planet barely habitable for the twins' paternal ancestors. Like the humans, the deep sea otters were originally immigrants from another world, and like Ronan and Murel, they could assume another shape – one vaguely squidlike, which the twins couldn't help thinking of as 'alien.' Their city was also designed as a sea- and spacefaring vessel. Once the twins had explained their urgent need for transport, since no other spaceworthy vessels were left on Petaybee, the aliens agreed to take them to *Versailles Station,* Marmion's home base. Once there, they hoped to alert Marmie's powerful friends to her illegal arrest, so the important people could make the company release her.

After all, Marmie was on the company's board and had a large financial interest in it. She was also an influential member of the Federation Council.

The twins knew that her arrest had been bogus, the result of her crossing a Corps colonel while rescuing Ke-ola's people and their aumakuas – or totem animals – the sea turtles and sharks. The colonel had done nothing to help the Kanakas while their colony was bombarded by meteors, and then accused Marmie in particular and Petaybee in general of kidnapping company employees and livestock and had his friends arrest her. If everyone else hadn't been busy with emergencies at sea, they might have been able to prevent it. But as it was, an open com link had alerted Mum – who was co-governor of Petaybee – and the village that after confiscating the *Piaf*, the company intended to send more troops to take Ke-ola and his people back and arrest Mum and Da and the villagers of Kilcoole as Marmie's accomplices.

The twins couldn't believe it when they first heard, but listening to the adults talk, they realized that there was more to internal Company Corps and Federation politics than they had ever wished to know. Mum said it was always a struggle to keep the most grasping, greedy, and inhumane interests from taking control. She had obeyed plenty of orders she didn't like while in the Corps, but now that she no longer worked for the company, she wasn't about to tamely accept outrageously high-handed tactics that flew in the face of previous Federation edicts regarding Petaybee and her people.

The thing was, once adults – including Mum – had been fully adapted by Petaybee to the planet's extremes, there was no leaving. Da had explained that complete adaptation to Petaybee's extreme cold involved actual physiological changes that made it impossible for assimilated Petaybeans to survive a space journey. To arrest a Petaybean adult – even one not born on the planet – and take him away from the planet was to sentence him to death. None of them, particularly Mum, intended to go tamely.

I hope we're doing the right thing, Murel thought to Ronan. *I was so wishing that this time maybe we could let the grown-ups take care of things, like they said, and stay hidden with the family and the rest of the village.*

Mum didn't leave us much choice, Ronan told her. *I am no more ready for another trip than you are. But if she and Johnny and Pet start a guerrilla war against the entire Company Corps and try to hijack their ship so Johnny, Pet, and Raj can get someone sensible to stick up for Marmie and for us, they could all be killed. Johnny and Pet are good, and that Raj guy is well armed, but hijacking a company ship? And then what happens to Mum if they succeed? Does she think the soldiers aren't going to notice their ship is gone and look around a little? She's bound to get caught and sent away. They might even be able to use drugs or something to make her tell where the others are hiding.*

Mum? Not likely! Murel replied, but she wiggled her whiskers back and forth, perplexed. *But they can't hide in the caves forever. Too many folk know about them now, and those who've failed Petaybee's entrance exam are not the sort who'd mind telling. Sooner or later they'll find our people and take what they think is their chance to be rid of us. But even if they weren't trying to arrest us too, we can't let the PTBs lock Marmie up in some horrible place. Da says she made a lot of the PTBs mad at her for championing us and Petaybee's cause, but she still has lots more friends who wouldn't let anybody touch her if they knew she was in trouble.*

Yeah, Ronan agreed, understanding PTBs as shorthand for powers that be. *And you can bet once she's free, her friends who are the good PTBs will make the rest of the company back off from trying to arrest everybody else on Petaybee too.*

22

Too right, Murel said. *I remember the lessons we had about the Federation Justice System, and the accusation and arrest both stink worse than week-old dead fish.*

When at last they could no longer see Petaybee, even as a bright spot in the sky, they began to explore the city a bit, keeping an eye out for Kushtaka, her daughter Tikka, and Ronan's new friends, Mraka and Puk. They swam in and out of the various rooms either through the door holes or by dissolving the walls. The colored lights in the city's towers spiraled and spun up and down.

2

Tikka found them. Though she was not as friendly with Murel and Ronan as she had been before the sharks killed her brother Jeel, Sky was still very much in her favor, and the two otters departed for the sliding areas that were built into the city.

Kushtaka's people were much like regular otters and seals in that they ate when they were hungry, not at fixed mealtimes. The fishing beam the twins had seen Mraka and Puk operate gathered many fish before the journey. Murel didn't know where the fish were stored, but they were almost as tasty as fresh caught. There were chutes in many places throughout the city where the otters could summon a snack, as Ronan and Murel had seen several of them do.

But although anyone was free to eat at any

time, the twins' hosts seemed to prefer to dine with convivial company.

First Mraka and Puk, then Kushtaka and a few friends, and finally Tikka and Sky, gathered together while Mraka operated the chute.

During a previous encounter with the two fishers, Ronan had taught them to balance fish on their noses and to juggle them. Now Mraka flung a fish to Puk, who caught it and quickly tossed it so Ronan caught it on his nose. The three of them juggled more and more fish, gathering a crowd that seemed to have nothing better to do than watch a couple of big otters and a frivolous seal play with their food. Sky ran from one to the other, wanting to catch a fish for himself, but he couldn't leap as high as the jugglers could throw. Finally, Murel had had enough and joined in the juggling circle to show them how it was really supposed to be done.

Every third catch, she threw a fish to one of the other onlookers so that the meal was being served rather than wasted.

There was no night or day in the flying city either, but the twins in seal form weren't especially disoriented by that. *Piaf* and *Versailles Station* both had waking and sleeping watches during which individual quarters or sections could be darkened or brightened to simulate dirtside conditions. However, deep undersea it was all much the same. The twins had learned that in seal form their eyesight, including night vision, was exceptionally good, besides which they had sonar. The city's lights were bright enough to see everything they needed to, and if they wanted to sleep, they had only to go into any of the rooms. The city had far more rooms than it had citizens, so although some of the deep sea otters preferred certain rooms, or dens, as Sky said, many just ducked into the hole nearest wherever they happened to stop when they were tired.

Most of the twins' hosts had specific duties. Some were particularly skilled at a particular function of the city, but all at least took turns doing most tasks.

The twins observed their hosts in several of the jobs but were never invited to help. They had tried asking tons of questions, but finally Kushtaka had asked them not to, because they were interfering with the work. Murel told her that they only wanted to know about the jobs in case they could help, but Kushtaka pointed out that as seals, they would find working many of the controls difficult, if not impossible.

When Murel and Ronan first arrived in the city, they were surprised to find that they did not change into human form. Kushtaka had explained that it was due to the extreme density of the air in the city-ship. Both the alien 'otters' and the twins could breathe it as well as swim in it: although it contained enough oxygen to sustain them, it was 'wet' enough that the twins retained their seal form while within the city's bubble and did not change as they normally did when out of the water. They didn't fully understand her explanation, but as long as the unusual atmosphere kept them alive, that was all that counted. However, not being able to help out was rather dull, so after the novelty of living as seals in a bubble in space wore off, the twins slept a lot, unless their particular friends among the alien crew were available.

The deep sea otters' city-ship must have been much faster than the *Piaf*, because it seemed to take them far less time to reach *Versailles Station* than when they'd traveled with Marmie on her ship.

The station looked just as it had when they'd first arrived. Like the deep sea otters' vessel, it had lights, but instead of swirling in spirals, they were gridded and symmetrical. They knew the top level was Marmie's main home, with its comfortable mansion, adjustable climate, and the artificial river and pool she had installed just for them. It was hard to imagine going back there and seeing the place without Marmie, Pet, or Johnny.

How are we going to dock? Murel asked.

We can't dock in a dry place, Mraka told her. *But our hunting device is actually a modified transport beam. We have reconfigured it to perform its original function, so it can insert you into the station once the hatch is open.*

If we can get them to open the docking bay, Ronan said. One thing that made this whole mission so awkward was that the city-vessel was truly *alien* in a galaxy whose people and technology all reflected post-Terran human colonization. The deep sea aliens couldn't communicate with regular humans, and had no devices that would allow the twins to do so either.

They are your species, are they not? Kushtaka said. *Can you not speak to their minds and tell them you need access?*

We don't do mind control, Murel said indignantly. *We only use telepathy to talk to other creatures when we're in seal form.*

You are now in seal form and they are certainly other creatures, Kushtaka pointed out. *I see no problem.*

We haven't tried to use telepathy with other humans except Da and sometimes Mum, Ronan told her. *Usually we just talk to them. I suppose it's worth a try, isn't it, sis? If you and me and Sky and maybe even Kushtaka's people focus on the idea of the hatch opening, maybe someone will decide it's time for routine maintenance.*

Kushtaka's people weren't interested, however, and weren't sure what was being asked of them. Ronan and Murel tried to concentrate, but it gave them a bit of a headache to try so hard to send to some unknown person over what was still a considerable distance, through the city's force field and the space station's hull.

Sky sat on his hind legs, shifting his upper body from side to side as he peered at the closed hatch, watching it closely to make sure it didn't open without him seeing it do so.

I hope nobody sees us and decides we're hostile and fires on us, Murel said.

I don't think they have any long-range weapons on the station, Ronan told her. *If they do, nobody mentioned it. And if they send a shuttle out to investigate, we may be able to use telepathy on whoever is aboard.*

Or wave at the robot cameras in a friendly fashion at least, Murel said, flapping her flipper up and down. *Yoohoo, we're sentient seals lost in space and could use a lift, thanks ever so much. I don't see how we're to manage this one.*

You need not concern yourselves over that, Kushtaka told them. *We have been cloaked since we first approached. Unfortunately, this does make it difficult to convey to the space station that we require them to open their shell so we can deliver you. Perhaps if we could take you somewhere that had a sea like our own? We cannot linger here long.*

Alert! The otter in the sursurvu announced to the city at large, *All personnel return to your duty stations. Another vessel approaches.*

It proved to be a large luxury liner, and it sailed right past the hovering home of the deep sea otters.

They could not intercept the communications between the new ship and the space station, but as soon as the ship was in position to dock, the hatch opened to admit it. The city-vessel followed right on the liner's tail, ready to insert the twins and Sky into the hatch with the whirlpool hunting/transport beam.

Couldn't you just zip past the other ship and enter ahead of it? Murel asked nervously. The idea of riding the beam seemingly unprotected through open space alarmed her.

There are several reasons why we cannot, Kushtaka told her. *We would have to accelerate in order to pass the ship but would have insufficient time and space to decelerate for a safe landing. Even if that were not a problem, there is the difficulty that the ship might ram us or land on top of us, though we would have to decloak when we land. But last and most important, if we go inside the station with the large ship behind us, we will be trapped there. The beam is the only way we can effect your entry.*

But how can it work? Murel wondered. *With no gravity or suits or anything? Won't the water freeze in space?*

The beam was originally designed for space, as we told you, sister seal, Puk assured her. *Our people use it all the time – or that's what the stories say, at least.*

You do understand we'll die if it doesn't work? Ronan asked. *I wouldn't like to be the main late lamented character in the story you tell later about how it didn't work after all.*

It is a slide, Sky told him, his sleek body quivering with anticipation. *Slides always work.*

We have to try, Murel decided. *We can't come this far and then give up because we are too scared. Marmie may not be scared, but I bet the little kids from Halau are.*

Too bad Kushtaka doesn't have a normal com system here that people could understand, Ronan said. *We could just hail the station, tell them what's happened, and go home.*

As they spoke, they were positioning themselves close to the pool of what looked like

31

ordinary water. That was where the beam would start once Mraka and Puk activated it.

The new ship is entering now, Kushtaka told them. *This is the proper time. Mraka, Puk, now!*

The pool emptied into a swirling light-filled column that snaked past the hull of the other ship and into the station's docking bay. It looked extremely insubstantial.

Count to three, Murel said.

You going first or shall I? Ronan asked.

A sleek brown form shot past them both. *Hah!* Sky cried. *Good sliiiiide!*

Ready, set, go! the twins said together, and jumped into the beam after him.

It had its own gravity and its own temperature control, and was overall a much more complex instrument than the tame whirlpool it seemed back on Petaybee. It supported them until they slid onto the deck, wet from the beam, bumping up against Sky, who had slid to a stop next to an already docked shuttle.

In the center of the bay, only one technician saw them as they flopped across the floor on flippers and belly to cover, where they could change into their dry suits.

He blinked once, then was called to task by a coworker and returned his attention to helping the big ship dock.

Peering around the docked shuttle, Murel

saw Sky watching the big ship get berthed. Once more the little otter stood on his hind legs and did his cute back and forth examination of the people who had finally come to look at the adorable otter. He kept saying 'Hah! Hah!'

That was when the twins decided to run out into the bay yelling, 'Sky! There he is! Bad otter, Sky, running away from us like that.'

'You kids need to get yourselves and your animal out of here,' the bay chief told them, striding up. 'This is no playground.'

'We know that, sir. Sorry, sir.'

'They got the otter, sir, but what about the seals?' the technician who had seen them asked.

'What seals?' his boss demanded. 'This is *Versailles Station*, Conrad. Not Sea World. Get a grip.'

The chief walked away shaking his head over the way some people let their kids run wild, but Conrad watched Ronan and Murel suspiciously as Sky hopped onto Murel's shoulder and they headed for the nearest com room to carry out their mission, rushing too fast to note the designation of the new ship or to see the first of the company brass disembark.

3

By the time the *Piaf* docked at Gwinnet Incarceration Colony, the ship's cat, Zuzu, and her mistress, Adrienne, had abandoned their attempts to have the cat act as morale officer for the Kanaka children trapped aboard the liner when the Company Corps impounded it.

Zuzu liked the children and did not like to hear them cry, but she wanted to cry too, seeing the soldiers' heavy boots stomp past and hearing them bark orders at her friends. She spent much of her time huddled beneath whatever bunk or chair Adrienne chose.

When the ship docked and the soldiers clamped restraints on Adrienne's hands and shackles on her feet before leading her and the other crew members away, Zuzu stayed huddled. A long time had passed without anyone returning before she crept out and slunk from one cabin to the next trying to find someone she knew.

Only the lounge seemed to be occupied. The children were there, but they were strangely quiet, where only a few minutes ago Zuzu had heard them screaming and crying for their mothers. None of the mothers were there, though three female soldiers stood among the small quiet bodies that lay on the bedding in the middle of the lounge, all breathing, Zuzu noticed, all apparently sleeping.

Zuzu slunk around the wall and the corner of the huge tank that had been used to hold first the sea turtles and then the sharks from Halau, where her crew had also rescued the children and their families. It was a good hiding place. She could watch without being seen, and felt safe enough to grab a quick nap before she heard the tramp of boots once more in the *Piaf*'s corridors.

Where was the crew? Adrienne, Steve, Madame, no one was returning? Only the soldiers? Zuzu wanted to cry. She had been with Adrienne since she was a tiny kitten. Adrienne loved, fed, and protected her. All of the crew were her friends, but Adrienne was her special friend, the closest to a mother she remembered. Like the children in the lounge, Zuzu was suddenly orphaned.

The *Piaf* had been her home most of her life too, but she could not stay here while the soldiers ran it. Many of them smelled bad, spoke loudly and angrily, and stomped around so much she was glad she didn't have a long flowing tail, like some cats.

Her tail was a tidy curl atop her rump, the legacy of ancestors who were Japanese bobtail cats, a very superior and elevated sort of feline. She had never met one, but Adrienne told her about them and assured her that hers was a distinguished lineage.

A little dark woman came aboard with the soldiers and marched from child to child, inspecting each one. Then, with something in her voice that sounded like Zuzu felt when the food in her dish was not her favorite flavor, the woman said, 'The transport is ready for these children. They may all go to the island.'

'Mama!' a kit barely old enough to say the word screamed, and hauled at the little dark woman's trousers with his grubby fist.

'Be still, child,' the woman said. 'Your mama is not coming back to the ship. If you want to see her again, you must follow the nice corporal and do exactly as she says. She will take you on a nice ride to somewhere that you can play while you wait.'

The female soldiers lined the children up and

herded them out of the lounge. This time Zuzu followed, slinking, crouching, hiding behind things and under things until the last child and then the little dark woman were leaving the ship. Taking her life in her own paws, Zuzu whispered out behind them. She did not follow the children to the waiting flitter, however. It would not be going where their mothers were, and so it would not go where Adrienne and the crew were. She did not like the little dark woman, but the woman seemed to know things. She strode toward a building with two tiers of lights from the portholes and a great many more lights strobing the ground between the building and a high fence.

At a gate, the small dark woman showed a tag she wore around her neck to the guard, and he opened the gate, not noticing anything so small and stealthy as a brown-and-gray mottled cat who slipped in at ground level on the heels of the woman. 'Welcome to Gwinnet, Dr Mabo,' he said politely.

When Aisling told him that she had seen his kids swimming out into the river, Sean Shongili swam as fast as a seal possibly could, but he was not fast enough. The kids had a substantial head start on him, hours since the time Aisling had seen them and Sean awoke to notice that they were gone. It was a long swim out to the coast, and though he called them repeatedly, he received no answer.

An hour or so before he reached the coast, he was suddenly pushed back by a high tide of salt water. He felt the alarm of other sea creatures in the vicinity, as well as Nanook and Coaxtl. Surfacing, he saw the cats, colored lights washing over their fur, lift their whiskered faces to watch the city-vessel of the alien otters spinning upward, brightly lit, into the still-dark sky.

He did not need to ask anyone whether Ronan and Murel were on board the departing vessel. He knew they were, even though he had vetoed the idea when they brought it up. When they returned, he would have a serious talk with them. Just because they had been sent on one mission on behalf of the planet didn't mean they were to rush off and try to solve every difficulty that arose without consulting their parents, particularly when their plan of action had already been disapproved.

Sean continued on to the coast, this time swimming in mid-channel, keeping in sight of Nanook and Coaxtl. Once there, he found Sky's otter relatives and learned the details of the situation that his intuition had already outlined. At Sky's request, the sea otters had gone to the deep sea otter den and asked them to come for the twins, who had enlisted the help of Petaybee's long-established but newly discovered residents.

Why did the deep sea otters go along with it? Sean asked. *Our family has already caused them quite a lot of bother, the children particularly so.*

For home, the otters said. *River seal children went for home. Deep sea otters went for home too.*

Naturally, Sean replied, wondering why he'd been so dense. He still wasn't thinking of Petaybee's oldest residents as having the same connection with the world that the others did, but they would, wouldn't they?

He turned and swam back upriver. There was nothing else to do about the kids now, except tell Yana, and he felt somehow she would already know by the time he returned.

Halfway back to the cave, he saw the company troop ship preparing to land. That was quick, but then this whole anti-Petaybean operation, including Marmion's arrest, was actually a political maneuver and quite illegal. They would want to achieve their objectives quickly before their actions could be discovered, questioned, or countermanded. The people of Kilcoole were hidden and had a further escape route through the caves if need be. Folk in the more remote villages would not be so well prepared. Electronic communications could be intercepted, with the ship having landed. When the PTBs didn't find the people they were seeking, they would not be above seeking other people to use as hostages.

An underground river system had guided him to outlying areas in the past. One entrance to it opened nearby.

Go to Clodagh, he told the cats. *Let no one follow you or see you enter the caves. Tell Clodagh I am going to warn the other villages that the troops have landed. No one else need go overland and risk themselves.*

You hide best of all men, Nanook agreed.

They would not leave him yet, however, and paced beside him as he swam upriver another hour and a half to the entrance to the cave. When he stuck his head out of the water long enough to say good-bye, Nanook was crouched on the bank as if ready to fish him out. Coaxtl sat on her haunches, looking up at a sky newly white with falling snow.

'The home hides us,' the snow leopard told him.

Marmion had seen only the presentable parts of the Gwinnet facility in the past. To the surprise of her escort, she had nevertheless been able to ask questions and make recommendations to better the lives of the souls incarcerated there. What only a very few trusted friends knew was that Marmion was not the stranger to prison they imagined.

Although her name was a venerable one, her father and mother had supported the wrong candidates in one of their world's many violent and bitter political feuds. Her parents' candidate had been murdered and all of his supporters killed, tortured, or imprisoned and their lands confiscated. The women's section of Nouveau Bastille Moonbase had figured in some of Marmion's earliest memories. She had lived there with her mother until she was seven years old. One day, a guard brought a man in the uniform of a fleet commander and his wife to her mother's cell. This couple could not have children of their own, so they proposed to take Marmie from the prison and raise her as their daughter, since her own parents had proved to have such poor judgment that they could no longer provide a decent life for her.

Just like that, Marmion was taken from her mother. And though her mother cried and protested bitterly, she also told her daughter to be on her best behavior, do as she was told, and try to use the advantages that had been put in her path.

Although her heart ached for her mother's embraces, and even for the kind of often-coarse attentions of the prostitutes, thieves, and murderers in adjacent cells, Marmion found it easy to give the appearance at least of being a good girl. Père Jean, the commander, was usually on duty, and when he was home, showed little interest in the daughter he had adopted largely to please his wife, Dominique LeClerc.

Maman Dominique, as she wished to be called, at first liked to take her pretty little girl shopping and show her off at parties other wives gave for their children. The other mothers, however, were not deceived about Marmie's origins, and some of the children were beastly enough to warrant a few of the self-defense moves her former cell mates had taught her. The party invitations stopped. After a while Maman Dominique began shopping alone, and the whispers among the servants were that what she was shopping for could not be purchased in the shops but certainly improved her temperament.

Once the novelty of her presence had worn off, then, Marmie's care and education were provided by paid servants and employees. The girl found them easy to manipulate, and she was mostly able to do as she pleased.

Then one day, when she was not yet thirteen years old, that world changed for her too. Père Jean came home after a year in space and saw not a daughter, but a blossoming young woman. He made a point of asking Marmie to do something with him alone – something intimate – but the girl's time in prison among worldly women had made her wiser than her years or her wide, innocent eyes indicated. She told Maman Dominique about Père Jean's request. Maman Dominique went to speak to her husband herself, and when she returned, the couple had apparently decided it was time for Marmie to be sent to boarding school.

There, exercising the charm and charisma that came from her genuine interest in the people around her, she made many new friends and forged alliances that she cherished still.

While living with her adoptive parents, she had tried to bribe servants and tradespeople to take messages to her real parents and perhaps get some word of them in return, but the political coup and its bloody aftermath were too fresh in everyone's minds. Once away from her second home, however, Marmie quickly found the connections she needed to let her mother and father know where she was and to tell them that she was well and had not forgotten about them. She eagerly awaited the first response from her messenger, but it was a sad one. Though her father still lived, her mother had died shortly after Marmion had been adopted.

For the first time since she left the prison, Marmie wept. Then, after a while, she set her grief aside in order to try to liberate her father. To that end, she strengthened her network with the prison, and in time was able to arrange to exchange messages with him almost weekly.

When her classmate Madelaine Algemeine invited her home for the holidays and Marmion met her handsome brother, Marmie's soon-to-be beloved Gabriel, her life changed drastically once more. Gabriel was heir to the Algemeine fortune, had inherited their business acumen, had a pragmatic attitude toward politics, and had many influential friends. On the other hand, he was enough of an idealist to find her tainted origins romantic, and made a personal quest of helping her free her father. Meanwhile he used family connections to buy the de Revers family properties, and on their wedding day, with Marmion's frail father there to give her away, presented her with the family lands as a wedding present. Père Jean was in space at the time, but Maman Dominique was invited, at her real father's suggestion, to serve as mother of the bride.

Marmie's protests that she did not wish to be disloyal were dismissed by her father. 'You and I know who your mother was,' he told her.

'But when they took me, it broke her heart,' Marmie said. 'She did not survive long afterward.'

'Perhaps, but your mother would have seen your adoption as your only hope to grow up in freedom and with some privilege. We both hated for you to be taken by strangers who were our enemies, but you have not fared badly. From all that you've told me, Madame LeClerc saw that you were cared for and when the time came, protected you in such a way that it led to your marriage to Gabriel. For this she deserves our thanks and respect.' When Marmion still looked doubtful, her father smiled a wry broken-toothed smile. 'Also, *ma chérie,* one must consider that although your good fiancé has freed me, I am still not a popular man with our leaders, and must depend upon the good-will of my adversaries to remain alive and free to see my grandchildren.'

And so Dominique LeClerc and Marmion's beloved father presided at her wedding. Madelaine Algemeine was the maid of honor; other classmates were bridesmaids. And the LeClerc servants and employees were all invited to the wedding feast. Also present, though less conspicuously, were the contacts, go-betweens, and messengers, including two prison guards, whom Marmie and Gabriel had used to free her father.

Oddly enough, her father and Gabriel's passed away within weeks of each other, leaving Gabriel as the head of his family and its business concerns. Madelaine married his closest friend, who entered into the Algemeine family business as well.

With her respectability assured, Marmion often returned with baskets of food, toiletries, and books for the prisoners in both the men's and women's sections of the Bastille. She was careful to always bring similar dainties for the guards and prison employees, and asked after their health and their families. This was not because, as she let the prisoners old enough to remember her know, she was grateful for the care given her as a child, but so they would permit the prisoners to keep and use her gifts. Many of these people were no more criminal than her parents, and had in fact been friends and comrades of her parents, but were not fortunate enough to have someone to see to their release.

Oh, yes, she was familiar with prisons, with guards and matrons and inmates alike, but once her own business acumen and the enterprises she had inherited from her husband made her wealthier than anyone had ever imagined possible, those who spoke of her origins mentioned only the original luster of the de Revers name. She thought it unnecessary to disillusion them about the less-than-glamorous aspects of her past.

So, although Marmion dreaded going back into captivity, she did not experience the fear or the humiliation Colonel Zachariah Cally no doubt hoped she would. Her main concern was for her crew and passengers.

When they arrived at what was euphemistically referred to as the reception area of the prison, they were separated by gender, but the initial order was the same. 'Shave 'em, strip 'em, hose 'em down, and suit 'em up.'

The Kanaka women accepted this mistreatment stoically, their misery showing only in their eyes, but some of Marmion's women crew members tried to fight. 'Tell them to cooperate,' Marmion whispered to Adrienne. 'Accept it as the local style. The shave seems brutal now, but it's that or involuntary dreadlocks and lice later. Don't fight, no matter what. You cannot win, and they will do you real damage if you resist.'

'Shut up, you,' the nearest guard said, yanking Marmion's head back by her flowing curls.

'You're no different than the rest of these sluts to us and you don't give orders here.' She shoved her toward one of the chairs surrounded by piles of hair. 'Take a load off, queenie.'

But a stern voice contradicted her. 'Not her, not yet. Put her in uniform and give her one of our VIP suites. Make sure she doesn't hurt herself.'

They led her down claustrophobic corridors between cold cell blocks to a tiny bare room with a hard slab for a bed and bench and a stinking hole in the floor to drain waste. The door had no bars, just a slot for food at the bottom. She was sure there would be cameras hidden somewhere in the ceiling or the door and that the door would have a one-way panel through which they could observe her without her being able to see them.

As the door closed and locked behind her, she heard other cell doors clanging shut.

4

Ronan, Murel, and Sky cleared the bay and burst into the port master's office. The port master, a whippetlike woman with a silver buzz cut, stood staring out into the bay and spun around to face the interlopers.

'What are you kids doing here?'

They didn't know her, but her name tag said, CHIEF C. BROWN.

'We came to warn you,' Murel told her. 'Marmie – Madame – has been arrested and taken to Gwinnet Incarceration Colony by some corrupt Company Corpsmen. We need help getting word to her friends and allies so they can get her released.'

'Why did they send kids to tell us? The *Piaf*—'

'They confiscated the *Piaf* and all of the crew and passengers,' Ronan told her. 'They may be headed here—'

The woman returned her attention to the docking bay, shaking her head. 'Nope. You're a little late. They just arrived.'

The twins followed her gaze. The big ship's hatch had opened and triple files of Company Corpsmen marched double-time over the gangplank down the bay, heading straight for them.

Come on, Mur, we gotta get out of here, Ronan said, pushing through the office's interior hatch.

Where to? Murel asked as they raced down the long corridor.

Marmie's house.

That's the first place they'll go! she protested.

I don't think so. Not with her in custody already. They'll be too busy taking over everything else. Meanwhile maybe we can use her com system to get word out about her arrest.

But they'll take over the com systems first, she argued.

They found the first lift that scaled all levels of the station and took it up to Marmie's penthouse. The weather was set on fine – a nice spring day. The house was open, being run by Marmie's housekeepers in her absence.

'Slainté, Mrs Fogarty,' Ronan called as they raced for the com room.

'You're back!' the housekeeper said. 'No one told me you were coming. And me without dinner for herself!' She followed them to the com room, where Murel sat at the keyboard composing a message to send to Marmie's entire list of contacts. There was no time now to sort out who was who. 'You're tracking water all over my floors again, and what *is* that animal with you, a big rat?'

Ronan said, 'No, Mrs Fogarty. He's an otter.'

'First seals, now an otter. This place is turning into an aquarium.'

'Never mind about that, Mrs Fogarty. Soldiers are on their way, probably to impound the station and arrest us all.'

'Why? I've done nothing wrong.'

'They've taken Marmie and are confiscating all of her stuff, arresting her staff as accomplices,' Ronan told her.

Bollocks! Murel swore, and turned around with tears of frustration in her eyes.

No luck? Ronan asked her.

I don't think so. Just as I hit Send, the system shut down.

The com screen came on and a uniformed man said in a deep gruff voice, 'Attention all personnel of the space station designated as *Versailles*. This property is under an impound and seizure order according to statute 68795-Zed and all personnel are subject to

51

questioning regarding the alleged criminal activities of the owner.'

'That's preposterous!' Mrs Fogarty exclaimed. 'They can't do that! That's piracy, that is.'

''Fraid they can, missus,' Ronan said. 'Look!'

The surveillance screens showed three flitters landing in the east garden. An improbable number of armed troops poured from each and fell in behind the last passenger, who wore the official robes of a Federation Councilman.

'That's just wrong,' Mrs Fogarty said, pointing to the councilman. 'They don't dress up like the Grim Reaper unless they're presiding in court or some such official function. It's myself should know, since there's many the time I've done up Madame's robes before and after she'd need of them.'

The twins didn't answer. 'Please don't tell them we're here, missus,' Murel said instead. 'They're after us too. We have to hide.'

'What I have to tell them is nothing they'll be happy to hear,' Mrs Fogarty said with a grim set to her lips. 'Excuse me. I've a brand-new broom around here somewhere that I bought before Madame installed the central vacuum to spare me back. I feel the need of it now.'

Ronan and Murel were already dashing for

the nearest access to the pool, Sky running circles around them. It wasn't actually a pool. Marmie had built it specifically for them, fashioned as a sort of artificial river that ran under the house and out around the grounds, among garden fountains and small ponds, before looping back inside again to form a lovely stream inside the great room. They felt they could hide there.

What if they catch us in seal form and make us change? Murel asked.

Why would they do that? Our secret may be a bit more public than it used to be but I doubt it's the gossip of the Corps. Besides, they're very noisy. We'll know they're coming long before they know we're there, and that will give us time to change.

Otters dig dens in water banks, Sky said. *Dens are good to hide in.*

I don't think we can dig into the stuff under Marmie's lawn, Sky, Murel told him. *It's not real. It would be like trying to den into the side of the spaceship.*

While their otter friend was thinking about that, they zipped out of their dry suits and tucked them into the pouches strapped to their backs. Then they dove into the pool, swimming quickly to the portion flowing under the house. To preserve their secret, Marmie had not set cameras near or within the banks of the waterway. Most views of the house and grounds included only glimpses of it.

Now what? Ronan wondered.

We *keep our ears peeled*, Murel said. *If my message was transmitted before they cut it off, this will all get sorted out soon.*

If not?

Perhaps we can sneak into the com center, disable the soldiers there, send again, and skedaddle?

And how would we do that?

I don't know. But we must do something or we might as well have stayed and waited to be arrested at home.

They'd kept their heads above water so they could hear what was happening above them. The house was well soundproofed, but their hearing was much better in seal form than the average human's.

'Children? I've no idea what you're talking about,' Mrs Fogarty was saying.

'You'd do well to cooperate, lady. Two children and a small brown mammal were seen running from the docking bay by our crew when we docked.'

'There are many children who live here. Madame runs a school, you know. And children do have pets.'

'They were seen entering the maintenance lift. That's off-limits to children, is it not?'

'As if that sort of thing ever stopped an inquisitive youngster!' Mrs Fogarty scoffed. 'But there are no children here, as you can see for yourselves. They must have popped off on one of the other levels.'

'Tear the place apart,' the soldier who'd been doing the questioning said.

'Here now!' Mrs Fogarty protested.

'Lay that broom down, lady, and step away from it,' the trooper demanded.

'I'll lay it up side of your head,' she threatened. There was a sizzling sound and a thump and no more from the housekeeper.

I hope they just stunned her, Ronan said.

Murel hoped so too, because she knew that not only was Mrs Fogarty loyally defending Marmie's property and privacy, she was also providing a distraction. Murel had never been stunned. She hoped it didn't hurt.

'Search the grounds,' the officer in command said. 'Look for the kids, the animal, or any fresh sign. Our orders are to remove all personnel, including children.'

'Right, Captain, sir. Uh – permission to ask a probably dumb question, sir?'

'Granted, but make it snappy.'

'If we remove all personnel, who's going to run this thing? It's a valuable piece of property.'

'Very astute of you, Private. You aspire to company management, do you?'

'Sir, no, sir. There is no higher aspiration than to serve the Corps, sir.'

'Damn straight. In answer to your question, however, Private, I don't suppose you happened to notice that ship that docked a short time after we did?'

'No, sir.'

'Filled with qualified Corps-trained station maintenance personnel. Now round up those kids and that animal so we can load and lock the prisoners up and leave. Is that clear?'

'Sir, yes, sir. One more thing, sir?'

'Anything for you, Private,' the officer said through what sounded like gritted teeth.

'Signs, sir?'

'Sign what?'

'You said to look for fresh signs? Sir?'

'Sign, Private, sign. Where's your sergeant anyway? Sergeant Montgomery!'

A distant voice barked in a tone that would have done credit to the twins' seal cousins. 'Here, sir!'

'Kindly explain to your man here what looking for a fresh sign means in reference to our current mission,' the captain called back.

'Otter shit!' the sergeant barked back, as if he were swearing.

Otters are not messy, Sky said. *Also, otters do not leave signs when they have not eaten for a long time, and I have not eaten since we left the deep sea otters.*

Glad to hear it, Sky, Ronan said. *Too bad nobody here keeps a dog. I bet most of these Corpsmen wouldn't know otter poo from doggie doo.*

I wouldn't be so sure of that, Ro, Murel told him. *The one in command sounded like he knew what he was talking about. Remember, the company gets a lot of its recruits from worlds like Petaybee and Halau. Maybe that soldier and even some of the others are from places where people and animals live close together. For all we know he could be as good as Aunty Sinead.*

Aunty Sinead would never track down kids – unless it was to help them, of course – or use stunners on ladies like Mrs Fogarty. And I'll bet Mum never in her entire career in the Corps did anything like they're doing.

Probably not. We don't really know what she did, though, do we? Or much about her. I never read that journal she wrote for us, did you?

Nope. I was too mad at her for sending us off-world. I wish we had the journals now.

I'm going to read mine first thing when we get home, Murel vowed.

Me too. I wonder what she'd do in our place

now, Ronan said. *I'll bet she'd have infiltrated the com center, neutralized the guards, and sent the message already. Or maybe taken over command.*

I don't think so, Ro, Murel replied. *I think she'd probably be doing pretty much what we are. What worries me is what she's doing at home now.*

The snow was so heavy that the invaders of Kilcoole could not see their hands in front of their faces. They put lanterns on their helmets, but the light bounced off the sheets of white and cast a glare even their goggles could not dispel.

The wind blew scarves from their necks and mittens from their hands, and knocked over the smaller men and women. Master Sergeant Missoni rescinded the order to burn the village for fear the wind would blow the fires out of control and injure his people. Instead they sank pitons into the buildings with cables attached, stringing the buildings together like beads. The lines served as they would in a gale at sea, something for the troops to hold on to in order to keep from being blown away as they plodded blindly from one shack to the next. Finally, Missoni called everyone off. The flitters were engineered for low temperatures but not for the gale-force winds, and besides, a driver couldn't see to navigate. Even posting guards was use-less until the wind died down and the snow lightened. They had no equipment of any kind that would let a mortal man or woman see a damn thing under the current conditions. Even with the best gear available, a guard was far more likely to die of exposure than to prevent, protect, or detect anything.

Since returning to the ship was also im-possible, they bivouacked in the town meeting hall, a long one-story job with a lot of carvings on the walls and the support beams. Missoni guessed that the long fire pit down the middle was for feasts of some sort. The hospital was larger, but they'd discovered that it was deserted and cold, the many windows already thick with the same frost that iced the inner walls. The long building was more centrally located, sturdily constructed, and free of frost inside,

They built a fire and the smoke rose through a hole in the roof that sucked it out better than Missoni would have guessed. These people had acquired some technology in the last few years, it seemed. Not enough to keep the wind from blowing the smoke back down to choke them and keep a permanent haze between the tops of their hooded helmets and the ceiling, but it helped. The air on Petaybee was supposed to be pure and clean, so they hadn't brought masks. Missoni used the tail of his muffler to filter out some of the smoke and the others followed suit.

They were an inhuman-looking bunch sitting there, smoke-reddened eyes glittering with tears as they watched the flames leap and dip, red, orange, yellow, white-blue, and some crackly green. The wind roared and shook the walls as if it would bring them down on top of the miserable collection of human beings. How the hell did people live here, and why would they even want to? Missoni wondered. He couldn't imagine how even fur-bearing animals would live through a storm like this. Well, they lived in holes, didn't they?

And that, he realized, had to be exactly what the people were doing. This whole place was supposed to be full of caves. People had gone into those caves and come out again thoroughly messed up. Maybe the reason some people stayed on this iceberg was that they had gone down there too and become even more messed up – enough that they actually thought Petaybee was fit for human habitation. Enough that they imagined they liked it.

'Okay,' he said through his helmet com. 'What did you come up with on the data search?'

'Stacks and stacks of forms, sir, but when I brought them out, the wind snatched all but these last few out of my hands,' Private Murkowski said.

Ordinarily Missoni would have yelled at him, but under the circumstances he just grunted. 'Parr?'

A soldier seated two down from Missoni withdrew a small case from his parka with a still-mittened hand and passed it to him. It held some chips that looked like they might work on the little computer Missoni carried in the breast pocket of his uniform blouse.

The mission had been aborted before the search was complete, but there were several handfuls of papers and a few more chips and drives. Mostly, Petaybean communications still seemed to be stuck in the hard-copy phase.

Missoni looked over the papers, not expecting to make much of them. He was right. Besides, even if he understood what was on them, there was a good chance he wasn't supposed to know about it. He stacked them neatly beside him and laid a big rock from the fire pit on top of the pile. If they ran out of fuel before this storm blew over, the papers might come in handy.

Meanwhile he pulled the little unit from his

pocket and popped in one of the chips from the container Parr had given him.

A woman with a clear concise voice said in a slightly embarrassed tone, 'I do not often sing this but record it now at Sean's insistence, for the sake of our children. He seems to think there will come a day when they'll ask, 'What did you do in the war, Ma?' and this way I won't have to sing it again in front of anyone. So here it goes. This is my song about what happened at *Bremport Station*.'

5

The twins and Sky stayed under Marmion's house until the grounds were searched, then cautiously, quietly, swam as far out as they could in the direction of the freight lift.

Very slowly they lifted their heads from the water to hear what was happening on land. The three flitters were still there; guards were posted near the mansion, but there was no evidence of anyone else nearby.

What do you think? Is it clear?

Without warning, Sky jumped out of the water and onto the bank, where he stood on his hind feet and shifted his torso and head back and forth, listening. *Men who eat river seals are not here,* he announced.

With that assurance, Ronan hoisted himself ashore and, propelled forward with flippers and claws, reached the cover of some shrubs where he could shake himself dry and change. When he was once more clad in his dry suit, he stood watch – squatted, actually – while Murel changed, too. Then, while Sky scampered across the fake landscape in his undulating run, the twins crawled to the freight lift, trying to stay out of range of the surveillance cameras. When the door opened, they all leaped inside and Ronan pushed the button for the com center level.

The door began to open as soon as they reached it. Before they could stop him, Sky bolted through to scout ahead.

He only had time to say 'Hah!' before they heard a sizzle, then a man's gruff voice: 'Got the little bugger. What do you think? Is there enough of him to make a pair of boots?'

Before the door had fully opened, Murel forced her way out, shouting, 'Hey, let him alone, you big bully!'

She just had time to see a short soldier holding a limp Sky aloft by the scruff of his neck when a hand whipped out and grabbed *her* neck, hauling her away from the lift. 'Ow!' she said. 'Cut it out. And let the otter alone!'

'Oh, is this yours?' the soldier asked in the same voice she'd heard from schoolyard bullies.

Behind her there was a scuffle, and Ronan was pulled from the lift as well.

The soldier holding her spoke into a hand-held com. 'This is the last of the children, sir.'

He listened to the reply, then clicked off the device.

'Lot of kids for a space installation,' Ronan's captor remarked.

'There was a school here. The brass is interested in knowing what exactly these kids were taught.'

'How about the critter?' the soldier holding Sky asked. The otter wiggled in his grasp, apparently recovering from the stun shot.

'He's their pet, apparently. Bring him along. He might be good to eat, or who knows, if these two know anything, they might get extra chatty if it means the animal keeps his skin on.'

Murel's captor had relaxed his grip, and she twisted away, rushing at the man shaking Sky. Because he was holding the otter in one fist and his weapon in the other, his front was wide open. She butted him first in the belly and then, when he doubled up, in the nose with her own head. Before she heard the sizzle and felt a jolt of pain shoot through her, she saw the man drop Sky, who twisted in midair and was halfway down the corridor before he landed.

★   ★   ★

When Murel came to, she had a horrible headache and everything around her smelled strange. She sat up in a tiny room occupied by several other girls. Most of them were pre-schoolers, too young to have been in classes with her, but two – Chesney Janko and Lan Huy – were familiar from her time at Marmie's school.

Lan Huy wept in a shockingly loud and heartbroken way that set the younger ones off. Between sobs, she made Murel understand that she had seen her father, one of Marmie's chief engineers, stunned and dragged away before the soldiers grabbed her as well. Murel remembered that Lan Huy had grown up on *Versailles Station*. It was the only home she knew.

Chesney Janko was younger than either Murel or Lan Huy, but she tried to comfort the older girl, making soothing shushing sounds and patting her quivering shoulder.

Murel could scarcely hear herself think over the wailing of the younger girls, but she called to her brother anyway. *Ro?*

I'm here, sis. Me and about ten other guys.

She looked around the little room. *Where are we? I don't recognize this part of the station.* While the two lived on *Versailles Station,* they had had an opportunity to explore most of it.

We're not on the station, sis. What with you

settin' such a fine example, I decided one of us with a sore head would be enough. So I whined instead and begged them, whatever they did to us, not to send us to Gwinnet Incarceration Colony. They enjoyed telling me that was exactly where we're going. Everyone from the station. At least if we're there, we can find out what's happening to Marmie.

Even if we're not in a position to do anything about it, Murel said. *What about Sky?*

I don't know. I didn't realize otters could play possum so well, but he had that eedjit of a soldier fooled and got away. There's plenty of places for him to hide till they leave.

Hah! came an otterly thought. *Sky otters are fierce fighters. I used my strong claws and big sharp teeth to get away, then followed the otter-eating men who took river seals. Otters are good hiders, and there are hundreds of places for otters to hide here.*

Oh, Sky, I'm glad you're okay, but you should have escaped when you could. They might hurt you, Murel said.

You will not let them, Sky said with perfect confidence. *You do not let wolves eat otters, or sharks or even other seals. River seals help their otter friends. Otters help river seals too.*

I hope none of us will regret that decision later, but I must say, right now I feel better knowing you're near, Murel said.

Me too, Ronan agreed. *But don't let them catch you again, no matter what.*

Otters are very cunning, Sky assured them. *And we have big sharp teeth.*

To their surprise and relief, their captors did not question anyone during the journey, or even speak to them. They didn't seem to care who anybody was, just so they were off the space station. The kids were fed Corps rations, the kind the soldiers ate in the field – all nutrition and no taste – and given water. Their cells had flush toilets with blue chemical stuff in them and they plugged up easily. The temperature was controlled, but the number of bodies in each room made it way too warm most of the time.

The girls had exhausted themselves crying, and gradually the noise simmered to a generalized whine of anxiety, discomfort, and boredom.

Nobody was mistreating them, but neither were they exerting any effort to make things easier for the young ones.

Needing some distraction herself, Murel decided to use the kind of tactics employed by Petaybean child minders and teachers of restless classes. 'If my snow leopard friend was here,' she said, 'she would eat all of those bad people and set us free.'

Huy's lips curled into a small smile, Chesney laughed, and the little girls who had heard her looked mildly interested.

'Also,' Murel added, 'she'd bring us all ice cream.'

'What's that?' asked the smallest girl, the one the others called Daf.

'It's sweet and smooth and cold and really yummy,' Murel told her. 'It comes in lots of flavors. Where I live, we make it out of snow mixed with milk from our horses.'

By the time she explained what a horse was, what snow was, what a snow *leopard* was, and how that leopard would manage to bring ice cream and kill bad people as well, Huy and Chesney caught on and launched into telling the tallest tales they could imagine or remember about their own worlds. Huy might have been raised on a space station, but her father had told her stories his own parents and grandparents passed down to him from the ancient cultures and peoples who settled their world.

'We had a dragon in my father's family, and if my ancestor knew what was happening to my father and me, he would come and carry us all away,' Huy said. 'If we pass by close enough to my father's world, I'll call him.'

'You can't yell that loud!' a six-year-old cynic told her.

'Don't have to. He can read my thoughts. He would be very displeased with these people, and before he took us away, he would scorch them with his fiery breath.'

The people who brought their food didn't scold or threaten them, but neither could they be persuaded to bring extra toilet paper or wash water. They didn't molest the girls in any way, which was a relief. On the contrary, they seemed totally indifferent to them, as if children were some inferior species beneath their notice.

'We're just hostages,' Huy said. 'They'll use us to make our parents do what they want them to. I hope they haven't hurt my dad.'

'My brother says they're taking us all to a prison colony. Maybe you'll get to see your dad there.'

'Will they try to make our parents say that Madame is a criminal, Murel? What did she do to make them mad at her?'

That was a story Murel knew all too well, so she told them about the trip she, Ronan, and Ke-ola had taken to Halau, how meteor showers destroyed the homes of Ke-ola's people, forcing them all underground, and how the soldiers would have just left them there with nothing if Marmion hadn't launched a rescue mission.

'If it hadn't been for Madame's ship picking

up the survivors, then going back to find other people still trapped, they'd have all died. The officer in charge must have got his ears laid back by his superiors. Somehow he convinced the company superiors that she had kidnapped the people of Halau and their sharks and sea turtles, and that's what she's charged with.'

'But that's so lame!' Chesney said.

'Of course it is. And the people in charge will realize that when Marmie's friends tell them what happened to her. The people who want to ruin her don't want anybody to know she's in trouble.' Murel explained about the magnetic field and volcanic activity on Petaybee making interplanetary communication impossible most of the time. She left out all the parts about her and Ronan being seals, and about Kushtaka's people and their history. Who knew what might be done to the kids to make them or their parents talk? She took a deep breath and gulped as a few possibilities crossed her mind, then put those thoughts firmly away. Need to know, Mum would say. She'd tell them when and if they had a need to know.

Ronan agreed that was the best way to handle it, though in the stories the boys told, they tended to massacre the entire ship's crew with their bare hands or, better yet, blow up the ship, once all the good people were safely ashore. Then they would storm the prison, and after battles that involved fencing with some sort of laser-beamed or edged weapons, overcome the guards, free the prisoners – well, the good ones, at least – and of course, for a happy ending, blow up the prison. When he shared some of these tales of valor with her, Murel said she thought there was an excess of blowing things up.

We males like explosions, he told her. *Especially when we're mad and helpless to do anything about it.*

Not as helpless as some people think, she replied staunchly. While she was glad Ro and the boys were keeping their spirits up, it hurt a bit to hear him referring to himself as one of 'we males.' Their twinship had always been the main 'we' in each of their lives – the selkie nature they shared with their father was the second-most important group to them. Family had come third. Now Ro seemed to think being male, a condition that excluded her, was also important. She had certainly not said 'we girls' or 'we females.' Although she was female and around the same age as the others, she felt – well, it wouldn't be nice to say better than they were, but different from them. Very different. So far the people their own age who knew about their secret had been fine with it, but she was sure some of these girls would be unable to handle it.

To keep things interesting, she tried to tell the girls the boys' stories, leaving out the explosions. She was a little surprised at the ferocity with which Huy and Chesney inserted their own torments for their captors. Chesney even knew something about setting explosions. When Murel told Ronan about that later, he agreed that it was something worth notice.

They relied on these nighttime conversations to push the boredom and fear away when everyone else finally quieted for sleep. They tried to remember and prompt each other's memories of the navigation and piloting lessons they'd had aboard the *Piaf*. Galactic geography and periodic tables filled more of the quiet time, then puns, then songs and more songs from the potlatches and night chants.

It's a good thing we can thought-talk, Murel said. *Otherwise I'd go bonkers from boredom. Huy and Chesney can come up with some good gossip from the station, but they don't know many songs, and the ones they know have words that don't tell stories. I'm supplying most of those.*

Rory's pretty interesting, her brother told her, *but the other boys, even the little ones, talk about games a lot. I saw some of them on vid when we were at Marmie's, but I can't say I understand the excitement.*

The scariest thing about the journey for the twins was when their captors decided the prisoners should have a shower. Fortunately, it turned out to be a sonic shower, so they were able to avoid the water exposure that would have forced their change into seal form. Other than that shower, they got no exercise, so it was hard to feel tired enough to sleep.

When Murel slept, however, she dreamed about the river at home with its clouds of ice overhead and the fish so plentiful all she had to do was open her mouth to catch some. Ronan was in the dream, and later, when he described his dream to her, it sounded like the same one.

The soldiers on the troop ship being rocked in its moorings by gusts of Petaybean blizzard wind were also bored. All except Spec 4 Greta Forcet. Fascinated by what she saw on the weather map, she put in a call to the bridge. 'Sir, I think you should see this,' she said.

Captain J. Wilbank replied, 'What's up?'

'This weather pattern, sir. I've never seen anything like it.'

'Yeah, this is quite a storm. I didn't know it was possible for snow to occur at temperatures this low.'

'It's not only that, sir. It's *where* the storm is.'

'What do you mean? Never mind, I'll come and see for myself.'

Not only the captain, but two other officers and three enlisted personnel came to see what she was talking about. The storm's ferocity made all of them feel under siege and eager for information.

'Look here, where the worst of it is – the heaviest snow and the highest winds are all right here, at the port and in Kilcoole. It's like we're being specifically targeted by the storm.'

'The river would act as a funnel—' the captain began.

'Yes, but the winds are not nearly so fierce along the river, nor is the snow so heavy.'

'Hmm. So if we penetrate the barrier of bad weather around the ship, we could send out another party to search for the locals.'

Forcet raised her eyebrows but said nothing. He might be right, but she wasn't going to volunteer for the expedition.

'I don't know, sir,' Lieutenant Chu said. 'It's

like this place is haunted *and* the ghost is really pissed off.'

'That's not it,' Spec 5 Ortiz said.

'Don't contradict me, soldier,' Chu said. He had just made rank and was touchy about his authority.

'Sorry, *sir*,' Ortiz barked, saluting smartly.

'Let her talk, Lieutenant,' Captain Wilbank said. 'Well, Ortiz?'

'It's just that I served with a couple of guys from here, sir. From what they said, the problem isn't anything dead. It's what's living. They say this world is alive and has a nasty temper.'

'Walk a little to the left, please, Yana,' Clodagh said as she reentered the cave. 'That groove you're wearing in the cavern floor should be wider so folk with bigger boots can still walk there.'

Yana knew her pacing was driving everyone else nuts, but once more her entire family had left her without saying where they'd gone. That drove *her* nuts. Waiting for news was very high on her list of things she hated to do. Or not do. It was the kind of thing her former superiors would have called 'a character-building experience.' She had certainly acquired the family

best designed to build her character. And now they were testing her patience by running off without a word at a time when she needed to think clearly and act without hesitation. Instead, concern for them left her feeling unable to make a decision about when to act.

Clodagh, dressed in winter gear, had been in the outer cave, holding a veritable reception for every land creature on Petaybee from the look of it. Pairs of wild eyes stared into the cave. In height they could have been anywhere from taller than a man – a bear perhaps? – to very small indeed. The only ones Yana could identify for certain were Clodagh's gold-striped cats, who came and went as if the snowstorm was of no concern to them. Like Coaxtl the snow leopard, they had extra-wide feet; tufts of fur padded their paws like snowshoes, and similar tufts warmed their ears.

'Has the storm let up at all?' Yana asked Clodagh.

'Here it has,' Clodagh replied with the enigmatic brevity that characterized most of her utterances in general and nearly all of her answers to other people's questions. Clodagh's tall, round body, clad in her furry snow pants and hooded parka, mittens, and mukluks, made her resemble a comical bear. This was especially true since over her parka she wore a kusbuk, a flounced, mid-thigh-length, hooded covering worn in summer as a lightweight top and in winter over the parka to protect the precious coat from damage. The villagers loved sewing their kusbuks out of the brightest fabrics they could find, making them easier to spot in a snowstorm and adding a bit of cheerful contrast to the often-bleak winter landscape.

'How about at sea?'

'Sean and the kids will be fine, Yana. But those company folk are socked in.'

'They are?'

'The ones in the village hid in the longhouse. The ones on the ship can't get out.'

Bunny Rourke, Sean's niece, said, 'I bet they wish we were still home to build fires for them and make them nice hot cups of rose hip tea.'

'Rrrright,' Yana growled. Johnny Green, Pet Chan, Raj Norman, and Rick O'Shay threw down the cards they'd been shoving back and forth in a desultory imitation of poker and looked at Yana expectantly. She smiled much as a wolf viewing a pen full of fat sheep might have. 'Ladies and gentlemen,' she said quietly, so as not to alert the other villagers, 'perhaps it's time to extend the planet's hospitality to our guests.'

'I'm going too,' said Sinead Shongili, Yana's sister-in-law.

'Shhh,' Yana said. She didn't want to risk any of the native Petaybeans being captured, since an adult who had adapted to the planet would die when removed from it. But Sinead was a hunter who knew the land as well as she knew her beloved Aisling. She was the game warden for their area – a cool head and a sure shot. They could use her. 'Fine, but keep back in the woods and cover us. We can't risk you getting caught.'

'Nor can we risk you, Yana, but I don't see that stopping you,' Sinead said tartly, pulling on her parka and shouldering her rifle.

Missoni and his troops listened to the woman on the recorder sing her song about a Corps legend – the massacre at *Bremport Station* – with interest that would have been astonishment were they not still so exhausted from fighting the storm. The voice was accompanied by a drum; in the background the wind howled, moaned, and whined around the building, now and then making a sound like the ruffling of the feathers of a gigantic bird.

When she'd finished, he cut off the recording, though there was room for plenty more data. 'How did she know about *Bremport*, Sarge?' Inuye asked. She was fairly new to the Corps.

'You heard the lady, Private. She was there. Before she was turned by the locals, Major Yanaba Maddock was one of us, a decorated officer who served with distinction at several bases. She was invalided out after *Bremport* and sent here for retirement. It's in the data banks on the ship. You can look it up.'

'I guess she had to stay here because the Corps wouldn't listen to her poetry,' Murkowski scoffed. 'Got herself a captive audience and didn't want to leave.'

'I heard it was because she fell for the head scientist here,' Parr said.

'Sex is a lot more likely a motive than poetry,' Inuye said.

'Shut it,' Missoni said. 'She was an exemplary officer before her injury. Show a little respect for the person she was. Any of us could be wounded and sent to where we'd be dependent on the goodwill of the locals to survive. When and if that happens to me, I hope to show more loyalty, but I've seen even worse things happen to even better people once they're no more use to the Corps. Break out your rations. We'll eat, sleep, and by then maybe the storm will have calmed down some.'

Murkowski grumbled, 'Should have confiscated some of the food in the cabins. It's not like they're going to be using it any time soon.'

They had each brought along only one ration packet, thinking to strike quickly, take their prisoners, and return to the ship. Screw that scenario. 'When the storm lets up, go back and collect whatever food you can find and bring it back here,' Missoni told them. 'We may need it, and we don't want them to have it. We may have to wait them out, and a siege doesn't work unless someone is starving. I'd rather that not be us.'

His com crackled, but he couldn't make out any kind of message. The verbal one was lost in the general howl, and when they tried a text message, it fragmented into an unintelligible sparkly geometric design. Pretty but useless.

When the men finished eating, Missoni posted a sentry at the longhouse's only door. 'If the storm lets up, wake me,' he told Murkowski. Then he and the others made themselves as comfortable as possible on the building's floor. He was asleep before his head touched the floor.

6

Murkowski grumbled to himself. He was tired too, and more than likely the storm would play out before his watch was up, so he'd have to help when the search resumed.

He paced himself to keep awake. He walked back to the fire and added another couple of logs from the pile near the pit. The smoke made a pewter haze that hung from the roof to just above the level of the floor. Several guys coughed and sneezed in their sleep. That storm had to break soon, or they'd all die of smoke inhalation. The wind sounded like it was trying to rip the roof off. What kind of a cold-blooded idiot would want to live in this freezer, anyway?

He slouched back to the door, and realized that in spite of the noise still coming from the roof, the storm seemed to have calmed a little. The door was flanked by two small windows, but each of them was black as space. He picked up the huge board toggle that barred the door, lifting it aside so he could see out. He hoped the draft would wake up some of the other guys.

The door opened inward, which was a good thing since three feet of snow was now drifted against it outside. Was it his imagination or had the wind finally deafened him? Either way, he couldn't hear it as well. He stuck his head and shoulders out over the snowdrift. Something landed on his back, forcing his face into the snow before he could yell for help.

Yana patted the track cat, Orca, on the broad black flat place between his ears. The cat sat down on his prey, draping one paw casually over the side of the man's face. The soldier's snow-encrusted eyes opened as he struggled to turn his head. He took in the slow extension and retraction of three-inch-long claws covering his left ear and tickling his left cheek and the corner of his left eye. Yana put her mittened forefinger to the portion of her muffler masking her lips, indicating that he should be quiet, and he responded with a flick of his eyelids since he was too intimidated by the claws to make a larger gesture.

Meanwhile, Raj, Pet, Johnny, and Rick

slipped past her and into the longhouse on padded mukluk feet. Each of them was better trained than most of the sleeping troops. They silently removed the rifles and sidearms, then returned to the doorway and joined Yana while Pet and Johnny carried armloads of snow to dump on the fire. They scuttled back to the door as the hiss and steam and sudden cold woke some of the soldiers, who grabbed at the air where their weapons used to be.

Yana, Raj, and Rick kept weapons trained on the soldiers until their friends were clear, then stepped back and signaled Orca to release his prey. The cat stood up after a long lazy stretch and bounded over the fallen man and off toward the woods.

The man on the ground reached for Yana's leg, but as soon as he used his body weight to support his reaching hand, he sank deeper into the snow and his mitten fell three inches short.

When he looked up, he found himself staring into the barrel of Raj's weapon.

Yana pointed to the other soldiers, and Raj barked, 'Crawl.'

When the man had backed through the snowdrift into the lodge, one of the soldiers called, 'You folks are making things worse for yourselves. It's not like we walked here on our own. There's a ship full of more like us waiting behind. You can't win this one. We just need to talk to the governors and straighten this thing out.'

'That's not how we heard it,' Johnny said. 'You came to haul them off to die in prison as you did Madame Marmion. We won't allow you to murder these people.'

'You don't want to go to war with the Company Corps, son,' the spokesman said.

'I'm not your son and at least two of us here outrank you,' Johnny told him, though he didn't explain how.

'You got weapons trained on my people, you all outrank me,' the man said.

'You do as we say and you've got nothing to worry about,' Johnny told him. He beckoned Yana, Pet, and the others inside, near the doorway.

'One by one, step forward, you first,' Pet Chan said to the spokesman. The man obeyed. 'Remove your parka and pants,' she told him.

'You're going to let us freeze?'

'Just trading,' Johnny answered. He took off his own parka and snow pants, borrowed from Sean, and put on the surrendered garments, noting the stripes on the parka sleeve. 'Thanks, Sarge.'

While he changed, Pet and Raj relieved the sergeant of his com, his knife, his ID tags, and his wallet. When they'd finished searching him, they allowed him to put on Johnny's clothing.

They searched the other soldiers in the same manner and forced two women in the party to trade with Yana and Pet, and two other men to swap with Raj and Rick.

Then they backed out, leaving the soldiers unharmed and unfettered, but unarmed as well. Johnny and Pet went to work constructing a bolt across the door, boarded up the windows, then called Sinead to come and stand guard, along with the villagers who'd insisted on coming with her.

The wind was gone, but it had blown all but a light skim of snow from the ice on the river, which had frozen solid enough to ski on. Yana and the others grabbed their skis, leaning against the wall of the longhouse, strapped them on, and headed upriver to where the ship was docked at the old Space Base.

The night was white with snow, and as they reached the head of the river, the wind rose up again, driving a horizontal wall of crystal darts across the snow-covered ice. The ship, the terminal, and everything beyond was invisible to them, just as they, Yana hoped, were invisible to the ship. From what she could recall, the Corps had no equipment capable of penetrating such a storm. A proposal to orbit a satellite around Petaybee to provide better communications and more conveniences was still on the table. If she, Sean, and the others had allowed the installation, they might have been able to foil the people who'd arrested Marmie. On the other hand, a satellite would have provided the company with better access to more-sophisticated equipment, including the kind that could have detected the presence of the five skiers approaching the ship.

Six of one, half a dozen of the other. Petaybeans lacked the technology that could cut both ways, working for or against them, but on the other hand, the planet's active participation in promoting their and its own welfare gave them a considerable edge as long as they could keep their feet on Petaybean soil, snow, ice, or water.

Disguised in the soldiers' winter clothing, they blundered through the storm to the ship under Rick O'Shay's guidance. Although Rick hadn't lived on Petaybee full-time since his youth, he had retained the Petaybean knack for navigating through the nastiest weather the planet dished up. They used the ID tag Johnny had taken from the sergeant to signal their desire to come aboard. Normally there would have been questions asked, but in the howling wind and knifing snow, using the com was impossible.

Once they were through the lock, where they brushed off their outer clothing but did not remove it, the sentry on the other end asked, 'You five are it?'

Johnny nodded.

'I thought you were bringing back prisoners. What's the matter? Couldn't find them in the whiteout?'

Johnny nodded again.

'The rest of your guys are still searching for them?'

Another nod. Yana resisted the impulse to roll her eyes in exasperation. If she were this kid's C.O., she'd have him on report as a security risk. Corps training and discipline – not to mention ethics – wasn't what it had been in her day, if he was any example.

He used the com unit to report their return and said, 'Captain wants to see you on the bridge.'

Unmolested, they walked past him into the belly of the beast.

7

It's time! Ronan's mental call broke into Murel's dream of the river. *They're unlocking our door now. Yours?*

Awakening, Murel listened. *Not yet. Sky?*

Hiding, Sky replied. *This place is not in space now. It is stopped on the ground, but the ground is not our ground.*

As Murel sat up, the door slid open. Two of the soldiers who sometimes brought the food stood outside. 'Okay, brats, your chariot awaits,' one of them said, unnecessarily waving her stunner at them.

They were herded to the docking bay and hustled aboard a shuttle. Ronan and the boys joined them as they were all jammed inside the small craft. From the main part of the ship they could hear barked orders, groans, and footsteps, and through the shuttle's viewport, just before they launched, Murel saw a great crowd of adults, some in Marmie's livery but most in civilian clothing, being forced into the bay by armed guards. She spotted Mrs Fogarty among them.

The shuttle lifted, maneuvered through the open hatch of the ship, and rose into the air above a bleak desertlike area whose sole distinguishing fixture was a massive city-sized fortified compound. As the shuttle gained altitude, Murel saw that the captive adults below were being offloaded directly to the surface, where they were marched down a short road through concertina-wire-topped walls and into the stark and barren grounds of what appeared to be a squat, rectangular building with several attached satellite buildings, each no more than two stories high. It reminded her of the hospital building on Kilcoole – if that building had grown to monstrous size and exuded brutality instead of a healing atmosphere. She tried to see as much as she could in the second or two before the shuttle pivoted in the air and headed out over open water. *So that's the prison,* she said to Ronan. *I'm glad we're not going in there, at least.*

Let's see where we are *going before you get too thrilled about it,* Ronan told her.

She wasn't the only one to notice the

destination of the adults. 'I want to go with my parents!' Rory demanded with a good imitation of his grandmother's haughtiest tones. 'You have no right to separate our family.'

'Sorry, kid, you're a little young for prison,' the shuttle copilot said. 'They'd eat a morsel like you alive.' He made a disgusting slurping sound.

But Rory's demand had unsettled the younger kids.

'Mom!' a boy wailed, and rushed to the viewport.

The copilot casually backhanded him and sent the child flying back into Rory's and Ronan's laps.

'Hey!' Huy objected.

'You want some too, girly?' the man asked. 'We're flyin' here, okay? And we're not taking you to see your mommies and daddies, so just forget that. Forget them.'

'Austin, shut up. You're scaring them,' the pilot said in a low voice, but one easily audible to the twins, who heard almost as well when they were human as when they were seals – unless, of course, it was someone forbidding them to do something they wanted to do. 'We have a job to do here, but there's no sense in being a jerk about it.'

For one brief moment Rory's eyes met

91

Ronan's. Murel didn't have to read her brother's thoughts to know the boys were wishing they could blow something up. But then Rory dropped his eyes, looking a bit sick.

I feel a little queasy myself, Murel admitted to Ronan. *What are they going to do to those people, just because they worked for Marmie? This is crazy!*

'If it was up to me, we'd drop the kids off with the rest of the criminals,' the copilot complained, then added in a lecturing voice, 'It's a well-known scientific fact that criminal tendencies are hereditary. If you ask me, there's no need to waste fuel taking them to some kiddie resort.'

'I didn't ask you. Orders are orders. The kids are processed differently. You know that.'

The shuttle left the buildings behind, crossed the barren land, and suddenly they were flying over what looked like an ocean.

Resort? That sounds hopeful, at least, Murel said.

Indeed, Ronan agreed. *Now if we can just figure out how to get from here to there and back again.*

'Two of those brats attacked our guys,' the copilot was continuing. 'Bit them. Seems to me it wouldn't hurt the little punks to let them see what they have to look forward to when they're older.'

As if the soldiers didn't attack us first! Ronan thought.

'Aw, shut up, Austin. You've started to enjoy this prison transport duty way too much,' the pilot said, still in a voice too low for most of the kids to hear. 'About time you transferred.'

'What the frag do you mean by that?' Austin asked.

'You're getting to where you're buying into the idea that these people exist for you to push around. That's not good for you, man,' the pilot told him.

'Huh. Not good for *them*, you mean,' Austin retorted.

'I mean *you*. One of these days you are going to be like me, ready to retire, go dirtside somewhere back where you came from or some other little vacation spot where the company decides to put you. Everybody around you is going to look like them, not like us, and you are going to be so fraggin' warped nobody will have anything to do with you. There's no home for old Corpsmen, son.'

'Spare me the fraggin' philosophy, Begay. You've got the same duty as me. What makes you think you know so much about what I'm going to be like when I leave the Corps? With what I've learned here, I might be runnin' the place, wherever I go.'

The pilot, Begay, shook his head and pursed his lips. 'I hope not. You're startin' to sound just like my old man.'

'He must have been okay. Here you are in the Corps and you've done okay for yourself.'

'Sure have. He's dirtside, *in* the dirt, and I'm here. Suits me fine.'

The shuttle descended and the twins saw more land, this with trees and a mountain in the middle of it.

Look! A volcano, Murel told Ronan.

Good, he replied.

Maybe, she said. *This isn't like home.* What she meant was that as far as they knew, this place wasn't alive, wasn't sentient, wasn't something that could be appealed to or reasoned with. Ronan knew that too, but he was more optimistic.

No, it looks to be a good deal warmer. It will be good for the Kanaka kids. Get them used to living in this kind of place for when they get back to Petaybee.

Murel was glad Ronan could be so positive about it. She didn't see how returning home was going to happen for any of them. Unless their messages had gone through, and she was by no means sure they had, she had no idea how they were going to get away.

The shuttle set down.

'This is your stop,' Begay told them, and with a press of a button opened the hatch. It was as if he had opened the door of an oven. The temperature outside was warmer than any they had ever experienced.

He then pushed another button that released the restraints that had kept them strapped to their benches.

From the open hatch, they saw a walled compound that looked far less grim than the first one. Though the wall was built of stones and topped with concertina wire, as the wall around the prison had been, what it enclosed looked like a village of shacks built of some sort of large rigid reed and thatched with broad tree fronds. They could see huge flowers and sprays of grasses growing in what looked like a garden, and there were even a few tall slender trees, their branches spreading like fern fronds circling the top.

Not too bad maybe, Murel thought optimistically.

That's not for us, silly. That must be where the guards live, Ronan told her. *Before we landed did you see over there, across the island, through the trees, where that dirt road from the village is going? That other stone wall with those buildings behind it? That would be where they're taking us.*

'What are you kids? Hard of hearing?' Austin demanded. 'Get out.'

Rory jumped down ahead of them, Dewey right behind him, then the twins; Huy and Chesney helped the younger ones.

Two more soldiers met them at the landing zone. They were a man and a woman a little younger than the twins' parents. The man was fairly slight, and the wind blew back his fatigue hat to reveal thinning brown hair. His gray eyes were as unfriendly and turbulent as storm clouds. Father's eyes were gray too, but tended to vary from the softness of the silkiest gray fur to sparkling silver when he was amused. The twins were told that their eyes had turned from the same gray as their father's to blue when they were toddlers.

The woman greeting them was a little taller than the man, with short blond hair, a trim build, and thin lips curved into the shape of a smile. She wore the visored cap version of the uniform hat, which shaded her eyes, so they couldn't see what color they were.

'Welcome to Camp Neverland,' the man said. 'I'm Captain Nobel Keester, medical doctor and commandant of the camp. This is my assistant, Second Lieutenant Portia Bunyon.'

'This way, children,' the woman said. 'Hurry

or you'll miss your meal for the day. You've still to be processed in.'

'What's that mean?' Rory asked.

'You'll see soon enough,' the man said in a way that Murel couldn't help feeling was ominous.

Catching the glance the twins exchanged, the woman dropped back and stepped between them, putting her arms over their shoulders in what looked like a maternal gesture but felt like a herding maneuver.

'It's nothing. A few vaccinations – you two are old enough not to mind a needle or two – and a delousing.'

'We don't have lice!' Murel told her.

'I'm not saying you do, but some here do. The haircut we give you will make sure you don't get them either. You'll find it's cooler too. Snap it up now, you don't want to miss your meal. Normally, incoming kids are bathed right away, but it's late, and if you don't eat now, you'll go hungry until mealtime tomorrow, so the doc is making an exception for you this time.'

The twins exchanged looks and a relieved *Whew!*

They allowed themselves to be herded through the gate, which closed behind them, blocking their view of the sea. Murel felt for a moment as if she were being smothered.

I know, me too, Ro told her. *But stifle it. The water will still be there when we need it. It doesn't look like they keep kids under lock and key, or even keep very good track of us so far. We'll get out when we have to.*

Murel thought maybe there'd be a dining hall with tables, but instead there was a long line of kids with bowls waiting for a soldier to ladle what looked like soup or thin stew into their bowls. An older boy handed each child a single slice of bread as they filed past and returned to the huts or tried to find somewhere to sit down and eat.

All of the kids except their group had shaved heads and wore loose tunics over bare legs. A few looked to be eleven or twelve but most appeared younger. Although it was hard to tell with the haircuts and outfits, Murel thought there seemed to be more girls than boys.

They joined the line, letting the smaller kids go first. By the time Murel got there, there was nothing left but rather putrid-looking watery stuff. She wasn't too worried. There was water nearby. If she and Ro could get close enough, they'd catch some fish.

Dewey, balancing his bread and bowl, was looking for a place to sit. 'Here, kid, I'll hold that for you while you take a seat,' an older girl said. She was tall and her build blocky, her skin about the same dark olive as theirs; the stubble on her head was black, and she looked familiar to Murel. She snatched Dewey's bread, which tore, and when Dewey tried to pull his bowl away from her, it flew out of both their grasps and hit the ground, spilling the soup.

'Fraggin' new kid!' the girl snarled. 'Look at that. He's so fat he can afford to waste food.'

Both of the people who had met the shuttle had disappeared, and the soldier who'd served the food did not look up from stowing his soup barrel and utensils aboard a small flitter.

'Hey,' Chesney said, dropping her empty bowl and rushing forward. 'Leave him alone, you. Isn't it bad enough we have to be here without picking on each other?'

Without answering, the other girl punched Chesney in the nose. Blood spurted.

Huy stood up and started toward her. Obviously, prison or no prison, camp or no camp, they were their own law and order here. Ronan and Murel and all of the space-station kids advanced on the bully girl, but she was quickly joined by what seemed to be every other kid in the camp.

But then another group, this one of smaller kids, stepped between the two. To Murel's surprise, one of them reached out and touched the big girl's hand and said something to her in a musical language Murel recognized, hearing her name and Ronan's in what the child said. The bully's fist uncurled, but she advanced again on Chesney, who was on the ground and bleeding. Kneeling, she reached her hand out and grumbled, 'Sorry, kid.' Then she turned to Dewey. 'Sorry about your food too. You can have mine tomorrow.'

She looked up at Ronan and Murel. 'Okay? No hard feelings?'

Before they could answer, she rose, jumped over Chesney's legs, and disappeared into one of the huts.

The girl who had touched the bully's hand said, 'Kai's just mad. She's been like that all her life, I guess. I'm Pele, by the way. Kai's my big sistah. I get scared, Maia gets her feelings hurt, Ke-ola wants to understand what's going on, and Keoki wants to argue. Kai gets mad.' She shrugged.

'You know Ke-ola and Keoki?' Ronan asked.

'They are my bruthas. Kai's too. And we all know you two. You're the se—' She stopped at Ronan's shushing motion. '—the twins,' she finished quickly. Dropping her voice, she asked, 'Have you come to save us again? Please save Kai too, even though she's a pain. She's not always like this, just when she gets upset.'

'She should learn to yell or hit a rock or something,' Murel said resentfully. 'Not pick on people who are littler than she is.'

'When we got here, some of the big kids took our food,' a round-faced little boy said belligerently. 'Kai's just doing it back.'

'It's brave – if stupid – to do it back to the people that pick on you,' Ronan told him. 'It's mean and not very logical to treat other people the way you hated to be treated yourself.'

Spoken like a true Petaybean shepherd seal, Murel told him. Maybe it sounded bossy to other people, but really, it was basic stuff. Other kids ought to *know* it already, she thought, but evidently it hadn't registered with some of them. She looked up and saw that the captain had come to the door of his hut and was watching them. He'd probably heard everything they said. It was a good thing Ronan had kept Pele from talking about their seal-selves.

As long as nobody knew they were selkies, they could use it to escape. Actually, the problem was that several people here already knew about them. Rory, for one, and all of the Kanaka kids had either seen them change or heard about it from the others, she was sure. If the powers that be here found out about them, she and Ro were likely to be in a bad way.

So far nobody had taken names or anything

like that, though she supposed if the soldiers did want to use certain kids to make certain parents confess or follow orders or whatever it was they were supposed to do, they'd find out who was who. They had to know where they'd collected the different groups of kids, and in that, she and Ro were lucky because so far the soldiers hadn't bothered to find out who they belonged to. She supposed they'd been too busy with the adults.

The captain was joined by Lieutenant Bunyon, who brought a whistle to her mouth and blew a short, piercing blast. All of the kids turned to look at her. 'For you newcomers, indoctrination will take place in a half hour in back of the admin hut, followed by a special treat for everyone,' she announced. 'We'll be showing a special film. I'm making popcorn for everyone who attends.'

The reaction was mixed. Those within sight of the officers made what Murel felt were exaggerated expressions of excitement and enthusiasm. Some were going for the popcorn, which was apparently some sort of treat, and extra rations whether you actually thought it was yummy or not.

The lieutenant added, 'For you newcomers, the film is mandatory. For the rest, curfew is extended until after it is over. Reassemble

102

behind the admin hut at the sound of my whistle.'

Ke-ola's little sister grabbed Murel's hand and tugged her toward a hut. Huy gave her a dirty look. Nobody was inviting the other new kids anywhere.

'Just a sec,' Murel told the girl, and turned back to Huy. 'Look, these kids can tell us what the situation is here. I need to find out what they know. It's not like I'm taking sides or anything.'

'Who cares?' Huy said. 'You're just looking out for yourself. You don't fool me. We'll find out soon enough what's going on here when they tell us. But you and your brother, living with Madame up in her mansion, you're used to special privileges. You certainly don't want to hang out with the rest of us.'

'That's not true,' Murel protested. 'But I can't explain right now. Okay? See you at indoctrination.'

She followed Pele into a hut filled with Kanaka relatives. There was no room for even one more person.

'Sorry,' Pele said. 'I didn't mean to get you in trouble with your friend, but we got to talk. You need to be warned.'

'What about?'

'Baths,' she said.

'Oh, yeah, that's going to be a problem,' Murel said glumly. The minute the water touched her or Ronan and they changed, it was going to be all over.

'Don't worry, big sistah. I have an idea,' Pele said, and with her brothers and sisters gathered around close so she could whisper, she told Murel.

Indoctrination was mostly about schedules. Mealtimes, curfews, bath days, immunizations, and other structured events that the orphans and children of social and criminal deviants should be happy the company chose to provide for them so their lives would not turn out as badly as those of their parents. Newcomers would not have to worry about finding a place to sleep until later. Tonight they were to sleep in an isolation hut. Tomorrow, after they were bathed, shaved, and immunized, they could be placed in quarters with longer-term residents who would assist in their assimilation to camp life.

All during her lecture there was a tantalizing smell of hot grease and grain that made the twins' mouths water. Just before the film started, a shaved-headed older boy wearing a cut-down version of the Company Corps uniform went among them with a carry sack and dribbled a few hot, salty kernels into each outstretched hand.

Then the film began, shown against the backdrop of a large white piece of cloth, the texture of the reed hut showing through it.

I can see why she offered extra food, Ronan told Murel after the film started. *This is so lame! It's nothing but a recruitment ad for the Corps.*

I know. Pele says they've shown one every other day since the Piaf *arrived. Bunyon doesn't always offer extra food. That seems to be for our benefit.*

Yeah, but I didn't get much, did you?

A couple of pieces. Why did she bother with the come-on, do you think?

Because we're new, I guess.

Soldiers marched, singing loud songs whose lyrics were lost in the voice-over of the narrator extolling the brilliant training and physical perfection that those who joined the Corps would achieve. Shots of them eating delicious-looking food and enjoying recreational facilities came next. Then all the thrilling occupational opportunities. Pilot, engineer, communications expert . . .

Hey, let's sign up to be one of those, Ro said. *Then we could contact Marmie's friends.*

Uh, I think they'd catch on, since they brought us from the station.

Probably.

She told him about the baths and what she had discussed with Pele and her family. *I don't trust that Kai, though.*

She's not taking this well, that's for sure, Ro agreed. *But she knows we're friends of Ke-ola's and trying to help her people, so I can't see why she'd mess with us.*

Me either, Murel agreed. *But I don't trust her, all the same.*

8

The next day they were roused by the shriek of the whistle, making them jump not only from the thin mats on the floor of their hut but almost out of their skins as well.

Rory pushed ahead of the others, whispering to Ronan as he passed him. 'I have to go first if we're going to make this believable.'

There was no breakfast and nobody expected any. One meal a day, in the evening, met the company's self-imposed obligation to care for the useless offspring of the Gwinnet prison inmates. If they wanted more to eat, there was always the opportunity to enlist offered in last night's film. Even those too young to enlist could sometimes find jobs working for the soldiers at the adjoining Corps installation. Pele was vague about what this work might involve except that older girls were sometimes used as laundresses.

As Pele had told them, a portion of shallows just offshore was roped off and strung with nets, three of them demarcating a small pool, a fourth stretched overhead. This, Bunyon had told them, was to keep the sea monsters from reaching across the net to grab the bathers, but Pele said she didn't think there were any sea monsters and that it was actually to keep the kids from jumping the net and trying to escape.

Some of the kids already in the water were apparently washing their clothes and themselves at the same time, as they were still wearing their tunics. Others went bare, vigorously splashing each other and soaping themselves. On a piece of driftwood on the beach, an older kid sat shearing the head of a smaller one, whose hair seemed to have grown out beyond the regulation stubble. Hard to tell the gender of either kid, Murel thought, though the older one's corded arms seemed masculine. None of the bathers appeared older than Huy, and none of the girls had developed noticeable breasts yet. Murel thought it was odd that everyone was so young.

Lieutenant Bunyon and Captain Keester strolled along behind the new kids, herding them toward the barber.

Did you see the moony looks on their faces when they're talking? Ronan asked. *Those two are mating. I'd bet the first catch of the day on it.*

They heard hurried footsteps approaching from the camp, and then a girl said, 'The vaccinations for the newcomers, Doctor.' Turning, they saw that she was in Corps uniform.

Rory, meanwhile, had reached the barber, and with uncharacteristic meekness submitted his head to the shears. His wild dark curls fell onto the sand. Through its rain across his face, he shot them a look Murel hoped the camp officers would fail to notice.

At a sharp nod from the doctor, the soldier girl marched forward and shoved a small roll of flimsy cloth into Rory's hands, then did an about-face and handed a similar roll to each of the other children, including the twins.

Ah, the fetching Camp Neverland uniform, Ronan said.

Murel started to shake it out.

'As I mentioned during indoctrination,' Lieutenant Bunyon said, taking her eyes away from Captain Keester long enough to lecture the new kids, 'the company, recognizing that you children were rescued from a variety of circumstances and climatic conditions, has thoughtfully provided these simple, easy-to-wear, and easy-to-care-for garments. They'll be much more comfortable than those hot ship

109

suits some of you are wearing. You can put them on once you've bathed.'

Rory laid his new uniform on the ground beside those of the other kids and jumped into the water, wading out a ways, then dog-paddling for a while before bringing his arms together in front of him in a surface dive.

Pele and her relatives ran in the water. Meanwhile Rory and the other kids from the space station lined up for the barber. He was very quick, and one by one they left their dark hair on the beach, tossed both old and new garments aside, and waded into the water.

Pele shot Murel and Ronan a look, and Kai's glance followed. As soon as Pele saw that Kai was watching, she pretended to be splashing her other brothers and sisters and washing vigorously.

Pele seemed to take it for granted that the twins would be able to rescue everyone, as they'd helped do on Halau. Some of the others, Murel felt sure, were thinking that if she and Ronan were prisoners themselves, they were in no position to rescue anybody. Kai was no longer openly hostile, but her hooded eyes seemed to Murel to say, 'Well, hero twins, not so clever now, are you? Got us off Halau so we could come to this dump and our families could go to prison.' Or worse, 'I wonder what they'll do with you here when you turn into seals like you did in the underground canals.'

Rory had told them he felt sure his grandmother, the shape-shifter-obsessed Dr Maria Mabo, had something to do with the families being transported from *Versailles Station*.

The thought that Dr Mabo might be involved made Murel shudder. Dr Mabo had lured Ronan into a situation where he'd been forced to change, and she knew about her as well. The doctor's fondest wish seemed to be to discover what made them and other shape shifters, like the Honus, transform. Neither Murel nor Ronan had any doubt that their former teacher would take them apart piece by piece in an effort to find the secret of their transformation.

But Dr Mabo had fled *Versailles Station* ahead of Marmie's security. As far as the twins knew, she was still lying low. If she was anywhere near here, it was probably as a prisoner.

'Ow!' Ronan cried, and before Murel could turn back to see what had made him holler, she felt the sting in her hip. Lieutenant Bunyon grabbed her shoulder so she didn't jerk away, but the doctor was already withdrawing the gun before she knew what was happening.

By then Ronan was sitting at the feet of the

barber and having his head shaved. Then it was her turn.

Come on, Mur, her brother urged as, bald-headed, he turned toward the water. She hung back, unexpectedly and totally irrationally unwilling to give up her hair and hating to be pushed into it. She didn't know why she felt that way. Her dark brown hair was no different from that of most of the people she knew at home, and she wore it cut just below her ears, but it was hers. She hardly recognized Ro now without his, and suddenly felt like she was losing who she was. She had given up being home, where she was loved, given up freedom, and now her hair? It was too much.

No! You look funny, she said, balking.

No, you look funny. I look like everybody else. We need to blend in if we're going to find a way out to help Marmie and the others.

As they'd planned the night before, Rory waded out of the water and dragged Ronan, still in his dry suit, into it. Rory yelled and whooped like he intended to drown Ronan, though Murel was sure he was only horsing around. Since they'd arrived together and had apparently been friends the night before, they hoped it would look like that to the camp officials too. They also hoped the camp officials would not see fit to intervene.

Rory grabbed Ronan around the neck and pulled him headfirst under the water. Ronan didn't seem to be struggling too much, and he wasn't calling for help.

'Come on, kid, you're my last for the day,' the barber said to Murel in a squeaky voice that couldn't decide if it was grown-up or not. He beckoned to her impatiently.

Cringing, Murel squatted at his feet, carefully keeping the weight off her punctured hip. The shears buzzed over her scalp, which at first felt cooler as the weight of her hair lifted and dropped to her shoulders and the ground. The truth was, the dry suit *was* hot, and perspiration made the falling hair stick itchily to her face and neck. The tunic uniforms would be much cooler to wear, and the water looked so refreshing.

The barber tapped her on the shoulder and pointed to the water. She rose reluctantly to her feet and took two slow steps toward the beach.

Two wet, dark-skinned Kanaka kids who appeared quite a bit younger than she ran out of the water and dragged her into it, dry suit and all. They were very strong, despite their size, and she couldn't pull away from them. But this was Pele's plan, and the jeering laughs didn't match the conspiratorial looks in their eyes when they deliberately met hers.

Where were Ronan and Rory? She couldn't see either of them now.

Ro?

To her relief, he responded immediately.

It's okay, sis. I'm clear and so far none of the advertised sea monsters have showed up, save yours truly. Rory helped me out of my dry suit so I could change on the other side of the net. He'll lift the net so you can get under without being seen while you're changing. It's open water out here, warm, but good and deep.

Good, well, here goes nothing. I hope there's enough of Ke-ola's kinfolk to keep the other kids from seeing me change. Except for Kai, they're all awfully little.

You'll be grand, sis, sure you will, Ro told her, sounding just like Da.

As the two Kanaka kids dragged Murel into the water, three more jumped on top of her as if trying to drown her, but they provided cover as her face changed and her hands became flippers, bound awkwardly by the confines of her dry suit. They swam as well as they walked. Murel found that odd, since Halau's water supply was underground and the Kanakas had gone there mostly to take shelter from the meteor showers. If the sea turtle people, Ke-ola's people, went down there to visit the Honus, and the shark people visited their

Mano'aumakuas in the subterranean lake, then perhaps that was where they also became so well accustomed to the water. There was an awful lot yet to learn about them.

Before Murel swam under the net, two of her 'attackers' peeled her dry suit over her flippers, freeing her body. Murel had explained the need for this to Pele during their talk. The little hands were quick and gentle, as they would have been with their Honus or Manos. They seemed to have even more of an affinity for her sea-creature self than they did for her as a fellow human, and to easily anticipate where she'd have difficulty with a sleeve or extricating a flipper. Since they had some interspecies communication with their seagoing aumakuas, as they called their clan's totem animals, it seemed to impart some general telepathic ability, or at least empathy, that extended to her and Ronan. You could take the kids out of the sea, but not the sea out of the kids, so to speak. Even after generations of separation from their original homeland, they were still attuned to it and its inhabitants.

They probably would have figured out what she needed even if they hadn't planned it all ahead of time, because it wouldn't be a common occurrence to see a seal struggling with human clothing.

Tiny hands stuffed her suit back into its pouch on her back, and with a final pat, the youngsters withdrew far enough to give her freedom of motion.

Rory suddenly appeared in front her and lifted the hem of a weighted net. She wondered briefly what good it did to have a net the kids only had to lift in order to swim to freedom. But freedom to do what? How many child inmates could turn into seals and swim as far as she and Ronan could? Maybe the net was supposed to keep other creatures out.

Pushing that thought aside, she swam under and joined Ronan, who waited for her a little offshore. They swam out to sea, diving and leaping over each other, feeling free for the first time since they had left the alien ship.

Each of them caught a strange-looking flat fish from a school swimming past. Murel felt refreshed enough to think again. *We should swim around the island and explore what's there,* she told Ronan.

And we explain our absence how? her brother asked.

We don't. We can't do anybody any good cooped up in the children's camp. We'll keep free till we find a way to release everyone else.

Okay, but we should also swim back to the main prison and see if we can find a way inside it from the shoreline. If we can, then we might be able to get our people out that way, as well. Hmmm, I'll bet there are sewers that empty into the sea. He said it as if he liked the idea of swimming in sewers.

Sewers? she asked with distaste.

Yes, in the stories I read while we were at Marmie's, fortresses always had sewers prisoners could use to escape.

I just hope the people who built the prison didn't read the same stories, Murel said. *What I was thinking is that we might be able to swim over to the soldiers' encampment at night and sneak into their com shed and use their equipment to call for help.*

Oh, well, yeah, if they have anything there that will go offworld, Ronan said. *I doubt they'd keep their long-range equipment here. It'll be back at the prison where the admin people are.*

You don't know that. You just want to swim in the sewer. Hey, Sky didn't come over here with us. She looked around and started using her sonar to call.

I hope he didn't get trapped on the ship. Ronan started calling too, but although their sonar didn't pick up any otter-shaped creatures of any variety, it did warn of the approach of something large and threatening.

They began swimming for all they were worth, sounding for obstacles in their path and dodging or diving to evade them.

This is no good, Murel said. *We can keep from getting eaten but we still can't see what's on the island. I want to look around.*

Fine, you check the surface and I'll swim underwater and check for trouble.

We have to stay in close to shore if we're going to see anything, she said, so they swam in until they were just beyond an area where the shoreline dropped off steeply into much deeper waters. They soon discovered that the net strung to contain the bathing children followed the line of a ledge that ran most of the way around the island. At its widest point, the ledge extended about twenty feet from shore.

On the far side, the island ended abruptly in cliffs rising almost two hundred feet above the waves crashing against its rocky base, with a ledge receding into steep cliffs.

There's a nice waterfall, Murel said, indicating a plume of water spurting from the cliff.

Maybe it's from a sewer, Ronan suggested hopefully.

You and your sewers. Everything seems to be on the other side of the island. It doesn't look to me like there's anyplace sewers would drain from. *It's just runoff from a stream or rainfall probably. But look over there at those rocks. They look like a fine place to rest and keep out of sight while we decide what to do next.*

They swam to the rocks and stretched out on the sun-warmed stones. Ronan sighed and settled down to nap. His fur started to disappear, and Murel jumped into the tepid water again, splashing him. He sat up, looking cross. *Cut it out!*

You were changing, she said.

So what? Who's going to know?

In the distance they heard the roar of a motor. A small boat had zipped out from shore, a vee-shaped wake spreading behind it like a flock of wild geese in flight. *They're looking for us,* Murel said. *I hope Rory and the Kanakas don't get in trouble because we didn't come back.*

Me too, but maybe they won't even notice, Ronan replied. *One kid with a shaved head probably looks like another to them. Did you notice our welcoming committee didn't even call us by name? Pretty sloppy, I'd say, but it's like they don't much care who we are. I hope the little tiff with Kai didn't call attention to us in particular.*

I don't think it did. They didn't intervene or anything. We all just seem to be a bunch of brats who for some reason may have our uses as far as they're concerned. Which is a good thing. I mean, what if Dr Mabo were here, as Rory seemed afraid she might be? She'd be over here in a flash to collect us and vivisect us. She had a worrying thought then. *I suppose they might have*

119

counted us and realized that two were missing.

Maybe, but I'm not sure they'd care if they thought we'd drowned, Ronan said.

Murel flopped back up onto the nearest rock and stretched out to bask. The sun made her drowsy. *I wonder if there are other seals in this ocean,* she mused. *If not, we may have a hard time blending in with the local sea life.*

We can always hide underwater, Ronan said.

I wish we hadn't had to change right away. We could have found out more about the camp if we had stayed there for a while.

We'll go back and check it out later, Ronan said.

How's that?

If they haven't missed us, we can always just go back next bath day and put on those tunics and make like nothing happened. Even if we don't go back into the compound, we can talk to Rory and learn more about what's happening in the camp.

I hope we've done the right thing, Murel fretted. *I hope they don't punish him or Pele's family because of us.*

9

Zuzu cringed in the stinking shadows, her mottled brown and gray fur standing at attention. The rat glared at her through its little red eyes, and she glared at it, her ears flat, her short curl of tail jerking. This was not only a kill-or-be-killed situation, it was an eat-or-be-eaten situation. The rats here were almost as large as she was. Her personal dish full of tasty and nutritious kibble and her bowl of clear water, always kept full and fresh, were only dreams now. Her formerly fluffy clean fur was matted and almost too filthy to clean. She had lost her firm plumpness, as catching her food and avoiding capture took a great deal of energy. She ate snake, lizard, rat, and roach, and their blood and fluids were her only drink.

She did not lack prey, at least. She would have had her choice among them, except that some, like this large rat, appeared to have chosen *her* for prey. His fangs were yellow and broken. Hers were pearly and sharp.

He snarled and charged at her.

She had nowhere to go but up. She leapt straight into the air, and when the rat reached the spot where she had been, she landed on his back and snapped his neck with one well-placed bite.

Her *maman* had trained her properly in vermin eradication. Although the *Piaf* had not been plagued by vermin, she kept her skills honed in mock battle with favored crew members, who covered their appendages with padding when they sparred with her.

She dabbed at the rat with a paw to make sure it was really dead. It was a very large rat, more than she could eat. A fine, fat rat, fit for either a cat or a queen. Zuzu was not especially hungry at the moment, but the rat smelled delicious, far too good to waste. She looked down the dim prison corridor. It was a long, long way to where her best friend was imprisoned, and dragging this huge brute of a rat would be quite a task, but perhaps Adrienne would be more sensible today.

Taking her kill's scruff firmly between her teeth as if he were a kitten, she dragged his carcass over the streaked and smelly plascrete floor, keeping to the shadows as much as she could while staying out of reach of anyone in the cells who might steal her prey or grab at her.

But if anyone saw her, they gave no indication. Her coloring allowed her to disappear into the walls and floor. If anyone saw her darting past, they might mistake her for another rat. No one was looking for a ship's cat in a prison, so nobody saw her. The guards stayed on the other side of the barred gates at each end of each corridor and often slept or played games. Sometimes they took a prisoner out there to play with, as she might play with a toy mouse.

Adrienne's cell was at the end of this corridor, so Zuzu would not have to haul her rat through one of the guard stations. It was heavy work nonetheless. The rat hung down so far beneath her she had trouble getting two opposing paws on the floor at the same time and had to waddle, propelling herself and her prey forward with her left forepaw and hind paw, then her right, while keeping alert for other rats or the guards.

At last she caught her friend's scent and dragged the prey through the bars separating them. Adrienne was sleeping. Zuzu laid her prize on the floor where her friend could hardly miss it, then hopped onto her chest, kneading the fabric of the ugly prison cover-all and peering into Adrienne's partly open mouth. Adrienne opened her eyes and let out a little yelp. Before Zuzu found her, Adrienne had been awakened by other creatures, not so friendly or familiar. Now, however, she smiled and reached up to touch Zuzu's coat. As soon as she did that, Zuzu jumped to the floor and stood by the rat, purring encouragingly.

Take it, she said silently to her friend, who had grown thin and pale since her imprisonment.

'Oh, *merde!*' Adrienne exclaimed, shoving the rat away with her bare foot. Zuzu calmly nudged it back at her.

Do be sensible and eat something, Zuzu tried to tell her. *You need to keep up your strength. I even killed it for you this time, though as I've repeatedly tried to tell you, you should start hunting for yourself. You're a bit slow, but you do have an advantage over them with your size. They're bigger than I am, but I manage, so you can too, if you'll only try.*

Adrienne did not touch the food but did lean over to stroke Zuzu's back. Before the cat could get a good purr rumbling, however, doors clanged open down the corridor and a pair of husky guards marched down it. The normal hum of activity in the cells quieted, making the guards' footsteps sound unnaturally loud.

Zuzu zipped beneath Adrienne's cot and shrank as small as she could in the most shadowy corner.

Just in time. The guards' heavy boots stopped outside Adrienne's cell and a scratchy female voice said, 'Okay, Robineau, let's go.'

Adrienne was frightened. Zuzu could smell it. She had seen other crew members returned to their cells looking as if they'd been caught in the middle of a dogfight. But Adrienne was angry, as well. If she had been a cat, her fur would have been ridged along her arched back and she'd have spit at the guards. It was all Zuzu could do to keep from hissing, but she kept as still as she did when hunting. The cell door opened and Adrienne stood. 'Where are you taking me?'

'To tea with the commandant, of course,' one woman sneered. 'He's ever so interested to hear all about your former career.'

'Don't worry, honey,' the other woman said. 'You're on the small side but sturdy looking. And everyone's been told not to leave any marks – just in case.'

'Dammit, Griz, you didn't have to tell her that. You and your compassionate nature!' The first guard snorted.

'I know. I know. 'Course, most electrical conversation starters don't leave marks to speak of. At least nothing that can be detected without an autopsy.'

Zuzu wanted to leap from her hiding place and claw their eyes out, but she knew the prison well enough now to know she was outnumbered. Best to keep still, stay low, and follow. Possibly there would be something she could do to help if she was close enough. But not too close. These guards were not cat lovers, she just knew it.

Shortly after Zuzu had slipped into the prison on Dr Mabo's heels, she had discovered a secret about it, about where the rats and other vermin came from and why the prison cells were so miserably hot. In spite of the solid look of the tough plascrete and metal bars – all of which gave the impression that the prison had stood there stinking for many years, rising out of the native stone – it was assembled from modular units. This floor contained four ranks of cells, two ranks each flanking the central corridors, which were secured with bars at either end. There were similar floors above and below this one. But where the stony-looking covering had been pried away by rats or eroded by wear and the horrible strong-smelling chemicals used by more manageable prisoners to clean the place, a small cat could also enter and, with a little maneuvering, run in the space behind the abutting cell modules, or slink along the top of the modules on each floor. There was no room for the smallest human, but for a rat-fed cat there was adequate space to follow her human's tormentors.

As Adrienne was led away, the other prisoners either jeered or called what encouragement they could, but their attention was diverted from the cell, which suited Zuzu. She squeezed through the bars and inched her way beneath the bars until she came to the nearest rat hole, which gave her access to the space between the floors of Adrienne's block and the ceilings of the block below. The thumping footsteps of the guards and Adrienne's lighter ones vibrated the underside of the corridor above her, and she followed them easily. The trick would be finding another opening farther along, so she could come out again.

Zuzu followed until she heard one of the guards order Adrienne into a room and then heard a door slamming. She crept to a spot right below the center of that room and crouched, waiting, but nothing happened. Her tight little curl of a tail twitched – not with impatience, because she was a supremely patient hunter and stalker, but from anxiety for Adrienne.

After a few moments she sat up on her

haunches and looked around. On her journey from Adrienne's cell, the cat had kept a lookout for light shining in from more rat holes. There were three, but she didn't know exactly where the holes were on this side of the bars. Rotating her ears to keep alert for any sound indicating that Adrienne was under interrogation or simply being chatted up, Zuzu cautiously strolled over to the gap between offices and looked down the length of the modules on her side, searching for more crude rat-shaped windows on the outer world.

Under the next room she heard voices – one familiar and beloved, one hateful and vicious. Her fur bristled at the sound of it, though the vicious voice was speaking so softly she could not make out the words. Madame Marmion, the other speaker, spoke calmly, but the cat sensed the tension underneath. 'I do not see what is to be gained by tormenting my crew, Major. We have no secrets and we have done nothing wrong. You cannot keep us here forever, and once we are free, you will be held responsible for any harm that befalls us.'

'Yes, but some of you will be just as dead, or inconvenienced by the absence of certain bodily parts or functions,' the man said. 'You overestimate your importance in the galactic scheme of things, Madame. You have more influential enemies than you realize.'

'And more friends, I trust, than you can fit into this prison.'

'Your first mate will be paying for your arrogance in a moment. I trust your ringside seat here allowed you to see and hear everything that happened there when the communications officer was questioned.'

Madame said nothing, but Zuzu sensed her pain and fear. Ears alert, she prowled her way under two more chambers, at last spotting another small hole leading into the corridor. Heading for it, she heard loud voices.

Zuzu peeked out of the hole but could see nothing. The voices were coming from a corridor perpendicular to the one she occupied, around a bend. She could smell something odd, though, something not rat, not human, yet familiar.

Squeezing through the hole, she crept down the vacant corridor, keeping close to the wall. To her relief, she passed a low grid improperly attached to the wall. It no doubt covered a duct, and it would do for a cat's bolt-hole if the need arose. She brushed past it, ears pricked.

'There it goes! Zap it! Zap it!' someone cried.

A sizzle like a laser blast sounded from farther inside the administration area. 'Damn, missed!' the apparent shooter exclaimed.

'What the hell was that?'

Claws scrabbled down the corridor.

'Biggest damn rat I ever saw. Come on, let's get it!'

Far down the corridor behind Zuzu, the door to Madame's chamber slammed open and shut. She hugged the wall. The man who had spoken to Madame stalked forward. 'What the frag is going on out there?' he demanded.

'Sorry, sir. Nagy shot at a rat.'

Madame's captor strode past her so closely he almost kicked her. She was very glad she did not have the usual sort of long loose tail for him to step on.

He marched up to the other men, and very quietly, very slowly, the creature began moving toward her again.

She heard its slightly labored breath and smelled a strong odor of fish.

A friend who is not an otter and not a seal!

Zuzu clearly heard its thoughts, and it didn't feel rat-shaped. Nevertheless, she hissed in warning. The not-rat ignored her, poking a long brown nose around the corner.

Zuzu raised a paw to stripe the nose, should it be so impertinent as to venture within her personal space, but before she could attack, the rest of the creature followed the nose, bending its brown self around the corner against the wall's dark molding and bowling her over in its joy to see her.

Cat? It was Sky, the otter. She had been too preoccupied to recognize him by his fish-breath, but now his other quite strong *parfum* was also in overpowering evidence. Much to her relief, he rolled off her.

Otter! she replied. *There is not a moment to waste,* mon ami. *We must conceal ourselves.* Allez.

She bolted back to the loose grid and squeezed through it, aided by the weight of the otter pushing behind her. With a whip of his long flat tail, he pulled the last of himself in behind her, while outside, Madame's tormentor and his evil minions stomped down the corridor, searching for their prey.

'What was it?' the officer demanded.

'Biggest rat I've ever seen, sir. The warden could have mounted the thing's head on his wall for a trophy.'

'What was it doing here?' the officer asked. 'Rats are not authorized in this section of the building. The warden doesn't mind them in the cell blocks – says it adds to the ambience – but they don't belong here. Unsanitary. Catch it.'

'Be glad to, but where'd the damn thing go?' guard number one said.

'It disappeared,' number two replied, not

without admiration. 'They do that, you know. Rats are smart, and that huge sucker had to be the king of all rats.'

'Didn't look like a rat to me,' number three insisted.

'Find it and exterminate it, and all of its little rat friends who can't stay where they belong,' the officer said. 'And be quiet about it. I have prisoners to interrogate.'

'Yes, sir.'

I know you, cat, the otter told Zuzu. *You are the space cat.*

Mais oui, *I am Zuzu, advisor to the first mate of the* Piaf. *And you also are known to me, although as yet we have not made the formal acquaintance.*

I am the sky otter who dens with the river seal twins. We are friends. Friends means relatives who are not otters. You are not an otter but you are pretty and clever. Otters notice these things.

Zuzu remembered the otter well. For a creature who was not feline, he had a certain *je ne sais quoi*. It would be good to have a four-legged ally with friends who were the allies of her friends.

Her welcoming purr was interrupted by a piercing scream.

Adrienne! she cried, recognizing her human's voice. It did not sound like pain so much as rage, but she felt that that would soon be altered.

Sharks? Sky asked anxiously.

Worse! Zuzu told him. Allez, allez, *sky otter. My Adrienne is about to be tortured.* But as she tried to run forward, she found that she and the otter were confined within a rectangular tube just big enough for each of them to pass through singly. *Alors! We find ourselves in the conduit for the air,* she told her companion. *This affords us less freedom of movement than I would wish, and is somewhat disorienting, but my sense of direction is very keen, and aboard the* Piaf, *I have often traveled in narrow places without losing my composure. The chamber de torture lies this way.*

What is torture? Sky asked, his long body rippling along behind hers.

When people claw and rend other people whose claws are sheathed so they cannot fight back. I saw Monsieur Steve when he had been tortured. He looked like a rat a moment before I am done with it, but they did not finish him with a quick bite to the neck.

Not sharks, then, Sky said, sounding relieved. *Sharks have hundreds of sharp teeth. They kill quick.*

They found the grid covering the opening of the vent into the chamber.

Within the room, they saw the bound feet of

Adrienne being circled by the deliberately slow and taunting footsteps of the interrogation officer. The cruel voice droned on and on, saying dreadful things. The essence of the tormentor's message was that Adrienne was a bad cat who peed upon upholstery and produced hair balls in inconvenient places, that nobody liked her and she deserved punishment from which she could only redeem herself by cooperating with her captors. Zuzu heard nothing from Adrienne but assumed her poor *amie* was capable of hearing or the voice would not continue droning.

That human is no friend, Sky observed.

The feline had no inclination to discuss the obvious. *We must act quickly, otter. But how to make them leave her alone? You saw how they pursued and threatened you, who had done them no harm. They have no respect for those with the correct number of legs. We must send them a message, but they do not speak our language.*

Otters send messages.

But how? How will you make them understand it? Make them leave?

They will not understand it because they are not otters and do not know the scent signs. But they will leave. He shook his tail and ripples ran down his sleek body as he expelled what was left in his digestive system.

The smell was overpowering in the enclosed space. From some central place within the system a fan enhanced the otter's odiferous efforts. Zuzu set to work augmenting the otterly offerings with her own.

The man's voice broke off. He sniffed, he gagged, he coughed, then the door slammed again and he bellowed down the hallway, calling for his underlings, demanding to know what stank so badly.

Zuzu feared that such bad men would lack the sensitivity to have their evil work disrupted by little more than noisome piles of poo, but as the man stomped into the hall, he called back to Adrienne. 'Sit there and choke on the stench, bitch. I'll deal with you later.'

Otter, you are a creature of great resourcefulness. Never did I know that otter excrement smelled bad enough to drive away evildoers.

It isn't just the scat, cat. Otters use scent for messages. I sent the man a very angry message and told him to stop hurting your friend. I do not think he understands otter scent messages, but he seems to have understood that one.

10

When Yana's team passed the engine room, they shed a member, Rick, who entered the room as if reporting for his shift, going straight to the duty station as they had planned and saluting the man already there. That man returned the salute, made an about-face, and headed gratefully for the crew's quarters. There would not be a lot going on in the engine room while the ship was docked, and they were counting on the crew being bored and somewhat slack.

After Rick left, the team had five minutes to reach the bridge. Yana had not been on a troop ship for more than a decade, but she was relieved to find that this was a vintage model that dated back to her days in the Corps. Same dingy beige paint, same sharp corners and textured metal corridors, same gridded stairs.

She would have expected to feel right at home here, on the same sort of vessel where she had spent much of her career, but despite the familiarity, she found it oppressive and confining. Her entire cabin on Petaybee would have fit in a small section of the ship's main corridor, but she'd grown used to windows and a door she could walk through to the outdoors.

Or maybe it just had to do with the fact that she was no longer on a ship full of comrades. Except for the four people with whom she'd boarded, she was surrounded by enemies. In her experience, that tended to make one feel confined.

Crew members had passed them without a second look so far, but she knew it was just a matter of time before someone who was looking for distraction from routine duties would realize they were not the people their name tags claimed them to be.

Pet Chan marched into the security control center, where cameras, monitors, and extra weapons were kept.

The bridge was in sight when Raj Norman took his planned detour and disappeared through a starboard hatch. This would be where the backup generators for the bridge were located.

Yana and Johnny stopped and positioned

themselves on either side of the entrance to the bridge as if standing sentry. With a slight crackle and a loud hum, the lights went out. A series of blips preceded someone on the bridge saying, 'Captain, the computers are down.'

It would take a few moments before they felt the temperature dropping. Meanwhile, they would have other problems.

With intercoms, computers, and lights down, as well as backup generators, Yana's team was betting it would take some time for the various sections to communicate with the bridge. The crew would be equipped with glows and battery-powered torches, and presumably had enough survival clothing to weather the storm. Their air supply was warm enough and should be sufficient for their needs. The team could not tamper with the ship's oxygen mixture without suiting up in full space kit, which would have aroused too much comment before they could put their plan into action. Besides, none of them wanted to kill anyone – at least, Yana thought grimly, it hadn't yet come to that – but they did need to distract the enemy crew and cause as many to leave the ship as possible.

The darkness would make finding the root of the malfunctions more difficult for the crew, and would also help conceal the hopeful saboteurs.

For further distraction, hoping to drag the command staff from the bridge, they relied on another old standby.

'Fire!' The bellow was Raj Norman's, with just the right degree of panic in it, enough to bring everyone running to where he had set a dramatic but not-too-harmful blaze.

People poured past Yana and Johnny into the corridor, their glows showing them to be the captain, first mate, navigator, and com officer. Good. That should be everybody. With the ship docked, there was no reason for anyone to remain on the bridge, though under normal circumstances protocol dictated that they do so.

Yana and Johnny slipped inside. Cursing came from down the hall as the officers and crew fought with the fire. Yana hoped Raj hadn't done too good a job of setting it. A shipboard fire was always dangerous, and if it got out of hand, even a little, it could damage something vital. They needed the ship operational when they were ready for it to be.

The crackling of flames was quickly drowned out by coughing, swearing, and one male voice saying, 'Too bad we had to put it out. It's starting to get bloody cold in here. What the frag is taking Engineering so long, anyway?'

'Sorry, Lieutenant, there was this fire . . .' a reedy voice, not without sarcasm, replied.

'And now there's not!' the officer bellowed. Uh-oh, one of those, Yana thought. At least his lousy disposition made him easy to hear from a distance.

She sat down at the comoff station, which she and Johnny had not rearranged, and recorded and directed several messages to be sent automatically at regular intervals once the ship was outside Petaybee's magnetic field. Such automatic messages were not something a com officer would ordinarily detect, since security software concentrated on incoming messages or possible tracking devices but not actual outgoing communications of a routine nature.

With that precaution in place, she joined Johnny under the consoles, where he was busily rearranging critical connections, swapping chips, disrupting circuits, wreaking selective and highly specific damage within the delicate web of wires. From the shadows cast on Johnny's face by her torch and his own, it seemed he was entangled, head first, in the trap of a giant arachnid.

Although they aimed to cause as much chaos as possible, Yana had a particular goal in mind. Dating from the days when Petaybee was the property of the company, equipment had been installed at Space Base to facilitate takeoffs from the usually frozen surface. Ships docked on Petaybee in specific places. The three docking bays contained sockets into which, in winter, the ships could insert their sterns and keep their hulls free of ice, thanks to built-in radiant thermal units. This arrangement was not unique to Petaybee. The company controlled many planetary properties with harsh and frigid conditions, and their installations on all of them contained the same sockets – nicknamed 'bun warmers' – so company ships and others with reasons to take off and land there were equipped with special controls to activate the coupling. The bun warmer's controls on company ships were linked both to the bridge and to engineering.

Locating the underside of the bridge-control panel, Yana disengaged the coupling, then pocketed the chip critical to its operation, grinning evilly to herself. This was the part of the plan that should empty the ship of personnel so her team could hijack it.

Rick and Pet were also busy making life difficult for the ship's crew. Raj's plan was to leave the firefighters to it while he merrily raided the ship's armory, diminishing its number of incendiary devices and purloining much of the ammunition. That should further slow the crew's undoing the damage the team was wreaking on their vessel without announcing the presence of intruders.

Pet now quietly reconnected the main corridor's security cameras and microphones. Without lights, the cameras picked up only the disembodied glows moving eerily if swiftly down the corridor in the direction of Engineering. Their havoc wreaked, Johnny, Pet, Raj, and Yana ran down the corridor to hide in plain sight amidst the crowd outside Engineering.

The crowd, including the officers, commented on the suddenness of the power outage, the lack of lights, the lack of heat and what to do about it, and cursed Petaybee roundly for its storm, its winter, and its general lack of hospitality. Funny how, although most of the troops had lived a good part of their lives in space, many of them born on stations or ships, there was still that atavistic part of human nature left over from long-ago Terra that associated bad storms with loss of power, or at least lost amenities such as heat and lights. In space, the ship was a biosphere, totally self-contained. When docked, except for the bun warmers, the same was also true. An earthquake might topple or swallow the ship, a flood could cover it, but blizzards normally would have no effect on internal functions. With all of them distracting one another while the captain attempted to deploy specific people to fix specific problems, no one was addressing the problem the saboteurs wanted them to worry about.

Yana gave a huff of impatience and saluted the captain, her borrowed uniform and correct military demeanor her best disguise. It was a bit risky but they could hardly wait for the crew to discover the larger problem for themselves. In the blizzard raging outside, the hull would be iced over in a few minutes and it would be impossible to leave the ship, much less the planet. 'Sir, the hull is freezing.'

'Engineer, get those generators back online. Our connection with the bun warmer must have been broken when the power went down. Meanwhile, all personnel not essential to reestablishing interior function suit up for the outdoors and bring all handheld torches and thermal devices you can find to thaw the hull.'

Troops ran in all directions, and Yana ran toward the air lock with them. This was the part of the plan where she was to return to Petaybee, while Johnny, Rick, Pet, and Raj took the ship and the few remaining crew members into space. For a hastily devised plan, it wasn't bad. It should work.

We have a couple of days until they bathe again, Murel said finally. *So we should plan what to do until then.*

After such a long stretch of doing nothing while in the brig aboard the ship, she felt anxious to get started with the heroic, rescuing part of their mission. But they needed to understand where they were and what went on here before they blundered back onto shore.

We could try infiltrating the soldiers' camp, Ronan suggested. *One bald kid probably looks pretty much like another to them, and we could suss out the com situation.*

Yes, but if we get caught doing that, it's all over. Besides, that camp is pretty remote and there doesn't seem to be a proper docking bay for a full-sized ship. Anyway, I didn't spot one from the air. I'll bet the long-distance relay equipment is back on the mainland. Instead of hanging out here until the next bath day, let's see how far it is from here to the mainland and if we can swim there and back before we try to meet Rory again. It didn't take all that long to get here by flitter, but it's probably farther than the average human can swim safely or it'd be no good for isolating the kids, would it?

144

Odd, when you think about it, she added. *Why are they keeping the kids so far from the parents? If they mean to use families as leverage to get information from prisoners, you'd think they'd want their hostages handy, wouldn't you? I don't think we* are *meant to be hostages, actually. I think they've got some other purpose, but I'm beached if I know what it is.*

We'll know more once we talk to Rory again, Ronan said, poising on the ledge and leaning forward, nose down and ready to dive. *For now, last one in is shark bait!*

Except for being warmer, the sea here was much like Petaybee's; it was especially similar to the part near Petaybee's new volcano. Only a few leagues from their rock the smell of sulfur grew strong as the sea floor began spiking black smokers, the chimneys made from the hardened mineral content of the subterranean gases escaping through the crust. The creatures dwelling there paid them no more mind than did the giant white clams and crabs on Petaybee. Bouquets of red and white tube worms blossomed on the outer slopes of some of them and lined crevasses in the floor. They evaded the worst of the superheated, acidic waters by swimming close to the surface, working their sonar, alert for sharks, whales, other seals, or schools of tasty fish.

There were a lot of fish, but they detected no other marine mammals whatsoever, much less sea monsters.

That's a bit odd, don't you think? Ronan said.

Not really, Murel replied. *Remember that everything – well, almost everything – that came to Petaybee was stocked there by the company. Maybe they didn't see any reason to put seals here, or whales or the other species.*

There goes our clever disguise.

Maybe, or *it could be everything migrates away from here about now, or there's mating going on elsewhere, or any number of reasons we don't know about.* Murel was actually relieved that they hadn't had to explain themselves to the resident sea creatures yet. That was always assuming the creatures shared thought patterns in similar language – she had read somewhere that long ago, on Terra, when the world had grown up of its own accord, the animals of the seas were thought to speak languages as varied as the peoples on the land. But she thought that if the company had stocked all of its client worlds, surely all of the creatures would speak a version of Standard, similar to the universal human tongue. She wondered if they'd think she and Ro spoke it with a Petaybean accent, or dialect. Even if they could understand each other, that didn't mean that the animals here, including seals, would be friendly. Most species were at least somewhat territorial, and families of seals would not necessarily welcome interlopers such as themselves.

Then there were the leopard seals. They didn't have them on the northern pole of Petaybee, but the southern pole did, and she had heard tales of how they ate other seals and anything else, including humans sometimes. What had the company been thinking to let them on Petaybee? Da would say everything had a place and a purpose, but she couldn't think of any reason for such nasty animals except maybe for parka covers.

They continued to swim across the water from the island in the direction of the mainland, hoping their headings would fetch them up there. The water was far warmer than they were used to and made them feel sluggish.

There's land around here somewhere, Ronan said, sounding exasperated. *We know that much, but I could use a nice little rocky island to sun on for a bit now. This is farther than I thought.*

It probably won't seem so long once we know our way, Murel answered.

Their sonar picked up the landmass long before they could see it across the heaving hillocks of the sea. On the whole, the water was reasonably calm. What swell there was they could easily circumvent most of the time by swimming beneath the surface, where the eating was better anyway. Also, staying underwater gave them the opportunity to study the topography of the sea bottom in order to identify reference points that would make finding their way back and forth less chancy.

There was actually a range of underwater mountains a couple of miles offshore, and a corresponding deep valley or trough. They dove down the far side of a mountain to suss it out.

Through the darkness and the murk they saw ghostly pale, waving tendrils with what looked like leaves on the ends of very long stems. As they drew nearer, they could see that the stalks grew from beds of shorter stalks, like grass, all of it waving, rising out of the deep ocean to meet them, seeming to reach for them.

Seeming nothing! Before they had quite seen enough to be able to count the number of blades in each cluster or how many clusters there were, they were staring into huge bulging eyes.

Hello, Ronan greeted them. *What are you called? We're selkies, seals right at the moment, as you see, but often human beings. We're from a planet called Petaybee and we don't have anyone like you there. What are you?*

Hungry. The thought was not in any language they knew but the sentiment was perfectly clear. The leaf ends of the long tentacles were close enough now for them to see the suckers on them, and the barbs in the suckers. Four pairs of huge unblinking eyes grew even more huge as the creatures rose up.

Okay, Murel said to Ronan, *we've seen that there are large animals. You've introduced us properly and said hello. Now let's get out of here, shall we?*

Why should they attack us when there are all of these lovely fish around? Ronan asked, but it was a rhetorical question, as he had already turned his nose toward the surface.

Before she could reply, she saw a whiplike movement from the corner of her eye, and a tentacle lashed out and dragged Ronan backward. He screamed.

His captor's other tentacle was engaged in fending off its three companions, who seemed momentarily more interested in demanding that it share Ronan than in capturing Murel. Nevertheless, she shot toward the surface. She couldn't do Ro any good if she was in the same position as he was. Two of the creatures abandoned the one who had Ro and followed her at a distance, but when she was about halfway to the surface they fell back.

She broke through the water, caught her breath, and dived again, but Ronan and his captors were nowhere to be found. Frightened, she called to him, using her sonar. *Hold on, Ro, I'm coming!*

It's dragging me down, he replied at last, and through him she sensed the painful suckers that held him in the constricting grip of the large tentacle pulling him toward the thing's beak.

Can't you slip out somehow?

No. It's like being bitten by a school of sharp-toothed fish hanging on for dear life.

Bite it!

Can't reach . . .

Murel's sonar homed in on him and helped her evade the tentacles that were attempting to snag her flippers or head. One passed close to her nose and she snapped at it, tearing away a rubbery writhing chunk. It tasted like cat pee smelled, strong and full of ammonia.

Another tentacle had begun reaching for her, but when she bit the first one, the second one contracted as if with the pain, and the creature gave off a squeaky-feeling subvocalization. So it had a central nervous system of some kind. Good. She meant to hurt it until it turned her brother loose.

Suddenly the water around her grew even darker and she could no longer see the creature, though her sonar told her it was there and she paid very close attention to where its appendages – and its friends – were.

She had to reach Ro before the monster pulled him to a depth where seals could not survive.

Swimming through the opaque water, she dove nose first into Ro, who was being dragged toward the creature and the bottom at the same time.

She wished she were in human form and had hands and maybe a knife or a harpoon as well.

Ronan felt her coming and sent a warning, full of pain and fear: *Look out for the hooks. If you bite it, the barbs will sink into your mouth and it'll have you too.*

Using her sonar more precisely than she ever had before, she maneuvered around the tentacles, out of reach of the waving arms and away from Ro, caught the creature's fin in her mouth, then pulled her flippers forward and raked the body with her claws. Petaybean seals had long, strong, curved claws at the ends of their flippers to break through the ice on rivers or haul themselves onto icebergs. Hers came in handy for climbing higher onto the squidlike creature, giving her teeth another place to bite it as she worked her way toward the eyes, clawing and biting tracks and holes in the soft flesh as she went. Its eyes were at the front of this solid bodylike part, and she knew that its brain probably was too. One long tentacle was occupied with trying to feed Ro to the body. She just had to stay out of the way of the remaining tentacle and the arms and tear her way through to something vital or sensitive enough to make it release Ro and—

Mine! Ro's captor broadcast the distinctly possessive thought.

The club end of the tentacle of another squid lashed down at Murel, but she threw her weight sideways, still hanging on with flippers and mouth. The barbed and suckered appendage grazed her face on the side. Her fur provided some small amount of protection, but pain still shot through her cheek and into her eye socket and head. She rolled over and over with the squid's body in her grasp, while the long, barbed tentacle rolled too, a loop of it wrapping around her shoulders, its suckers latching onto her hide.

Mine! the second squid echoed as it unwound itself slightly. Murel felt Ronan's relief as he slipped from its slackened grasp. It flailed out to recapture him, the tentacle bobbing and weaving like a huge snake confused about where to strike, but he propelled himself upward and avoided the clubbed feeder tentacle, which instead connected with the other attacking squid.

Let go, sis, I'm free. Ro's thought-voice penetrated her concentration. *Let go and surface. It's diving!*

Can't. I'm caught, she said. Between the tentacle and alien body compressing her throat and the pressure of the dive, the breath she'd stored was being squeezed out of her. *Bite the one attacking me in the butt, Ro, but look out for other tentacles.*

Let go of her, you multiarmed freak! She heard Ro's challenge as if it came from far away. Another tentacle lashed out from somewhere but she was so weak she could no longer tell which of the two monsters it belonged to.

Soon she would not have enough breath to surface. Could seals drown? She felt light-headed already. For a moment longer she was dimly aware of Ro's thought-voice, and then her mind suddenly went as dark as the ink-stained water.

Floating on the surface, drifting on the sluggish tide, riding the crest of the swells and wallowing in the troughs without volition, the two battered seals washed slowly toward the shore. One had patches of fur ripped from his side, the other had a bare raw patch on the side of her face and angry-looking circular sores across her upper back. One of her claws was gone, while the male was missing a piece of a rear flipper.

Sis?

She opened one eye. The other was swollen shut. *Ro? I had the worst nightmare.*

Sorry, wish it was, but we're not out of it yet.

Something was dragging us down. I was about to pop for want of air and – ow, my face and back! I remember. The monsters.

Squid, I think, he said. *Like in* 20,000 Leagues Under the Sea, *remember? We watched it at Marmie's once. Then I read the book. Now we've been attacked by some. I must say I preferred both the vid and the book to the actual experience, but at least we're alive to make the comparison.*

I remember the squid, but how did we get away? You had to be as weak as I was.

Pretty much, yeah, though I didn't get choked like you did and I managed to bring my hind flipper up enough to keep the tentacle from crushing me before you made it let me go. It was the other squid attacking that freed us. Well, I did have to bite through the tentacle the second squid had wrapped around you, but it was busy fighting off the one that had had me, so it wasn't really paying attention. I think squid one thought squid two attacked it to take its prey – that would be me, and probably you for afters. When you attacked it and then the other squid nailed it too, it released its grip on me enough that I bit myself free. Those things taste like cat piss, did you notice?

Yeah, she agreed, and if she'd been in human form she would have made a face.

Then while they were slapping at each other, I got you loose and swam for it with you. The others had lost interest in us or were placing bets on who'd win the fight, I don't know, but nothing followed us to the surface.

She spotted something and rolled to one side. *I think you're wrong about that. Look.* Two bloated-looking bodies, one with scratch and bite marks along the length of it, the other with similar but not as severe marks, bobbed up a few feet away from where the twins floated. The arms and feeder tentacles drifted listlessly, washing to and fro with the roll of the waves.

Either squid can play possum or they're dead, Ro said. *Do you think we killed them, or did they kill each other?*

I don't think we made much of an impression. But maybe their struggles with each other wounded them, or maybe they tried to follow us too close to the surface. Other ones started to but turned back before they caught me the first time I surfaced. They're deep water creatures. Must be. If they live down in that abyss, they may not have been able to withstand the depressurization of lesser depths.

I wonder if they're really dead, he said, and started to swim toward them.

Ro, don't you dare! Murel told him.

He flipped in the water and came back up beside her. *Just teasin' you, lassie. I wasn't really going to.*

I'm in no shape to rescue your slippery butt this time, she told him, then added with a groan, *I hate to think what we're going to look like as humans. Everything hurts.*

I'm just glad shaving our heads didn't make us furless seals. If it wasn't for our fur, we'd have been hurt a lot worse. As it is, I hope losing this chunk out of my flipper doesn't make me walk funny.

We found where the large animals were hiding anyway, she said. *Maybe they ate everything else.*

Or maybe the company only imported these as a kind of living barrier – the prisoners might escape from the prison but not from the squid.

As if to confirm that last guess, they heard a boat motor and the water around them began thrashing, splashing over them counter to its natural heave and roll.

'Cap'n, would you look at that?' a man hollered across the waves. 'There's two that'll never dine on Gwinnet brisket again.'

'Musta got a piece of Clem Packer,' the

captain guessed in a more thoughtful tone. 'A guy who massacred everybody on a freighter and ate them when the nutrient bars ran out probably tasted pretty rank, and may have picked up some kinda poison from those dead bodies too.'

'Could be,' the crewman agreed. 'Wouldn't have killed a demon like Packer, but played hell with the sensitive innards of our underwater garbage disposals here. They're wildlife, y'know, and them things got delicate innards.'

'Yeah, well, I don't blame 'em. It made me sick just looking at the slimeball,' the captain said. Then he added, 'Speaking of wildlife, what are those?'

Before the wounded seal twins could dive, the bow of the utilitarian-looking boat sliced through the water, bearing down on them.

11

The ship's outer hatch had to be opened manually from the other side of the air lock. Normally it kept space out; now, when it opened, the blizzard rushed in, powdering the floor and topping the heavy winter gear of the people nearest the opening with a new coat of snow. Yana saw two crew members raise their faces skyward with expressions of wonder and anticipation. But this was no weather for even the greenest newcomer to the white stuff to learn about making snow angels or snowmen or note the difference between each flake and the next. The freezing wind that accompanied the snow caused everyone to cover their heads, faces, and necks with thermal balaclavas. Ears and noses could freeze to white brittle lumps in a matter of moments at this temperature.

The captain gave the command, and one by one the crew disappeared behind the howling white torrent.

Yana followed them, somewhere near the middle of the queue, as they left the ship to brave the blizzard with handheld torches, hand warmers, generators, and anything else that they could imagine might help free the hull of ice and keep it that way. She could have told them the generators wouldn't work in the cold, but of course she kept silent.

Keeping one mitten against the hull, she found a position between the ship and where the river should be, although she couldn't see it. She couldn't see anyone or anything, which was the bad part, but the good part was that none of them could see her either. So while everyone else focused on their own small sections of icy hull, she turned her back to the ship and, bent against the wind like a charging moose, walked deliberately forward. Unless the storm had spread since she and the others had entered the ship, it was still only a narrow band between the ship and a relatively calm walk back up the river.

Johnny, Rick, Pet, and Raj, none of whom were Petaybean enough to be damaged by a trip offplanet, stayed behind, using the ship's malfunctions to cover their movements. They would restore power and, once the elements that thawed the hull had done their job, take the ship into space, stranding the crew. Sinead should be dispatching a Petaybean welcoming committee, armed with the captured firearms of the soldiers in the longhouse to escort the crew to the longhouse as well. They would all be the guests of honor at the first-ever All Corps Latchkay, Yana thought with amusement. She sure hoped they'd like smoked salmon.

As she expected, within two dozen steps she was through the wind and the rest of the snow. Overhead, the ghostly green, pink, gold, blue, and red of the aurora played crack-the-whip across the sky above Kilcoole.

Her feet sank thigh-deep into the snow with every step, and footing on the river was treacherous. Ice lay beneath the new snow, which was too dry and powdery to pack well. Yana wished she could have brought snowshoes or skis, but that would have attracted undue attention, so she trudged forward, her hips and thighs aching with the effort of pulling each foot high out of the drift before setting it down ahead of the other.

She had made it halfway to Kilcoole when she heard the rumble of the ship's engines and the surprised voices exclaiming just a little louder than the rumble or the wind howling around them. She turned to see the ship rise into the air, piercing the storm, showering melting ice from its surface as it climbed toward the aurora.

As if the ship's ascent were a signal to the storm, it slackened. The wind blew off in another direction, and the snow sifted away to nothing, exposing a crowd of pointing and shouting crew members railing against the hijackers of their ship and the collusion of the planet they'd come to conquer.

Grinning beneath her balaclava, Yana watched them and took a step back. Her heavy boot plunged easily through the snow and downward. There was a slight resistance and a cracking sound where the ice should have been. She felt something give beneath her foot, and then a splash and a rushing sensation against her heavy clothing. Icy water seeped over the top of her boot, slid down her tucked-in waterproof snowsuit leg, and soaked her sock. The freezing water attacked her formerly protected flesh with only a momentary sensation of cold, then knifed into her, sending a shock all the way up her body and deep into her marrow. Trying to pull her foot out, she overbalanced and stumbled, driving her wet leg deeper into the river. Unable to maneuver her free foot, she fell backward. *Damn Aidan and his fishing hole,* she thought as she slid over the edge of the freshly cut hole and plunged toward the bottom of the river.

Her life didn't flash before her. Nothing flashed before her but water and the disgusted notion that of all the people in her family, she, the one who didn't go sealy when wet, was the one to fall into the freezing river.

Her clothing was heavy but waterproof, so for a moment or two the covered parts were somewhat protected. The balaclava rode up on her face during her plunge and blinded her, and she reached up a clublike mittened hand to dislodge the wet wool. Above her was a cloudscape of ice, eerily lit by an odd phosphorescence coming from the inner banks of the river that cast a green glow upon it. She kicked toward it, trying against all instinct not to gasp for air. All that hadn't been knocked out of her when she fell was the single breath she'd managed to gulp in before her face submerged.

The ice did not freeze in a solid sheet underneath but in clusters separated by little dips, which she knew – from both her Corps survival training and from listening to Sean and the kids discuss seal matters – formed little air pockets. Not that air was going to help her much if her lungs froze before she found the way out. She tried not to think what life might be like if she did survive without feet, or ears, or a nose, and sternly told her inner coward to shut the frag up.

Taking in air through cold-numbed lips, she held her breath in and raised her mittens to feel along the bottom of the ice. The unevenness that held her air supply made it much more difficult to find the hole, which was hidden behind an inverted hillock.

She stuck her head up into the hole she had just made and hauled the incredible weight of one of her arms out of the water and onto the ice. She followed with the other arm. Because it had been so very cold and the hole was cut, not thawed, the ice held under her mittens, but the mittens became ice almost at once too, as did the sleeves of her coat.

She was grateful to be breathing, to see the aurora dancing in a now-clear sky as if all were right with the world. And indeed the world was doing fine. She was the one with a big problem. How to get out?

She had been able to hear the ship's crew. Would they hear her if she cried for help? Would they help? There should be a group of villagers coming to take charge of the soldiers any time now. Couldn't they see the ship was gone and hurry it up a bit?

As those thoughts ran through her head she tried to call for help, but all she could produce was a feeble cough. Her voice wasn't the only thing that was weak. Her hands were slipping, and pretty soon she'd have to fight her way back up again.

She looked up again at the frozen sky, which seemed to have grown icicles. No, those would be her lashes, probably her eyelids, crusted with ice.

Oh well, she'd heard freezing to death was not a bad way to die. Already she couldn't feel anything except vaguely sleepy. That was how it started, she knew. You went to sleep and died, and they found your frozen corpse at breakup.

Sean swam upstream for five miles in open water warmed by the geothermal current that formed something of a circulatory system for Petaybee's northern pole. The aboveground tributary ended at a mostly frozen lake, and he had to dive under the ice, swimming through uncomfortably shallow water. This place was a sink, hollowed out early in Petaybee's form- ation, perhaps even before terraformation, by a natural volcanic event. Sean wasn't certain exactly how it had happened. He was a biologist, not a geologist, and at the moment he was a seal who did not much care how the water came to run the way it did as long as it was there to transport him where he wished to go, without more danger than he could afford to brave.

This passage was a bit tricky, but unless it had changed, which it certainly could do without notice, it should be safe enough.

There was a high ridge in the bottom of the sink before it deepened until it sank down into its source, an underground spring, not as warm as the one at the communion cave but almost always open, even in the coldest weather, because of the magma channels flowing beneath the rock. This was also subject to change, of course. However, Petaybee seemed to have some control over where its fluids ran, and by now it surely understood what he and the others were trying to do to protect it, so he rather expected it would arrange itself to his best advantage – that is, stay as he remembered it – and he was not disappointed.

The opening to the underground waterway, a spring at the surface but a broad and deep underground river below, was exactly where it had been on his previous journey by the same route, and in case he had forgotten, inorganic-looking arrowlike clusters of bioluminescent material along the bottom marked the way.

He'd run into this before on an underwater errand for the planet, and he was relieved to see that it had its considerable attention at least partially focused on his mission.

The force of the water increased as he neared the place where the spring bubbled into the pool, but he pressed forward, passing from the cave under the thin ice frosting the lake's surface to the hole in the side of the bank where lukewarm water gushed into the lake bed. This hole was at the edge of the sink, boring into higher ground that rose overhead as he swam into the stream.

The warm water made him sleepy and sluggish, but he had to actively swim against the current to reach his goal, the lower level of the communion cave at Kilgalen. The river swept past it on its way to the sea, but there had been a good level place to land and change in the past. He blessed the dry suit Marmie had provided. For that matter, he blessed Marmie, and although he knew that she and they all had enemies, found it difficult to fathom why anyone would go to so much effort to create trouble for such a marvelous woman. She was herself one of the PTBs – and yet she had used her influence and money generously for the benefit of the planet and its people – and other planets and other people, from what he could tell – without worrying about what she'd be getting out of it. He was concerned about his kids, of course, but if he had been in their flippers, he'd have done the same.

There was plenty of room overhead and plenty of oxygen there, but he had spent so long in administrative chores he was not as accustomed to swimming hard as his children were, and his chest, back, and the joints where his flippers met his body ached with the effort.

When the channel narrowed again, Sean watched for more arrows, and there they were, larger and larger until the entire underground passage was filled with the bioluminescence and he could clearly see his destination.

He was almost too tired to pull himself out of the stream before he was carried backward, but gained strength from knowing it was the end of the journey for now.

He shook himself dry and, when he was fully human, put on the dry suit, with booties, gloves, and hood, and climbed up into the back end of the communion cave.

Siobhan Chugliak, the village's shanachie, and her husband, Floyd, met him inside the cave.

'What is it, Sean?' she asked.

He told her. 'The town is under siege and we're worried the PTBs will use the central com system to monitor and trace any calls we make on the portable ones. So I've come to warn you myself.'

'Very good of you, I'm sure, and we'll start a relay to all the villages, so you needn't trouble yourself. Come on back to the cabin with us – have a cuppa to warm up.'

'Ta very much, Siobhan. I won't say the swim wasn't tiring.'

'We could take you home by sled if you wish.'

'No, that's more easily spotted, and besides, it's downstream clear to the river on the way back. I'll be grand.'

Over tea, he went into more detail about the arrest of Marmie and the coming of the troop ship. He had not yet drained his cup when he began to feel that he had other places to be. Floyd had already alerted the rest of the village, and six dogsled teams were dispatched to three other villages to begin the relay. They traveled in pairs in case of mishap.

'I need to return home now, Siobhan,' he told her. Another hostess would have protested that he hadn't finished his tea, that the scones were still in the oven and would be out at any moment, and that his hair had not yet dried from the melting of the ice on the way from cave to cabin. But Siobhan, like Clodagh, though perhaps not so strong in her skills as yet, was a shanachie and knew that such impulses were best heeded.

As soon as he reached the landing spot, he slipped from the dry suit and stowed it, re-entered the water, and was on his way.

The trip back should have been as easy as he'd told Siobhan, but his sense of urgency was increasing, and he swam with the current to make faster progress.

He was back in the river in a third of the time it had taken him to leave it, but did not feel the relief he expected. Instead he swam as quickly as he could upstream. No ice impeded him here, because of the warm current from the hot spring. He turned his head toward the spring and the cave, but something pulled him back into the current and he continued to swim upstream until, as he neared the village, the ice closed in from both sides of the shore and he finally was forced to dive beneath it, knowing he'd have to claw open a hole when he wanted to emerge.

Underwater in the dark, he still knew his way using his sonar. There was the boat ramp right outside Kilcoole – he knew it by the posts sticking through the ice. But what pulled him onward was still ahead of him. His signals preceded him, bouncing, returning, telling him the lay of the river bottom, banks, the ice, and what was in between.

Up ahead, between the village and the spaceport, something large suddenly entered the water, sinking, flailing, then rising beneath the ice. Two legs, a body, something human.

A soldier who had inadvertently fallen through the ice? A villager? It didn't matter. He had to help, of course. He had been pacing himself, but now he pushed forward, pumping his long gray body in a smooth continuous series of powerful undulations.

It would take him only a few minutes to reach the victim at this rate, but he also knew that immersion in the frigid river had a good chance of killing the hapless human, or if not that, then frostbite would likely injure him beyond even Clodagh's ability to heal.

Suddenly above him the ice groaned and cracked and the water sloshed beneath it as if the river were being shaken. A quake? Possible, though they were less frequent once winter set in.

He drove himself forward. The body was upright in the water and seemed to have found an airhole, but with the quake, its movements changed from feeble to frantic. The ice would probably be cracking around it too, threatening it with submersion again. Sean was now swimming as hard as he could, but he didn't see how he could possibly reach the person in time to save him.

As he passed Kilcoole, however, he suddenly became aware of a thin stream of warm sulfurous water like that from the hot spring shooting down the middle of the river. That was different!

A little farther on and the area between the ice and the flowing water was filled with steam. Ice cracked and parted with the new heat. He sent his sonar signals forth at faster intervals, so as not to lose the victim in the steam, but the noise of the breaking ice confused his senses.

He only knew he'd reached his goal when a heel connected with the top of his head.

12

Bien! Mon ami, Zuzu told her new partner in crime, *we seem to have begun a four-legged underground in this place of despair. We are a two-creature Résistance. But the man will return and finish his evil work. How shall we further deter him?*

We could bite him.

Other men would come and chase us, possibly kill us. And me, I am not ready to die. The universe still has need of such a cat as Zuzu. As it is, I fear we must vacate this ventilation passage tout suite before those evil men pump into it vapors of a nature most poisonous to our kinds.

But your friend who is not a cat remains caged.

Vraiment. She raised and lowered her ears and whiskers to signify that there was little she could do about such a hopeless situation.

Sky squeezed around her and looked into the

room at her poor Adrienne bound so helplessly to the chair. The otter leaned against the grate with his body. Zuzu heard a creak and a crack as it gave under his weight. *This door would open for the right otter.*

By all means, be my guest, she said graciously. She backed away to give him room, careful to keep her back paws and tail free of the pile of scat.

The otter chittered and squeaked and shoved and heaved, and presently Zuzu heard a cracking sound and a triumphant 'Hah!'

He then proceeded to use his teeth and front feet to tear an even larger hole, and slid himself into the room. Zuzu daintily followed.

'Zuzu!' Adrienne's whisper bordered on the sort of hiss that the cat, as her esteemed companion, might have found offensive had it not been so laden with concern for her welfare. 'Oh, sweetie, they mustn't catch you here. They would kill you in some awful way just to torment me.'

Zuzu hopped onto her shoulder, purring comfort and reassurance that she could be back in that hole and out the other side before those clumsy oafs saw so much as a single hair on her curly tail. Meanwhile Sky used his big sharp otter teeth to attack the tapes binding her friend's hands and feet.

Adrienne sagged with relief as her limbs were freed but jerked to alertness, putting her wrists and ankles together again as the door to her room rattled.

Allez, M'sieu *Sky!* the cat warned, and sprinted back through the opening, barely clearing the pile of poo as she raced for the exit. The otter was almost as swift as she and was halfway through the opening when the door opened and a voice cried, 'Gotcha!'

Zuzu did not see what happened next because her view was blocked by a shrieking otter. When he suddenly disappeared back into the room, her tail twitched twice before she sprinted back through the pipe and out into the corridor for the brief dash to the rat hole.

Adrienne's tormentor had carelessly left a tray containing implements for the infliction of pain near her chair. When he barged into the room and saw the hind end of the otter, he disregarded his prisoner to try to capture the animal. Adrienne's feet were asleep, but she grabbed the back of her chair with one hand, planted both feet on the ground, grabbed the tray with the other hand and began flinging instruments, pointy end first, at her captor. Her hands weren't in much better shape than her feet, so her aim was off despite the nearness of her target, and most of the instruments bounced harmlessly off the man.

Evidently he was a single-minded kind of guy, because he was so determined to capture the otter that he ignored her. He had hold of the creature's tail and was yelling threats about skinning it alive. The otter turned, teeth bared, and sank them into the man, who tried to take aim with his sidearm. Adrienne was steady enough to grab her chair and crack him over the head with it. He went down, but his arm came back up with something pointy in his hand. He stabbed at the otter but immediately had a face full of spitting Zuzu, who had erupted from the duct like an avenging demon.

He tried to pry the cat away from his face with the hand that was not being chewed on by the otter. Roaring as Zuzu's claws dug into him, he pried her loose and flung her across the room. Grabbing the nearest sharp implement, Adrienne stabbed him in the neck and he went limp. Sirens were sounding and footsteps were running down the hall. She was free, but how was she going to get out? And Zuzu . . .

The otter crossed the room in one slinky motion and nudged the cat, who raised her head, shook it, and with another nudge was back on her paws and racing behind him into the vent.

Adrienne, gripping her torturer's gun, stood beside the door, waiting for it to open.

Dive! the twins told each other in unison as the pointy prow split the water between them.

They did, swimming around the boat on either side, intending to meet at the stern.

But as Murel swam halfway the length of the craft, something dropped on top of her, and when she tried to dive lower to evade it, it went with her. Her flipper was caught in it. It continued dropping on top of and all around her until she found herself enveloped, unable to move. *A net! Ro, I've been netted.*

Her teeth snapped down on the nearest section, but the material didn't give and the boat's forward motion trapped her upper jaw in it. She pulled backward to try to free herself, shaking her head, and snared something else.

Hold on, sis. I'm coming.

No, no! Don't! she began. If her teeth couldn't free her, his wouldn't be able to either, and he could be caught as well. Better if they wait until the boat docked wherever it was going to dock. He might be able to board, turn human, and use fingers and tools to free her.

Her sonar was confused by the boat's noise and motion, and she knew Ro's was too when she heard him swear, *Fraggitall anyway! They got me too. Can't bite through this stuff either.*

Don't try, she warned him. She calmed down enough to slowly maneuver her head free of its square rope prison and put her jaws back together. *Ah, better. If they don't haul us up again before long, we could drown.*

I know. Nets aren't made for flippers to climb, but maybe if we can find the middle so we're not entangled, we could surface inside the net. Mine's a whole lot bigger than I am.

This one too. It's worth a try.

But the nets closed over their heads as they were dragged up out of the water to dangle on either side of the boat.

Whiskery faces peered through the nets at the catch of the day.

'Well, well, lookee here. Seals! I didn't know we had any in these waters.'

'Me, neither, Captain. You think they killed those squids?'

'Doesn't seem likely. They're not all that big. Some species are larger than others, though, I know that. Not a heck of a lot else, though. Not many planets have them anymore.'

'Are they good eating?'

'Not especially. They were hunted for their

177

fur coats a long time ago and were practically exterminated back on Terra because they eat a lot of fish and ruined the waters for commercial fishermen.'

'You think we ought to just kill them, then?'

The twins shivered in nets still too wet for them to change. And if they did change, then what? That didn't bear thinking about either.

'Did I say that?' the captain asked. 'They were only a threat because there were too many of them – and frankly, too many fishermen too. My mama's side of the family had this kind of hereditary hatred of any nonhuman thing that took the fish, but on my daddy's side, they would have just as soon killed the fishermen for taking the fish away from the wild critters. My folks had this kinda Romeo and Juliet-type courtship without the suicide.'

Murel, who was the seal he was regarding while discussing their fate, tried to look as big-eyed and adorable as possible, to appeal to the instincts from his father's side of the family.

The captain grinned at her suddenly. 'Cute little thing. Go below and grab my camera, Lloyd. Let's get some pictures of them and the dead squid, mark the bearings, and release the little buggers. The two of them aren't going to take enough fish between them to upset anybody. And we sure don't have any use for fur coats around here.'

'But how'd they get here, Captain?'

'I dunno.' The captain shrugged. 'Nobody mentioned anything to me. Maybe the company is introducing a new species. Maybe something else is.'

'Something else?'

'Well, I've heard that on some of these worlds the company terraformed to use for one thing or another, unauthorized species have popped up and nobody can figure out why. Maybe the same thing is happening here.'

'Won't the brass want to examine them, then?' Lloyd called as he ducked into the cabin and emerged with a little waterproof orange package.

'Maybe so,' the captain said, holding the package toward Murel and clicking a button that made a little whirring sound. 'If they do, we can probably recapture these, or if there are more, catch them too. On the other hand, if these guys were planted here as part of some new program by the company they've neglected to tell us about, they're not going to be real happy about us disturbing their seed stock.' He crossed to the other side of the boat, his seaman's legs maintaining their balance on the rocking deck. He took several photos of Ronan too. 'I'll try to suss it out with the brass, but meanwhile, don't say anything about this.'

'Aye aye, Cap'n, sir,' Lloyd said, flipping him an exaggerated salute. 'My lips are sealed.'

'Very funny, Lloyd. Let's lower the nets before these little fellas get sunburned. Then we can offload our cargo.'

They did that, lowering the nets so they were a foot or two beneath the surface, then opening them so the twins could swim out. Because the nets were so close to the surface, Ronan and Murel had to swim with their heads and backs out of the water to avoid being reentangled. It was lovely to be able to breathe without being bowed in two while the net cut a checkerboard grid into their hides. The captain was still snapping pictures of them.

Once beyond their nets, they dived and swam away from the bow of the boat.

Two near misses in one day! Murel said. *Lucky for us the captain took after his da's side of the family.*

Seemed a nice chap, actually, Ronan agreed. *It's odd to find a fishing boat out here, though, don't you think? Surely they don't catch fresh fish for the prisoners.*

Behind them there was a splash, and their sonar picked up something heavy plunging through the water. They turned and saw a naked gray-white body, its feet bound in heavy chain attached to a stone as large as its head. Its eyes stared blankly, and its thin hair waved like seaweed as it sank. Another human corpse followed that one, and another.

Far below, their sonar told them, the squids rose to snatch their prey.

13

A second boat plied the waters of Gwinnet's sea. It left the main compound at the same time the twins were fighting the squid for their lives, so although a small dark figure stood on the bow with binoculars, and the exploratory boat's sonar scanned the seas for large mammals swimming near the surface, it missed the twins. Instead, it landed at the island containing the children's compound, where, with a disgruntled sigh, the small dark figure went ashore to find her grandson and see what he might accidentally tell her of her true quarry.

'Professor Mabo, what are you doing here?' Rory asked when he saw her in the visitor's hut to which he'd been summoned by Lieutenant Bunyon. When Professor Mabo had taught at *Versailles Station*, she had insisted that he call her by the same title the other kids used. He'd learned to be wary of his grandmother, so even though she seemed to be regarding him with sadness and sympathy, he didn't trust her.

'I am here not as your teacher but as your grandmother,' she said. 'I know you feel I was harsh with you when I taught at the station, but I acted as I did for your own good. You would not have wanted the other children to feel that I singled you out for favoritism. Children can be very cruel, Rory.'

'So can family,' Rory retorted. She was not going to win him over so easily. It was her fault that he and his folks had been treated like criminals and brought here.

'I'm sorry you feel that way,' she said. 'But since you do, perhaps it will make what I have to say easier. I'm sorry to tell you that my daughter and her husband did not survive the flight.'

'You're lying!' he exclaimed, shocked. 'Why wouldn't they survive? You had them bring us here. I heard the soldiers talking about it before we were put on the ship.'

'Rory, prison duty changes people. Soldiers who have had otherwise exemplary records become hardened, even to their own people, and show no mercy. Your parents attempted escape – I feel certain they were trying to locate you. The guards overreacted. I have had them punished.'

'Yeah, you're good at that,' Rory said. 'What were you punishing us for exactly?'

'I had no intention of punishing you. On the contrary, I simply was trying to protect my loved ones from being implicated in the crimes committed by Marmion de Revers Algemeine. Your parents' association with her has become hazardous for them and embarrassing for me.'

'I guess so, since you say they're dead and everything,' he said bitterly. But the news was too new for him to truly grieve for the loss of his parents. He was just reacting to her with the distrust and dislike he'd learned she deserved. Later, alone, he'd think about what she said, but now he was not going to give her the satisfaction of seeing him upset. 'Good thing you took measures so we won't embarrass you anymore.'

She opened her arms and reached for him, apparently intending to hug him, but he sat back in his chair. The two of them were alone in one of the huts, seated on comfortable cushioned chairs, with a pitcher of fruit punch and a plate of little cakes between them. He'd been wondering since they'd arrived how to swipe the cakes to use as bribes with the other kids.

'I'm sorry you feel that way, Rory. I have tried to tell you this as gently as possible, before you find out some other way.'

She sounded to him like she thought she was the one being abused. He would have been more upset if he hadn't overheard the guards' conversation aboard the shuttle from the mainland. They'd said nothing about his parents being killed, and he felt sure that that Austin guy would have tormented him with it if he could have.

'Oh dear, the other news probably will not be received any better.'

'What other news?' he asked in a skeptical tone.

'The people from Halau aboard the ship from Petaybee. None of them survived either. The prison officials had decided not to tell the children, but I feel that that is unfair to them. They should know that they've been orphaned so they can make choices appropriate to their status when looking to the future.'

'That's real thoughty of you, Gran,' he said as disrespectfully as he dared. 'How did they happen to die?'

'Well, dear, the elders were frail, and the young mothers, some of them, pregnant – you have been a very sheltered child and cannot possibly know what that prison is like. They perished very quickly.'

'Sounds like it. Any other good news?'

'Not for you, but I understand that children

whose description matched that of Ronan and his sister were found on the space station and brought here at the same time you were. We did not part on a very good note, but I do think they should know – could you bring them here, please? The matron did not seem able to locate them.'

'I haven't seen them since the first day,' he said.

'They may have used their shape-shifting ability to try to escape,' she said. 'It won't do them any good, and the ocean here is extremely dangerous for those who are unaware of its peculiarities. I came by boat specifically to search for them. Oh, well, I'm sure that if they are still out there, they will learn soon enough that Petaybee is under martial law and the inhabitants of their village are to be transferred here in connection with the charges against the de Revers woman.'

'Is that so?' he asked.

'Yes, indeed. Now on to other matters. I know my news about your family and friends will have upset you and you'll probably need to go cry or whatever it is children do under such circumstances, but as your next of kin, I feel I must also mention that you should start thinking about your future. One of the benefits of children being on this island is that it shares the premises with a Corps training facility.'

'That's a good thing, is it?'

'Of course. The soldiers there often lend a hand in the care and maintenance of this facility and assist in searches for runaways and that sort of thing. And they provide role models and a source of future employment. A belligerent young man such as yourself ought to do well in the Cadet Corps training program if you learn to channel your animosity appropriately.' The last was said with no smarmy attempt at sympathy, just the same nasty mocking tone he remembered from last time. 'It's not like an orphan here has a great deal of choice in the matter.'

She turned and left the hut. Relieved that she had not tried to hug him again, he snatched up the cakes, folding the napkin containing them over the tops. The tunics he and the others wore had no place to conceal anything, but he thought he knew where he could stash the cakes for the time being.

In their haste to get away from the corpse-disposal boat and the squids, Ronan and Murel completely forgot to check their undersea markers and simply swam until exhaustion from their struggles overcame them and they drifted in an unfamiliar sea under unfamiliar stars.

I haven't a clue where we are or how to return to the island, do you? Ronan asked.

Murel, whose lethargy alarmed him, since he had no idea how severe her wounds were, answered, *No idea whatsoever.*

I've heard of whales getting beached, but never seals getting lost, Ronan said. *This never would have happened on Petaybee.*

I don't actually need any more reasons to wish I was home instead of here, thank you, Murel said tartly. *Even the stars are different here, which makes sense since it's a different solar system, isn't it? And I could use a proper moon. No wonder the tide is so sluggish. That little thing they have up there is pathetic. And no doubt has 'Property of Intergalactic Enterprises' stamped on the bottom.*

Night came upon them quickly. It seemed they had just dived below the surface into the darkness of deeper water, and when they surfaced the sky was nearly as dark as the water. The stars out here were enormously bright. If only they knew what the usual positions were supposed to be, it would tell them a bit more about where they were and how to proceed.

It doesn't actually matter that they're different stars, though, does it? Ronan said. *We know where they are now, and we ought to be able to gauge our position relative to them wherever we go.*

Murel hated to admit she didn't understand all that much about it. Ronan had had a crush on First Officer Adrienne Robineau, so he'd paid closer attention during their navigation lessons than she had.

However, he proceeded to talk himself out of it. *The only problem is that we don't know which direction this planet rotates.*

Shhh, she said. *Hear that?*

It was a boat's motor roaring in the distance. It did not sound like the same one that had captured and released them earlier. According to their sonar, it was a good distance away.

It must be leaving the island, headed back to the mainland, Ronan said. *There doesn't seem to be any other place for it to go. Probably a supply vessel.*

Maybe, she replied.

If we find it, we should be able to get our bearings from it, at least, Ronan told her, and she began swimming beside him, toward the boat. Before long they intercepted its wake and from it were able to backtrack – or back-paddle – until they found the island again and the beach containing the children's compound.

The rock will be around that way, Murel said, relieved to be back in familiar territory, even if it meant being closer to captivity.

Yes, but look – there's a light on the other side of the beach.

It could be a trap, Murel said nervously.

Maybe, but I don't think anyone who is out to get us would think a little light like that would be a good way to trap us. I mean, we're selkies, not weremoths. Ten to one it's Rory trying to get our attention. I'll swim in. You stay out here in case there is a trap and you need to help me out.

But he found no nets, no traps, just a miserable-looking, bald-headed, scantily dressed Rory, holding a glow light.

When Ronan flopped onto the beach, Rory walked down the slight, sandy slope to meet him, speaking softly. 'Ronan? Murel? I was hoping you'd come. I seriously have to talk to you two. I've had a visit from my loving gran.'

Murel swam in and they both dried off and slipped into their dry suits.

'Want a cake?' Rory offered. 'They're a little squooshed, but I saved you guys some. I had to bribe the beach monitor to look the other way, and another kid to get me the glow. I think the beach monitor will keep up her end of things, but you'd better stay close to the water all the same. She thinks I just needed to come out here and be alone to brood about suddenly being an orphan.'

'You're an orphan?'

'Yeah, me and just about everybody else, according to dear old Granny. She told me my parents were killed trying to escape and the only thing left for me to do is join the company Cadet Corps.'

'That's harsh, Rory. I'm so sorry,' Murel said.

'You ought to be. She claims they've captured your village and your folks and everybody is being brought here. But she knows you're here too, or at least suspects it, and I'm pretty sure she's lying, trying to draw you out.'

Ronan and Murel, recalling their mother's plans, exchanged stricken looks. 'Yeah, but what if she's not?'

'She had to be – her mouth was moving,' Rory said bitterly. 'But I was thinking, maybe it's not such a bad idea if I play along and try to join up. I could find out stuff we need to know.'

'Do you think you might get into their com shed and contact Marmie's friends to tell them what's happened to her?' Murel asked.

'Oughtn't to be a problem,' he said, sounding a bit brighter.

'Because if you could do that, it would solve everything. They'd get her released and she'd free everyone else.'

'That settles it, then. I'll do it,' he said. 'Maybe I can borrow their com system and maybe not, but I'm far more likely to get a chance as a recruit, aren't I?'

The twins agreed.

'Too bad they don't have a submarine corps you two could join,' Rory joked. He sounded absolutely bubbly now. He felt bad about his grandmother being such a villainous old bat, so if he could be the one to free everybody else, Murel reckoned it would help him feel better.

'Just make sure you remember you're just playing a part,' Ronan said. 'You don't want to actually become one of them. Not that they're all bad, of course – take Mum or Rick O'Shay. But you don't want to end up a total bossy git like that Austin guy.'

'Don't worry. I won't. So we'll rendezvous again tomorrow, same time, same place?'

'Say,' Ronan said, 'do you reckon if you're over there you might be able to steal us a print-out of a chart of this ocean?'

'I thought you guys could navigate by instinct.'

'On our world, sure, but this ocean is so empty and the stars are all wrong. If we could even get a look at the layout of the landmasses, we'd have a better idea about where to go.'

'Fair enough,' Rory said.

An adult female called out, 'You there, on the beach. You're in violation of curfew.'

'Just admiring the moonlight, miss,' Rory said, while Ronan and Murel stripped off their dry suits in one well-practiced motion, packed them into each other's pouches, and dove into the water.

'Who's that with you, then? All of you come up here where I can see you.'

But by then the twins were underwater, swimming toward the rocks.

14

Yana was so numb she could not feel the hands that grasped her arms to haul her out of the river. She thought she was probably dying already. It was said that the cold began to feel almost warm when one was truly freezing, and the water beneath her had suddenly begun feeling that way. It was a relief. Then there was the olfactory hallucination that told her she was smelling the sulfurous odor of the communion cave. She had the oddest sensation of something slipping between the legs of her snowsuit, bearing her up. Perhaps that was the case, since she didn't fall back into the river even though her stiff and iced-over mittens could no longer maintain a hold on the ice. Her arms simply lay splayed in front of her like a pair of useless logs. Though she vaguely felt that she needed to survive for Sean, the kids, and even Kilcoole, she was so drowsy she couldn't be bothered to care about all that at the moment.

The brightness of the snow dimmed beneath the shadow of a large form that reached down and grabbed her arms, while her parka was jerked upward by the hood.

'Well, well, we seem to have caught a big fish,' a gruff male voice said, and the part of Yana that was still alert to her surroundings knew she was not out of trouble. This was one of the troops from the ship.

But then another voice, a familiar one, said, 'Yes, well, she'll need tending to, and so will some of your people, so we'd best return to the village and then we'll see who's caught whom.'

Yana was facing the wrong direction to see the speaker, but she could almost feel Sinead's rifle leveled at the ship's crew. At any rate, she was pulled more gently upward and back. She felt almost weightless, as if buoyed up toward her rescuers.

Then the ice chose to break under her and splinter back under Sinead's feet, forcing her sister-in-law and the village rescuers to retreat.

'Ladder!' Sinead called. Then, close to her ear, Yana heard, 'Hang on. This is going to be slow, but we'll have you ashore soon.'

In front of her the soldiers were scrambling off the river and up onto the banks as the ice crack chased them from her hole back in the direction of the ship.

Sinead shifted her grip, and Yana dipped back down to her chin momentarily as the ice under her split even further. Then suddenly she was borne up and a new current carried her back toward her rescuers, stopping only when the ice remained firm enough for her to be hauled upward.

She looked up and saw Sinead's eyes dancing with amusement behind their iced-over lashes. 'Thanks, Sean,' Sinead said.

They hauled Yana onto the bank and bundled her onto a sled, but not before she saw the sleek dark head pop out from beneath the ice and regard her with an *Okay, now?* look before the seal dived back into the river.

'Adrienne, *c'est moi.*' Marmie's voice preceded her through the door. Adrienne sagged with relief until she saw the laser pistol pointed at Marmie's back, followed by a tall young Corpsman.

Shoving Madame aside, Adrienne growled, 'Drop it,' but Madame reached up and grabbed the man's wrist. He looked down at her with alarm.

'This is Christian, Adrienne. He's a friend. Quickly, we must leave this room. Everything here can be seen from the adjoining one.'

Adrienne glanced over to where the animals had been making their escape. Not one hair remained of either of them. She didn't like to leave Zuzu behind, but her formerly pampered feline friend had given ample proof that she could take care of herself when necessary. And now Zuzu also had an ally.

Sky and Zuzu watched from one of the rat holes as Marmie, Adrienne, and the soldier passed.

The fur along Sky's spine rippled all the way to the tip of his tail. *Caged again.*

Zuzu's whiskers twitched thoughtfully. *I think not. Neither Adrienne nor Madame are afraid.*

Cats know when humans are afraid? How?

Elementary, mon cher *otter,* Zuzu told him. *It is a matter of scent and posture. Their shoulders are not tensed in fear of his weapon, their hands are relaxed, and most of all, they do not smell afraid. Then too, I overheard Madame whisper,* 'Et maintenant, Christian?' *to the gendarme. From this I deduce that they are on cordial terms. He will no doubt help them escape.*

Sky considered this. *Good. I will escape too.*

You cannot go with them. You will draw attention to their unsuitable amiability.

How then? My friends who are river seal children do not know where to find me, so I must go to them.

How will you find them?

We talk in our heads, in the same way that cats and otters talk. When I am near to them, they will hear me call and come.

And if they cannot come?

Then they will guide me to them and I will save them. Friends save friends. We have done this hundreds of times.

In that case, follow me. I know a way out for otters and cats. Unfortunately, it is too petite for humans, even dainty ones such as Adrienne and Madame.

Otters are very slinky and can fit through very small places.

Indeed. If it transpires that Madame and Adrienne have escaped, I may decide to come with you on your search.

Oh? Do cats swim fast like otters?

I am fond of water, oui, Zuzu said with a proud lick to her shoulder. *I am, I confess, unique among my species in that I swim very well indeed. Er – how much swimming would be involved in your search?*

There is a sea. I saw that the river seal children were carried across it in a sky ship. This otter can ride in sky ships but cannot make them go. Though otter paws are very useful, they work better for swimming than for making things fly. Even the paws of sky otters, he added regretfully.

Ah, Zuzu said with regret as well, *I comprehend perfectly. You wish to help your friends, as I do mine. Still, it seems a shame, does it not, to disband our alliance when we have discovered how much more useful even my brains and beauty and vast experience of this place can be with the assistance of your excellent teeth, paws, and exquisite slinkiness.*

Sky preened. *Otters* are *excellent, it's true. Excellent is good, isn't it?*

Zuzu said, *Excellent is very good indeed, my friend. So, shall we embark on this mission together as far as we can before splitting up?*

Sky agreed happily. Sky otters were smart and brave, and learned to do things quickly, but having a cat for a friend was almost like having another otter or a river seal helping.

Zuzu led the way through the dark, rat-infested passages. Sky heard the scrabble of claws and, worst of all, the nasty scent messages the rats left, telling how they would use their rat nails and their big sharp teeth, if given a chance. Twice Zuzu walked straight up to a group of the rodents, and their red eyes gleamed. They thought they could gang up on the cat and kill her, but Sky edged up as close as he could to his companion and made his own eyes small and mean and said, *Hah! Cats eat rats. Rats do not eat cats. I think otters eat rats too!*

The rats fled. They were very big rats, Zuzu said, but Sky was twice the size of the largest and he let forth a scent message that told them he was extremely fierce and that his claws and teeth were twice as big and sharp as any rat's. He might have said something about the hundreds of relatives who were right behind him and Zuzu too, but if he did, he had no way of knowing if the rats believed him or not.

At last the rat droppings and remnants of his own scent messages and the latrines of the prison cells above and below them diminished and the passages grew less dim. Sky sniffed eagerly. Salt water! He smelled salt water. He was not a sea otter, but according to the Father River Seal, he was an estuarial otter who could swim in salt water as well as fresh. He did not like it as much as fresh water, but he was getting used to it the more he did it. The cat led him to an opening through which a morning sky was tapering from the pink of the inside of a lovely otter's mouth to the blue of the river seal twins' eyes, and he quivered with happiness as he looked forward to swimming in the dark blue-gray waters washing up against the outside of the prison, directly below the hole.

It is a long way down, Zuzu said. *Farther than I thought.*

It would be better if there was a slide, Sky agreed. *But otters are good divers. Are cats?*

Zuzu considered. She did not like admitting that cats in general were in any way inferior to otters, or that she in particular was less skilled at something than he was. So she said, *Cats are made to climb and leap. You dive and I'll climb down, then leap in to join you.*

Sky leaned forward, pushed with his back feet and muscular tail, and entered the water with a feeling of freedom he had been missing for what seemed hundreds of hours, or the otterly equivalent.

15

The twins swam toward the rocks where they had lain before, but as the sun limned the formation, they saw that its outlines had changed. A tall bit with a rounded point had been added to the highest point of the little island.

Someone is there! Murel said. *Waiting for us, it looks like.*

I doubt it's anyone friendly, Ronan replied. *If Mabo knows we're here, I'd bet my right flipper she's behind it.*

I wouldn't take the bet, Murel said. *She'll be looking for us, and she knows what seal habitat looks like. Unfortunately, our rocks are a pretty classic example. She'd guess that we might well fetch up there when we're in seal form. Keep your head down and let's swim back the way we came.*

Once they were out of sight of the rocks, Murel stopped swimming. *Now what?* she asked. *It seems like we flew all this way to swim around aimlessly in the sea. And I don't know about you, but I really need to rest somewhere. I've got all these sore spots from fighting the squid and the net.*

Me too, but I think the best thing, since Mabo is looking for us here, is for us to go back to the prison, Ronan said.

But what about the squid? And if that boat sees us again, the crew might get more curious.

I think the boat took care of the squid by at least diminishing their appetites. Besides, you said yourself that they have to stay down deep. We'll just keep near the surface and we should be fine. I saw some other offshore rocks closer in. If we can reach those, we can decide what to do next.

Murel was so weary and sore, she wasn't sure she could make it all the way back to the prison. But following her brother, she slid beneath the waves.

I wish there were some other way, she complained.

What do you suggest? Ro's voice carried a sarcastic edge to it. *We don't have arms and legs until we can dry out on land. We can hardly overpower that sentry as seals. Unless you think we could flop him down and flipper-slap him into submission?*

No need to be mean. Who saved your blubber

butt when you were stupid enough to get grabbed by the squid?

Saving blubber butts from squids went two ways, to the best of my recollection.

There has to be a way, she insisted. She felt even less cooperative than she had before Ronan made his smart remark. Then, as if inspired by her annoyance, she thought of something. *We can't attack him on the land, but we could in the water. Hands and legs are only an asset on land.*

Unless the hands are holding a harpoon? Ronan suggested mulishly.

That's where being smarter than the average seal comes in – er – handy, she replied. *If he has one, once we get him in the water we can take it away from him. We can fight sharks, whales, and squids. One measly person shouldn't be that hard. Here's what we do – we'll split up and one of us will attract his attention from the water. If he's really after us, we should be able to lure him in. If not, the one attracting his attention will have to hold it and make a lot of splashing to cover for the other one climbing out onto the lower rocks, drying off, and getting the better of him.*

Rrright. Then what?

Well, we find out what he's doing on our rocks, for one, and keep him busy while we rest up enough to go somewhere else. For starters.

Ronan grunted. *Brilliant.*

Ro, I absolutely cannot make that swim again.

But you've enough fight left in you to take on a possibly armed human?

If I must.

Very well then, he caved unexpectedly. *I'll do the fancy swimming and you flop ashore once I've got his attention and either push or bump him into the water if he's not gone for it already. Then I'll take care of him.*

See that you do, she said, her tartness hiding the gratitude she felt that he'd found a way to do the energetic bits. *I don't want to have to rescue you again.*

No worries on that account, he said. *In case anyone is watching from shore, you go 'round to the back so you can change without being seen. Let me know once you're in position and I'll start the show.*

It wasn't a bad plan. It almost worked. But the moment the person on the rocks spotted Ro, he raised a whistle to his lips and let out a long blast.

That doesn't sound good, Ro said. *Show cancelled. I think you're going to have to go for that swim after all.*

He dived again, but before Murel could beach herself, the watcher from the rocks dived too. Murel backflipped in the water and headed back to the portside to help Ronan. But long before she rounded the rocks she heard a motor roaring toward them and heard Ro cry, *They've set nets! Swim out to sea, sis.*

And leave you?

I'm caught! Get away. You can't get caught too. You're going to have to save my blubber butt again.

Zuzu was an excellent swimmer, as cats went, but cats were not made for life in the sea. Sky capered around her, splashing, diving, and laughing with otter chittering and chattering, but the amusement value of his antics quickly dwindled.

She liked water, but this was far too much of a good thing.

This water is very warm, Sky told the cat. *And there are many fish, but so far none with shells.*

Merci *for the information, but I have enjoyed enough of this water. I believe I will return now to the land.*

But we only started swimming! Sky protested.

For otters this may be the beginning of swimming, but for cats, even a cat of aquatic inclinations such as moi, *it is time for the swimming to end. Je suis fatigué, otter.*

Tired of swimming? Sky could scarcely see how that was possible. *Maybe if you just sleep for a while.*

Do not be ridiculous! I cannot sleep and swim at the same time!

You do not have to swim. Just wrap yourself in kelp to anchor yourself and float until you are rested.

Cats who float are deceased, otter.

You did not blow enough bubbles into your fur when you groomed, he chided.

I do not blow bubbles into my fur on any occasion whatsoever, she replied indignantly. *Cats do not* blow *the bubbles, you comprehend.*

I did not know that. No wonder more cats don't live in the water. Okay then. Return to land. I must find the river seal children.

Zuzu turned her sodden and skinny corkscrew tail to him and began paddling in the opposite direction. But nowhere did she see the land the otter claimed they had only just left.

She kept paddling, but land still hid itself from her. Her paws felt like anchors and her body sagged in the middle. Although the waves were neither high nor rough, water kept splashing into her face and she had to snort to clear her nose. Her tongue tasted of salt and her mouth was very dry. Her eyes also felt hot and dry. She grew so tired she could not think and could scarcely feel. And then a large series of waves began pounding against her and she could no longer keep her head above the water.

Adieu, *otter!* she thought, and felt herself sinking, drowning, and had visions of her lovely bed on the *Piaf*, of her food dish in the galley, of Adrienne waving her peacock feather for her to hunt, of cuddling in Adrienne's arms and being stroked, of sleeping peacefully beside her friend. Of her battles with the prison rats with their sharp claws and teeth.

She had always won those battles, but suddenly she felt the teeth dig into her neck and carry her off – *merde!* The rat of death had come to claim her!

The sled carrying Yana arrived in Kilcoole just in time for Sean to meet it. As soon as he'd gotten his feet under him, he'd ducked into the cabin and took his and Yana's beaded latchkay parkas and mukluks from the storage chest, and her best snow pants and an extra sweater and a change of thermal underwear. Belatedly he grabbed the fancy patterned mittens and hats Clodagh had knitted for the two of them with portraits of seals and track cats in black, white, gray, and beige curly-coat wool.

Soaked and frozen, Yana would be needing her layers. He could only hope her adaptation and acclimatization to Petaybee had reached the point where it would protect her from the worst effects of her dunking. He thought it would. Maybe the ice had thinned because of that new warm channel opened by the quake and that was why she fell in, but he suspected the channel had been opened to protect her from the worst effects of her polar plunge. The planet was certainly sentient enough to know that she was a valuable ally. As for himself, the dry suit kept him perfectly warm, but he didn't want some inquisitive uniformed lad or lass to start wondering why he was dressed so differently from the others.

He handed Yana's spare clothing to Aisling, who was hovering around the sled, unfastened the blankets bundling his wife into the basket, and lifted her out, then turned to Clodagh's cabin. As he entered, the soldiers were being herded by the rifle-toting villagers into the longhouse.

Clodagh, being Clodagh, had somehow known she was needed and had a fire going in her stove and a kettle boiling on top. The kettle was dented, and he saw that many of the bunches of herbs she had hung from the rafters to dry were strewn around on the floor and crushed. The kitchen table was still overturned, and one of the villagers dashed past him to set it right, propping up a broken table leg with a spare log.

Deirdre, Clodagh's apprentice, dragged her bed close to the fire, and Sean laid Yana down on it. She promptly sat upright, brushing off with wet mittens all offers of assistance but his and Clodagh's. The ice melted from her hair and lashes and made her look as if she'd been caught out in the rain.

He peeled off her mittens, and Clodagh cut off the heavy military boots that for some reason she was wearing instead of her mukluks, which were lighter and worked much better during Petaybean winter than the Corps-issued ones. He meanwhile shrugged off his own outer gear and peeled the dry suit off to halfway down his chest, then took her bare hands in his and placed them between the suit and his skin. Her hands were as cold as the ice itself, but he felt the warmth coming back into them in answer to his own body's heat.

Clodagh examined Yana's feet, then took Yana's hands off Sean's chest one at a time and examined them. The blue-white of frostbite had already begun fading. She put Yana's hands back against his chest. 'You'll mend,' she said with her usual economy of speech. Then she beamed at Sean. She had a beautiful smile and a beautiful voice, and her huge roundness had always seemed to Sean to be Petaybee personified. Healing, comforting, protective, even maternal. Without saying anything, she was clearly telling him it was a good thing they had a selkie in the village.

Yana caught the look and shook her head, disgusted at herself. 'Once more the little human in the family needed rescuing. Thanks, love. Some hijacker I turned out to be.'

'I don't see a ship on the pad, and the crew are under guard in the longhouse. I'd say you did a pretty good job, acushla.'

'I could kill Aidan,' Yana muttered.

'What did I do?' her threatened homicide victim asked in a wounded tone.

'Why did you need to cut a fishing hole in the ice so early in the season?' she asked.

He turned a stricken face to Sinead, who entered with much stamping of boots and slapping together of mittens to rid them of snow before hanging them on hooks beside the fire. No doubt she had tended to the dogs before coming in from the cold herself. Aisling helped her with her parka and brushed the snow from her short dark hair, saying, 'Yana's mad at Aidan about the ice hole.'

'My fault, Yana. He's not to blame.'

'See, you can keep murder in your own family,' Aidan said, holding up his hands as if in surrender, 'I was just following orders.'

'I had our people set a few little surprises for

our guests,' Sinead said. 'I'd have mentioned it, but things were moving a bit fast by then and there was no chance to warn you.'

'Petaybee knew,' Sean said. 'I felt a quake, and a warm channel opened up from one of the springs, right past where Yana was. I had been thinking it was the warm current that thinned the ice and caused her to go bathing so early in the season, and with her clothes on too.'

'Very funny,' Yana said. She stuck her tongue out at Sean, but since she was within two inches of his face already, he took advantage of the gesture to give her a lengthy demonstration of how glad he was that she was safe.

'Well, then,' Sinead said, 'I think it's high time for the rest of us to interrogate our prisoners. Come along, you lot.'

Clodagh pulled on her parka too.

'We'll be good, Clodagh,' Sean said.

'Shush,' the big woman replied, following the others. 'I'm needed elsewhere.'

Sky flipped onto his back with great difficulty, his jaws aching with their burden. Land was far away. Hundreds of waves. Hundreds and more hundreds. Otters swam well, but wet cats were very heavy.

He knew she was alive because he could hear

her crying inside. Also, she did not smell dead. There was a very sharp difference between alive smell and dead smell, and she still smelled alive, mostly.

The waves washed over them fast and slapping. Then Sky, who had been focused on his passenger, heard the engine, and then he did not.

Someone with a human voice called, 'Shut 'er down, Lloyd, and come and have a look at this. I swear, this planet must be in retrograde today or some such foolishness, because as long as I've lived here I've never seen anything but stiffs and squid. Now all of a sudden there's seals and this! Look to the stern.'

'What is it, sir? I can't make it out,' the other voice said.

'I couldn't swear to it, but I think it's a river otter carrying a drowned rat or something.'

River otter? This man obviously did not know a river otter from a sky otter!

'Isn't that something. Looks like they're headed for shore. I'll steer around them, shall I?'

'No – no, Lloyd, I know you're not going to believe it, but that's no rat, it's a pussycat, and look at how that otter is struggling to keep her head above the water. Either that otter is trying to save that cat or this tub is a luxury cruise liner.'

'No kidding?'

Sky swam toward their voices, which were friendly and also coming from the right direction. Then he stopped. The boat smelled like old death.

'It's okay, little feller, bring the kitty here. Ol' Cap'n Terry won't hurt you or your little buddy. I like cats. Never liked otters all that much, but one that would try to rescue a drowning cat is an otter I'd like to meet.' His voice had a pleasing rumbly singsong to it, the same sort of tone as Father River Seal and his sister and other humans who did not eat otters. The boat smelled bad, but Sky's sense of smell was very good at picking odors apart from each other. He could read all of the secret meanings of a scent poem or even an otter scent epic. These were usually travel tales of places visited but also told who the otter leaving the epic was, as well as his parentage, ancestry, mate, offspring, and how many fish each had caught lately.

Cap'n Terry's scent was good, like Father River Seal's, and Lloyd's scent was also good. Sky swam to the death boat.

'Dip net!' the captain commanded. A round hoop with a net in it came into the water. At first Sky tried to turn and just put Zuzu into the net, but her head went under, so he swam backward himself, into the net.

It raised him into the air. He told himself that that was fine. Sky otters were used to the air. He wasn't sure about cats, but he thought that at this moment Zuzu was probably glad to be anywhere but in the water.

They were hauled over the side of the boat and lowered to the deck. One of the men reached for Zuzu, and Sky unclenched his jaws, which were aching from holding on to her with the right amount of pressure to keep her skin between his teeth while not biting through it.

With Zuzu on her tummy, the man pushed on her back and water poured out of her nose and mouth, but still she didn't move. Putting her on her back, the man tilted her small wet head to one side. Water did not actually make cats look good. Zuzu's fur did not look sleek like an otter's – it glued itself to her body and made her look thinner than she was, so that every cat bone showed. Her whiskers drooped and her curly tail looked tiny and sad without its fluff. It was good they had been swimming in warm water. On Petaybee she would have frozen. With one finger the width of a large eel, the man gently pushed the cat's jaws apart and pulled out a bit of seaweed. More water followed. Then he put that finger on her chest and began moving it up and down. After the first hundred finger pushes, he bent very low.

'Hah!' Sky exclaimed, and scrambled to his paws. It looked as if the man was trying to eat Zuzu. He covered her mouth and nose with his own mouth, but he did not bite. He puffed with his own chest, then removed his mouth and pushed her chest some more.

The third time he did this, Zuzu's paws flailed the air and she thought, *Stop! Do not eat me alive.*

He is not eating, cat. He is giving you breath. Instead of blowing bubbles into your fur, as an otter would do, he is blowing them into you so you will have some to keep the water out.

Otter? I have now achieved a sufficiency of the bubbles. Tell him to stop.

Sky could not transmit his thoughts to humans who were not river seals – no thoughts except those expressed in scent notes, at least. The note he and Zuzu left for Adrienne's tormentor had been very clear, but this one had too many parts to it, so he would have to show the human what to do instead. He leaped onto his back, put his front paws into the curly hair under the back of the head covering the man wore, and pulled back.

'What the frag?' The man sat up and dumped Sky to the deck. Sky could have hung on to the man's hair, but he didn't wish to use his mighty otter strength to harm the helpful human. He only wished to get his attention.

Freed of the man's finger and other attempts to revive her, Zuzu weakly rolled onto her paws and began to busy her tongue with trying to lick her fur back into shape. Sky rushed forward to get a few salty licks in.

Zuzu's fur was not amenable to having bubbles blown into it, but with the hot sun pouring onto the deck, her fur quickly started drying.

It itches! she complained, scratching herself with first her left hind foot, then her right. Sky resumed licking the salt from her body.

Just as his mouth was tasting very dry from all of the salt, a small can of water appeared nearby. It was fresh, and both he and Zuzu drank. Seawater was good to swim in, but sky otters preferred fresh water to drink. So did Zuzu.

Something smacked the deck, and the delicious aroma of fish filled the otter's senses. Zuzu had recovered herself enough to be hungry and attacked the middle of the fish with relish. Sky waited politely for her to step aside and let him have some too, but it had been a long time since her last meal, and a half-starved rat in no way compared with a fresh tasty fish.

So Sky told her, *Other fish are in the sea, cat. You cannot swim far enough to find the river seal* children. *These men like cats and they have this boat for you to ride on. I must find the river seal children. I wish you luck.*

But, otter, we are a team!

Yes, but not a swimming team.

And he jumped back into the water, swam, and caught his own fish.

'If that don't beat all.' The captain's voice rumbled down to the water as Sky struck out once more away from shore. 'That's not just any otter we're dealing with here, Lloyd.'

Behind him Sky heard the boat's motor roar. Soon, he knew, he would leave it behind, would be far from shore and all alone.

But when he looked up to see if there was land in front of him yet, the boat was a short distance behind, Zuzu sitting at the bow while the captain stared forward through a metal thing with two bright shiny eyes.

Hundreds of waves later, when he looked up again, the boat was still there, Zuzu was still in place, and the captain was still watching.

This kept happening. Sky got used to it.

He was the leader and the boat was following him. He was its alpha otter. It would follow him anywhere.

But the next time he looked up he had to wonder. Where in anywhere was he, and where did he want to go? Where the river seal twins were, of course. But where was that? There was nothing but sea here. He was a river otter first, an estuary otter with sea otter cousins second, and then a Sky otter. He liked to see a bit of coast, especially when he was alone.

So when he looked up again and saw the boat, Zuzu, and the captain with his glassy eyes thing, he felt, not lost exactly, but undecided. The captain lowered his glassy eyes and spoke to the other man. Then, walking toward Zuzu, the captain put a hand on her shoulders and Sky heard her thought-purr.

The man raised the glassy eyes to his own again with one hand, took the hand off Zuzu, and waved his arm in a direction. He did it once, twice, three times. The boat turned toward where his arm pointed. Then he waved to Sky and made a beckoning motion.

It was good to be alpha otter, but tag was a good game too. Sky struck out with renewed energy, anxious to get ahead of the boat in this new direction so he could once more be in the lead.

16

Christian led Marmie and Adrienne down long corridors, past the cells, down flights of steps into a low-ceilinged ill-lit plascrete bunker whose narrow hallways branched and rebranched until Marmie was sure they had walked at least the same distance through this underground area as they had walked through the prison above.

'Is this the dungeon?' Adrienne asked in a whisper.

'It's a multipurpose area. There are cells down here and some interrogation rooms.'

'No doubt,' Marmie murmured. From the tunnel-like passageways to the left and right issued the scents of mold, decay, whiffs of human excrement and urine, and something worse. She tried very hard to recall her association with Christian and his mother, hoping it had been entirely positive and that he had no reason to seek retribution against her. If she had given offense, she certainly didn't see how, but then she seldom did. She was not herself a petty person and did not understand the petty grudges some individuals seemed to collect as if they were objects of beauty.

'Also hard copy files and storage,' he added after they had turned into a new aisle. He stopped outside the third door and turned an old-fashioned key in an old-fashioned lock.

They entered what looked like another long cell block, but behind the bars were shelves of moldering cardboard boxes.

'This is the oldest part of the prison,' Christian told them. 'Anyone who has particularly displeased his or her superiors gets assigned to do a little filing down here. Starting back there.' He nodded to the point where the corridor and its cells disappeared despite the codelike flashing of the extremely unstable-looking overhead lights.

A desk with piles of printouts sat between the door and the first two cells in the place where a guard station would normally be situated.

He picked up a clipboard and tapped the paper. 'Any files not mentioned here specifically are to be hauled forward, to be picked up for disposal in the incinerator. That is also on this level, adjacent to the interrogation rooms.'

'So we will pretend to be naughty soldiers and keep our faces in the files,' Marmie said, nodding and holding out her hand for the clipboard.

'Yes. There is only one surveillance camera in each cell, but many of them are covered with files or dust, and besides, the screens for these rooms are turned off most of the time. No audio surveillance that I know of. I will lock you in and come for you or send someone to fetch you as soon as possible.'

Opening one of the cells, he pulled down two boxes. Inside each was a guard uniform, a bottle of water, and a packet of nutrient bars. He gave Marmion a key. 'Please, if something goes wrong and you are recaptured, don't be caught with this on you. I have no idea how long I'll be gone, and if I am much delayed, you will eventually want to try to escape on your own. I don't advise it. This place is a maze, and in many ways the most brutal and dangerous part of the prison.'

'How long do you estimate?' Marmion asked.

He pointed to the dusty concrete wall where a large clock that was marked in twenty-four-hour Standard time hung. The face was almost obscured by dust and cobwebs, but the second hand was moving. 'At least twenty-four hours.'

He started to turn to leave, but Marmion stood on tiptoe and kissed him on each cheek. 'This is very good of you, Christian. Be careful of yourself. They are bound to miss us soon, and you will be questioned.'

'I plan to be unavailable for questioning,' he told her.

'Good luck with that,' Adrienne said dryly. 'You've put yourself in a lot of danger for us.'

He smiled. 'Perhaps, but there are many among us who have cause to do a favor for Madame Marmion. I know of one man, at least, who can take you away from here, though, alas, not in a spaceship.'

'No sense compromising more people than necessary,' Adrienne said. 'We have only to alert some of Madame's powerful allies and they will put an end to this nonsense. They'll open the cells and release our people and put those who arrested us inside instead.'

Christian had been heading for the door, but then stopped and looked back at them, a worried frown on his face. 'The officials here are good at covering their tracks. People who talk about what happens at Gwinnet have a way of disappearing. They're fine with scaring the prisoners by letting them know what goes on here, and they don't mind some reports of the brutality leaking to the outside, just as long as it frightens people powerless to stop them. The officials and politicos claim a hard reputation is a deterrent to crime, but some of what happens—' He shook his head and looked down. '—is so inhuman it could be classified as war crime.' His eyes were tormented as he looked back up at them. 'They have terrible things planned for you, Madame, and for your crew as well. Revenge for the inconvenience you have caused them, but also to make an example of you to other powerful people who would get in their way. They have stayed their hands so far only because they are still rounding up those who are loyal to you, and because they do not wish your friends to find out about your arrest in the meantime and upon investigation find you damaged before they have full control of the situation.'

'We'll see who is damaged,' Adrienne muttered, but at this stage she knew it was a vain threat, coupled with wistful thinking.

'Have they – damaged – any of my crew thus far?' Marmie asked. 'They have kept me in solitary, and other than poor food and sanitation and a bit of jeering, today is the first time I have felt actually threatened.'

'They've roughed up a few of the men, claiming they resisted arrest. I can't stay any longer, ladies. I have to try to make arrangements before I'm expected for my next shift.'

'Wait,' Adrienne said. 'If someone else comes instead of you, how will we know it's safe to go with them? Shouldn't we have a password?'

'What do you suggest?'

'Have them say they've come with orders from General Bonaparte regarding the retreat,' Marmie suggested with a smile. 'And Christian?'

'Madame?'

'*Merci beaucoup.*'

Ro! Murel sent her thoughts and her sonar after her brother as far and as loudly as she could for as long as she could, but although he answered at first, and her sonar found his shape in the water, she could no longer hear him, no longer find him. She swam out beyond Kai's reach but then had to dive and swim in the opposite direction from that of the boat that had captured Ronan. Fortunately, neither that boat nor the other vessel they had spotted near the squid trough seemed to be equipped with complex tracking devices. And why should they? Other than the squid, there were no large animals in this ocean, and there didn't seem to be a lot of marine traffic either. Her own sonar was apparently more sophisticated than what the boats used.

She was much farther from shore than she wanted to be by the time her sonar no longer detected the boat – or her brother.

She thought he might be unconscious now, since he didn't answer, but she kept trying. But when she finally did hear another thought-voice, it wasn't Ronan's.

Murel river seal? It's me, your friend, Sky. Why are you calling Ronan river seal? Is he not with you? Is he hiding? Are you playing a game? Can I play too?

Sky? We thought – we didn't know what happened to you. Are you okay?

I am good. The cat is also good, now that she is not drowned. She said she was good at swimming, but she is not an otter so she rides in the boat with the men. But she likes hiding and seeking. I do not know if she knows how to count hundreds, but she is very clever. Not as clever as an otter, but very clever for a cat.

What boat? What men? Do you mean the ship's cat, Zuzu, from the Piaf?

Yes! Sky said. *Where is Ronan river seal hiding?*

He's not hiding, Sky. He's been taken, netted.

We were netted, Murel, Sky said. *It was not*

bad. They scooped us into a big net and put us down on the boat and then the man with the eel fingers touched the cat's chest over and over and almost ate her, but not really, it was more like grooming. Very strange. But then she got up and washed. That is the reason she is not swimming now.

Sky drew nearer while telling her this, and she swam closer to him. Her sonar 'saw' his image at last.

Over here, Sky, but dive and I'll meet you underwater.

But if I dive, the men will not know where to bring the boat and Zuzu to find me.

That's the general idea, Murel told him, too weary to keep the impatience from her thoughts.

But they are good men. Their boat smells bad but they are good. They fixed the cat.

Just because people are nice to cats and otters doesn't mean they'll be nice to river seals, Sky. I have to keep hidden from these men.

Hah! We are playing hide and seek again! the otter replied. *The cat and I played hide and seek too, with the cat's human female, Adrienne, and the nice human female from the ship, Marmie. The bad men had them, but the cat and I hid and sent them a scent warning and they left. Then a good man came for the females.*

227

Were Marmie and Adrienne okay? Are you saying they escaped?

Mostly escaped. But maybe only hiding from the bad men.

All of Murel's impatience with the otter and some of her tiredness vanished. *That's good news, Sky. You did good. You and the cat showed a lot of ingenuity and courage to help them.*

No, Sky said. *We didn't show them anything. But we loosed a strong scent message on them and they smelled that and ran away! Scent messages are like swimming. Cats do it, but not as good as otters.*

Sky?

Murel heard an anxious and somewhat nasal thought-tone calling her friend.

Mon ami, *you are lost. Where are you?*

I am playing hide and seek. Murel river seal and I are hiding from the boat.

But why? Mon capitaine *demonstrates great anxiety on your behalf. Everywhere he searches for you.*

That is the point of hide and seek, cat, Sky pointed out.

Zuzu, those men are trying to capture or kill my brother and me, Murel told the cat.

Nonsense! Zuzu said. *They are purrfectly pleasant men, if a bit smelly. They are very kind. They feed the local sea creatures with refuse from the prison.*

Is that *the boat that picked you up? The one that dumps the bodies of the dead prisoners into the squid canyon?*

Ah! So that *is the smell. The dead prisoners you refer to – no one we know, I trust?*

Not so far.

What is a squid canyon? Sky and Zuzu asked together.

It's a deep abyss in the sea where squid live.

And squid are what? Zuzu asked.

Remember the sharks?

How could I forget? Sky asked with a quiver of his whiskers.

They're like sharks, only with lots of arms.

Hmph. More than four seems excessive, Zuzu said.

Murel told them about the squid attack and got so involved in the story she didn't realize she was surfacing for air as she communicated. The surfacing, unless there was some reason to do it sooner or later, was almost reflexive.

As she surfaced, she felt a paw on her hind flipper and looked back to see Sky.

Tag! he said.

She took in her air, and as she did, saw the boat. It was almost upon them, and Zuzu was sitting like a figurehead on the bow. As Murel dipped back beneath the surface, the ship lowered its net. She tried to swim away but felt confused – she didn't want to be alone again, to leave Sky and Zuzu, and that, coupled with her exhaustion, caused her to dither in trying to decide which direction to swim. By the time she decided to dive below the net, it was touching her nose. She twirled around and around in it, trying to get out, but Sky held her with his paws saying, *Be still, Murel river seal. These men save cats and otters and feed squids. I think they will save a river seal too.*

As they were hauled into the air, Murel recalled that the men had let them go before. So why had they netted her a second time? Did they know what she was now? Were they trying to catch Sky again?

A long heavy metal hook came straight at her through the net. She flinched, but it only threaded itself over two sections of the rope that made the net and pulled the entire thing toward the boat's deck, where it was lowered, then opened, dumping her and Sky hard onto the wooden planks that smelled of death. At least the boat was not presently hauling its customary cargo.

Zuzu, we are here! Sky announced, jumping up, ready to scamper off.

So I observed, Zuzu said with a yawn. *Did you perhaps bring fish with you? I am once more famished.*

Murel hoisted herself onto her front flippers and started to shake herself dry, then thought better of it. Perhaps she could jump overboard again before the sun dried her, and the men would never know of her dual nature.

But the sun was hot and there was no place to hide. Sky, who had watched her transformation countless times, ran around her, trying to obscure the process with a blur of otterly speed. Zuzu was not so helpful. To Murel's chagrin, the cat stalked the transforming bits.

Qu'est-ce que c'est? the cat exclaimed. *Where did the fur go?* Alors! Un nez! *And fingers!*

Zuzu, please *stop making such a big deal out of it,* Murel begged. *I'd like to finish my change and dive back overboard before the men notice.*

But this is so interesting! How do you do this thing? Zuzu asked, sniffing at Murel's shins, where the flippers were just narrowing and pinkening into feet.

I do it all the time. So does my brother and my dad. We're selkies. I thought you knew.

Non, the cat said, sitting back and washing a paw. *Me, I mind my own business. What is it to me who turns into seals and who does not? Or who turns into humans or does not, for that matter? To me it has been much better to be always the cat.*

The clomp of heavy, smelly boots and a

shadow fell across Murel and her friends. The captain hunkered down beside them. He reached out a hand to touch her and she flinched. 'So you're the dangerous alien escaped prisoner with seagoing superpowers we were all supposed to watch out for. How about that?'

Murel didn't know how to respond. She wanted to say she wasn't dangerous, but then thought it might be better if he thought she was. Finally she said, 'I'm just a kid. My guardian was sent to prison and they rounded all of us up. I haven't done anything wrong.'

'You were one of the seals we caught earlier, weren't you?'

'Yes, and you let us go then. Let me go now. My brother needs my help.'

'He was the other seal?'

Again Murel didn't know if she should admit that or not. While she was hesitating, the captain turned around and bellowed to his mate, 'Lloyd, dig my civvies out of my sea chest so our catch of the day doesn't get herself a nasty sunburn.'

When Murel put it on, his T-shirt, in shades of blue intended to blend with the sea and camouflage him, came past her knees and elbows. Sitting with her knees to her chest, she pulled it down to cover all the rest of her too. The captain slapped a visored uniform cap on her head.

'Your nose was getting a little red,' he said. 'Now then, you want to tell old Cap'n Terry all about it, or shall I just call into the base now and let them tell me what to do with you? Or maybe I should wait and see what the otter and the cat turn into?'

The reassuring thing about him was that although he was smiling, he didn't look or sound overly nice, the way adults did when they were trying to cajole a kid into doing something, all soft smiles and gentle eyes and even baby talk till they were ready to pounce. He looked at her like he expected an answer, needed an answer, or he'd do exactly what he said and report her. Whereas if she answered? 'You already know my secret,' she said. 'But I don't know anything about you. What's the point in telling you how we got here or where we're from if you're just going to turn us in? I'd be wasting my breath.'

'I'm curious,' he said. 'And the last time I boned up on interplanetary law, there wasn't one against little girls turning into seals or vice versa.'

'Yeah, but you work for the company. You throw the dead bodies to those squids. Anyway, I hope all the bodies are dead.'

'Me too,' he said. 'I can't figure out how you killed those two we saw yesterday.'

'We didn't,' she said. 'They attacked us and we fought back, but then they started fighting with each other and we got away.'

He nodded. When he spoke again, she thought he was going to ask a question, but he said, 'Fair enough, you want to know about me – and Lloyd too, I guess. We used to have a space vessel, but I had a slight dispute with a company official over my fees and whether or not he should pay them, and the next thing you know, my ship was confiscated and Lloyd and I were arrested.'

'So you're a prisoner too?'

He shook his head. 'Nah, though we could still be. Later that year there was some new blood in the Federation court system and on the company board, and all of the cases were reviewed. Anybody could see the charges against us were pure fumes, but by the time we were released, our ship had been chopped up for parts.'

'Didn't the new court offer to pay for it?'

'Honey, letting prisoners go and letting money go are two totally different issues to a corporate entity. They did give me some compensation, and later I invested part of it in this boat. And they offered me a job.'

'This one?'

'No, I worked as a locksmith for a while early on, then later helped set up security systems. Gwinnet was the last place I worked on.'

'But – how come you're working out here now?'

'I didn't like it inside. I saw stuff that turned my stomach.' He gestured to the boat's deck. 'At least the stiffs I throw to the squids aren't suffering anymore.'

His voice was bitter, with a fierce edge that rang more true to Murel than any gentler pity. He sounded like her mother might have if she were doing the same job. Da, he would try for scientific detachment from what he couldn't help, but when Mum said how she felt about something, you knew that for her, that was how it was – the long and the short of it, as Aunty Aisling might say. Da was the family diplomat. Mum, with her long career in the military, was more inclined to direct action, and if that was not possible, frustration. And in some cases subversion, the kind she had been plotting when Ronan and Murel decided they needed to take matters into their own appendages.

'Couldn't you leave?' she asked. 'Do you have to do this?'

He took a deep breath and gnawed the end of his fluffy white mustache, which reminded

Murel a bit of one of Sky's sea otter cousins. 'I tried to transfer offworld again, but there was never space for me on the transport ships, somehow or other. I think they're afraid I'll blow the whistle. But I couldn't just stay inside and watch. I knew that sooner or later I'd go nuclear on one of those bastards and end up back on the wrong side of the bars. So when this boat was brought in as part of a seizure from a big drug bust, I bought it. Then I put on my cheery corporate guy face and convinced the brass to let me transport the bodies out to the deep part of the ocean instead of dumping them right offshore, where they were creating a health hazard for the guards and admin personnel, as well as the other prisoners who, you know, didn't actually count.'

He jerked his thumb back at the mate. 'Lloyd came with me. One of these days we'll get him back home to see his kids, or maybe it's grandkids by now, but in the meantime I need him around. He's the only one who can put up with me for any length of time.'

'Have you got a family?' she asked.

'Several,' he replied. 'In different places, from different times in my life. I used to hear from one of my sons once in a while, but that was before I landed here. I don't think any communication is allowed through.'

'None? Are you sure?'

'I haven't received any demands for money from any of my exes since I've been here. Which just goes to show you that even a sewer like this has a silver lining.'

'Are you going to turn me in?' she asked.

'If I don't, I don't know what to do with you. We're not exactly outfitted as a cruise ship here.'

'Just let me go, then.'

'You were never here,' he said. 'Only – if you go back in, what are you going to do? You said they caught your brother. Seems like it's not going to be long until they catch you too. I have a suggestion for you – and it's just a suggestion, mind you. Why don't you and your otter buddy dive back in the drink but hang around with us? That way I'll know you're safe or can help you out if you get into trouble.'

'Or know where I am when your friends come to collect me,' she said.

'If that's what I'm up to, I could just net you again.'

'True. You could do that,' she said. 'But I can't just hang around here and be safe. I have to try to help Ro and Marmie and the others.'

'We got a message asking us to assist with your capture, and it warned us about the net stretched along the bottom. There will still be people waiting for you to spring it. Your safest bet is to go ashore with us, but we're going to need a reason to land on the island. If someone asks us what we're doing here now, we can claim we're doing some recreational fishing. You'd better keep out of sight.'

'I can do that easier in the water, but I have to help Ro.'

He nodded. 'We'll see what we can find out from this end, but we've got to make it all look like business as usual. Can you hear it if I tap on the hull?'

'Sure, but it's easier if you just tell the cat.'

'Of course it is,' he said, clearly trying not to laugh. 'Silly me not to think of that. You're all telepathic, right?'

Murel nodded.

'You talk to the squids too?'

'They were about to have supper so we couldn't stay and chat,' she said.

He grinned but made no further comment.

She pulled off the hat and jumped overboard, letting the water pull the T-shirt up around her neck. Sky used his otter paws, more flexible than her flippers, and helped her remove it the rest of the way. They left it floating, and the dip net descended and scooped it up.

She wished she could relax and just let the

238

adults handle this, but it was beginning to seem like those days were over. This man might help and he might not. Her impression was that he sincerely wanted to, but from what he said, he was almost as much a prisoner as she was.

Nevertheless, instead of turning back toward the mainland, he turned his bow toward the island.

17

Ronan's struggles with the net ended when his head knocked against the side of the boat. Dimly, he heard Murel calling him, but he could not answer. Then the calling stopped, as did all other impressions until he found himself awake, on a beach, naked and in human form, surrounded by feet both bare and booted.

'The freak's waking up,' someone said, half threatening and half scared.

'Let's throw it back in the water again and watch it change back,' someone else said.

'Are you kidding? The old bat would kill us if we let him go. As it is, extra rations all around.'

'And a promotion for me,' a girl said. Ronan looked up into Kai's triumphant face. 'I'm the one who helped catch him. If I catch his sister too, I'll get off this planet and have a berth aboard a ship before the rest of you finish basic training.'

Ronan scanned the faces around him while keeping his own as still as he could, trying not to give anything away. Rory was there, his expression also carefully blank. Kai was the only one of the Kanaka kids in the crowd. Ronan had never seen any of the others, who were mostly older and wore, in addition to their camp tunics, bits of Corps uniforms. Among them stood adult soldiers, wearing uniforms and self-satisfied expressions.

Presently Dr Mabo arrived. She patted Rory's shoulder approvingly as she passed him, a most un-Mabolike gesture.

Rory must have joined up fast, Ronan realized, maybe right after he talked to him and Murel. He recognized that he was on the beach near the military encampment, not the one near the children's prison. There were no nice little huts or bamboo walls, just blocky prefabs and the company colors flying below the Federation ones on a pole in the middle. That was all he could see, looking between heads and feet. Mabo prodded him with her toe.

'Get up, boy, and come with me. We have important work to do, the two of us.'

Ronan sat up. 'Can I borrow a shirt or something?' he asked.

'Clothing is for human beings,' Mabo said. 'Don't worry. You won't be staying in human form long.'

She leaned forward, and he thought for one incredulous moment that she was going to help him up, but instead she reached around his neck and clamped on a collar. 'You'll be wearing this at all times, in whatever form.'

It was soft and nonchafing, but when he touched it, he felt some sort of webbing throughout the surface. 'What is it? A dog collar?'

'As long as you are a good creature and co-operative, it is simply a monitoring device.' She pulled something out of a pocket in her trousers. 'If not . . .'

Pain shot directly into his head and all the way down to his toes. He wet himself with the shock and the onlookers snickered or made disgusted sounds.

'If you fail to follow orders, that will happen. I can make it worse. If you attempt to escape, I can track you. There is a lethal setting, by the way. Come along.'

'Can I wash off first?' he asked.

'You'll be wet again soon enough,' she said.

Murel? he called, but his sister didn't answer. He was sure she hadn't been captured or she'd be there too. How was he going to get out of this? He wished he could communicate with Rory the same way he could with Murel, but he couldn't. Rory was smart. If there was a way he could help, he would. Unfortunately, Ronan was sure Mabo knew that too.

The others had parted before Mabo. When Ronan didn't follow quickly enough, the collar gave him smaller shocks that made him twitch and jerk and threw him off balance. Derisive laughter followed his naked behind as he trailed behind Mabo until she entered one of the pre-fab huts.

He heard footsteps behind him and turned his head for a second. Kai was following them into the hut.

Mabo gave him a grandmotherly smile and stroked the side of the collar's control device with her thumb. 'I realize, Ronan, that since you served as my research assistant previously, you are the most qualified applicant for the present opening. However, since you are to be the subject of the current experiments, I need a new assistant. This girl has showed initiative and furthermore seems to have some sort of a grudge against you. But don't worry. I won't let her harm you any more than necessary.'

When he had first stepped in from the sun-light, the inside of the small structure seemed dark and featureless, but now he saw that besides a desk, chair, and a metal table, there was a sturdy stand supporting a clear-sided tank about the size of a deep bathtub. It was filled with water, and for a moment he thought there might be fish in it – snacks for him? He didn't think so. Mabo didn't strike him as the considerate type.

'Get in,' she said, pointing to the tank.

He frowned at the tank, and another bolt of pain ran through him. 'I can't!' he said, hating the whine in his voice. 'It's too high.'

Kai walked to a shadowed corner and pulled out a ladder, which she attached to the top of the tank, then pointed to him and the ladder.

He didn't want more agony. He climbed in, mooning Mabo and Kai as he lowered himself into the tank.

His feet began changing into his flippered tail as soon as they touched water, and he slid down, eager to cover himself with water and fur.

'Stop right there,' Mabo said before he could sit in the water. So there he was, tail to the knees, bare human thighs bound at the knees by his own transition. Mabo climbed the ladder and leaned over the edge of the tank, holding something other than the control to the collar. Despite the heat, Ronan shivered as the back of her hand brushed his skin. He felt a sharp sting just where his tail met his leg, then another one, and jumped, knocking into Mabo. She turned her face slowly sideways to meet his gaze, allowing her eyes to flick meaningfully to her hand. He held perfectly still as she straightened herself on the ladder and climbed down it. Then, while she turned to prepare some slides, he examined the sore spot. The water was bloody.

'Ow,' he said.

'I never promised it wouldn't hurt,' she said. 'I have to take specimens. You'll get used to it.'

'Have you tried it on yourself?' he asked.

'Of course not. I'm a human being all the time.'

'So?'

'So if you don't quit whining and leave me to conduct my work in peace, I'll give you more of this to whine about.' The pain slashed through him again. He cried out before he could keep his vow to not give her the satisfaction. It didn't matter. She wasn't even paying attention to him anymore. Kai was out of his range of vision, behind him somewhere, which didn't thrill him either.

He wished he could train himself to think past the pain caused by the collar. Whatever Mabo said, he knew she didn't want to damage him, because then she wouldn't have a live specimen, so even though the collar hurt like mad, it probably wasn't doing him any real harm.

What hurt most was his tail. It was not designed to have his dry body standing on it. He eased himself slowly, slowly, down the side of the tank so he could sit. He didn't want another taste of the collar, but he didn't want to crush his tail either, which would mean his legs and feet would be broken when the tail changed into them again.

'Doctor, Doctor!' Kai said.

Mabo looked over and her eyes narrowed. He expected another stab of pain from the collar, but instead she stood, both hands closed, and said, 'I was going to do this a bit slower, but now that you're down that far, stick your head under too. Not your shoulders and torso, mind you, just your head. And leave it there until I tell you otherwise.'

He meant to obey, tried to obey, but the tank was too narrow and the water too deep if he tried it one way and too shallow another.

Finally Mabo said, 'Fine then, Kai, you hold him around the waist and stick his head under.'

The big Kanaka girl climbed the steps, her heavy gravity body making the tank slosh and shake with each rung. She grabbed Ronan by the hair, then under the armpits, and hauled him up until she could get an arm around his body where his waist met his tail.

Though it seemed to him she lifted him as he would one of Clodagh's cats, though he'd have been gentler, she complained, 'Ugh. He's really heavy.'

He started to return the compliment, but before he could, she took hold of the back of his head and bent him double, shoving his face into the water.

Murel called and called, both mentally and by using her sonar song, but she heard nothing from Ronan. Not a peep. Surely they wouldn't just kill him? They might not mean to, but accidentally? The thought panicked her until she realized with an inner certainty so concrete that if it had been an anchor it would have sunk to the bottom of the sea: *If he were dead, I'd know.* Followed by: *Wouldn't I?*

Sky popped his head above the surface and said, *Ronan river seal is not here. He is hiding?*

I wish! Someone is hiding him.

We can find him! Sky said. *Where are the best hiding places here?*

They're ashore, Sky, but there are nets between us and the shore. I think we're going to have to trust the people on the boat to take us ashore – maybe in disguise.

What is disguise?

Pretending to be someone you are not.

I will pretend to be another otter? Which one? There is only one sky otter and I am the one.

I didn't mean you. I meant me. I will pretend to be another human. There are no other otters of any kind here that I've found, so you'd better just hide. Come on, she said, and began swimming toward the boat, only to find it was no longer where they had left it.

She sang her sonar song again and found it, but it was very far away. *Cat?* she said. *I thought the boat was going to stay with us?*

The capitaine *thought that you were going to stay near to the boat. We received a message that is causing us to return to the prison.*

I thought he was going to tell you to let us know if there was a change in plans.

He did, but first I was eating and now I perform my toilette. I cannot do it all at once. So I tell you now. We return to the shore of the prison. If you wish to be with the boat, you must also come. The otter swims very quickly. He can catch up, of this I am certain.

Sky found nothing to quibble with about the cat's attitude, and Murel, raised with Nanook and Coaxtl and Clodagh's orange-tabby pride, realized she was very tired and worried indeed. Of course, the cat had better things to do than take messages for them. She was a cat, after all.

No matter. Before long the boat was in sight again and the captain spied them with his binoculars. Soon they were back on board. Murel changed, and wore the now-dry T-shirt and cap once more. Sky, with Zuzu's assistance, was eating a fish.

'I guess I don't have to ask if you had any luck,' the captain said.

'No luck. And if we had, I think I'm too tired to do anything about it.'

'Take a nap in the cabin. We've about two and a half hours until we reach shore and have business to take care of. We may need your help then.'

She took him up on his suggestion, curling into a ball on the sticky, ripped plastic cushion of the long, curved bench inside the cabin. Just before she dropped off, she was aware of two furry bodies joining her, one snuggling into the place behind her knees and one climbing on top of her to sit on her upturned hip.

'What are we going to do with them?' Sinead asked, nodding in the direction of the long-house, where armed villagers – the few not currently crowded into Clodagh's cabin – guarded the soldiers. The temperature outside had risen and the blizzard had blown away, leaving deep drifts and silence as its legacy. Clodagh's stove pumped heat into the room, and steam rose from the snow melting from mittens, hats, and boots.

'Keep them there, I guess,' Aidan replied, extending his bare hands toward the stove to warm them. 'They're really gonna cool their heels, though, with no fire.'

'Sorry,' Yana said. 'But they're still wearing good winter gear, and I don't trust them not to burn the place down around themselves to force us to release them. It's the sort of thing I'd have done if I were in their place.'

'It's not that so much,' Sinead said wryly. 'But I worked hard helping build the longhouse and it's got some brilliant carvings on the beams and posts. I'd hate to see it burned down. Still, we can't keep them there indefinitely.'

Sean, who had been away for the first part of the meeting, announced his arrival by stamping his boots on the stoop outside. His entry sent one of Clodagh's orange-striped cats leaping up from its nap on the coats piled beside the door onto one of the rafters, where it glared disapprovingly at the humans taking up all the other good nap spots not currently occupied by other orange cats. Its hind paws and tail disturbed bunches of the remaining dried plants strung upside down along the beams. Flakes of leaves, petals, and grasses sifted down onto the heads and shoulders of those below, along with a whisper of herbal fragrance that caused Eamon Oogliuk to sneeze into his mitten.

'Sean, we were talking about how safe it is for the soldiers to have them in the longhouse with no fire, and how dangerous we were afraid it would be to let them build one,' Sinead said, filling him in.

'It's been sorted out,' he said cheerily. 'I've been talking on the com to some of the distant villages. They're sending sleds and snocles to collect their share of our honored guests.'

'You're splitting them up, then?' Sinead asked.

'That I am,' he replied. 'First they'll be going to each village's Stranger Cave to make their manners with Petaybee, then those who are accepted will have a latchkay in their honor and those who don't will receive the appropriate treatment. By dividing them, even if we don't exactly conquer, at least we'll prevent them from planning any mischief together. I think this is one strategy they'll not be counting on.'

Clodagh smiled and began stuffing medicinal items in a bag made of woven rabbit skins.

'Did you try the com farther afield, Sean?' Yana asked when the general comment had died down. 'Any news of the kids, or from Johnny and the others?'

He shook his head. 'No, but I didn't try. I was busy contacting the villages to take care of the current problem. I'll try to reach Johnny now, shall I, and see if they've been able to get a message to Marmie's allies.'

'Try the relay to *Versailles Station* too, if you can get offworld,' she said. 'That's the logical place for the kids to look for Marmie's allies.'

'For that matter, I could try a few of them from here, if I can get out at all,' he said.

Clodagh shot a look at Yana and said to Sean, 'But stay and warm up a moment first, love.'

'No, no, I need to get back to the cave and let the others know what's going on here. The rock flock are supposed to be helping our newest citizens, but you know how transported they can get in the communion cave. No need to alarm the others any more than they are already. They'll want to know when it's safe to come home again.'

'I'd wait,' Clodagh said.

'Yeah,' Aidan agreed. 'They're a good enough lot, but they're new and we've no idea where their loyalties may lie. No sense burdening them with more information than they might want to have. Another ship might land soon, and we're down to just the one hijacker.' He dipped the tassel on his hat in Yana's direction. 'We don't want to put the newcomers in the way of bein' interrogated.'

'Nor any of us,' Aisling added.

'Indeed. So they'll need to stay in the cave a bit longer?'

'Aye, and the rest of us will need to be gettin' back there as well,' Sinead said. 'At least to sleep. We won't want to be caught out if another troop ship lands. They'll not be happy about us hostin' their personnel.'

'Back to the com station with me it is, then,' Sean said. 'The first sleds and snocles should be here in a couple of hours, so keep an eye out for them.'

Sean trudged back out to the com station. It was the old com shed with a Nakatira cube added. The soldiers had sacked it, but hadn't damaged anything of importance, probably thinking they might have a need for it themselves later on.

For a change he got a clear signal. He tried *Versailles Station* first, since the hijacked troop ship had only departed a short time ago. He'd become very familiar with the station's routing procedure while the kids were in school there and expected to hear one of the voices he'd come to know.

Instead he was answered by an unfamiliar female voice that gave the station's registration number but not its name or corporate affiliation, as previous comoffs had. 'Please identify yourself and state your business,' she said.

'You first,' Sean replied, putting a bit of the Irish blarney in his tone to sound flirtatious and perhaps as if he'd been into the blurry. 'You've a lovely voice.'

'Please identify yourself and state your business,' she said.

'You don't sound like the usual operator. Let me talk to Yasmine. She knows me, and you see, I'm a bit shy.'

'Identify yourself,' she repeated, then added, 'I can trace this, you know. Only authorized communications are acceptable.'

'How about putting me through to Colonel Cally then?' Sean asked. 'This is a classified situation.'

'There is no Colonel Cally at this station. Colonel Montgomery is the officer in charge. But he will not speak to unidentified callers.'

Sean broke contact. The station was under Corps control. He hailed the troop ship next. Again a clear signal, which was a great relief, since he felt an urgent need to talk to an off-planet ally.

'Good to hear from you, Sean,' Rick O'Shay,

manning the com, said in answer to his hail. 'How did it go on that end? Yana get away okay?'

'She took a bit of a dunking, but that was our fault. Sinead set a few surprises for our guests.'

'And how are your guests? Added some, did you?'

'Yes, the crew joined the rest of their party in our largest and most deluxe accommodation. Since heating presents a bit of a problem, however, they'll be touring the pole with some of our most experienced guides.'

'Ah. We're doing grand here too. A bit understaffed, but we're all excellent multi-taskers, so that's no bother.'

'I'd a special reason for wanting to chat, Richard.'

'And that would be?'

'It seems there's new management at *Versailles Station,* which is most likely where our young ones had their new friends take them. Is there any way you can find out what happened? They may be needing assistance, and we've no other way to reach them.'

'I'll speak with the charming Petula and get back to you, Sean.'

'You know what it's been like here, Rick. You might get us again and you might not. I'm sure the kids are fine, but if I don't do something to reassure their mother, she may declare war on the Company Corps, and while they're being a bother at the moment, I'd hate to see that happen to them. They do have their uses.'

'Understood. Ah, here is our Ms. Chan now. Pet, pet, Governor Shongili himself would like a word.'

'Chan,' she said in a clipped voice that reminded him of Yana on a bad day. 'What's up, Governor?'

'As you may be aware, my children took an alternate form of transport and we think they may have gone to *Versailles Station* to seek help for Marmie. I just tried the regular channels to locate them at the station, and it seems to have undergone a hostile takeover.'

'But all you've tried is the direct method?'

'Aye. Is there another you might employ?'

'Perhaps,' she said.

Sean sat there waiting, planning how to handle Kilcoole's share of the invasion party. He felt unusually impatient and restless. How long could it take them to contact the station? Surely Pet still had contacts there. She'd been Marmie's security chief for years, after all. When he tried to imagine what could be happening to cause such a long delay, he could think of all too many disturbing scenarios.

Contacting the station could tip off their enemies that the ship was not where it was supposed to be and that the crew was not what it was supposed to be. The station might notify others in the Corps who were closer, and they would recapture the ship and Petaybee's space-borne allies and send another ship with more invasion troops to complete the mission.

That was a long shot, though. Johnny, Rick, Pet, and the new guy, Raj, were all Corps veterans themselves and had experience dealing with the protocol and all that. As a native Petaybean, Sean had never served in the Corps or even been offworld, which sometimes made him wonder what a well-versed woman like Yana saw in him. But then, she couldn't turn into a seal and enjoy roaming the rivers and ocean as he and the kids could.

The kids . . . Where *were* the little hooligans anyway? What if they weren't at *Versailles Station*? Where would the aliens have taken them then? And almost scarier, with *Versailles* apparently under martial law, what if they *were* there?

He found himself tapping his foot and drumming his fingers against the instrument panel to the beat of one of the Irish tunes used for latchkay songs. Why didn't Pet answer him? He watched the instruments carefully, but there were no red spots or blips on the screens indicating that the planet's magnetic forces were playing merry hell with communications again. He realized that that was partially why he was so impatient. He had no idea how long this clear spot would last.

At last Pet's face reappeared on the screen, wearing a grim expression. 'I'm sorry, Sean. I couldn't reach anyone I could trust to find out more. We're monitoring the station's communications now to see if any mention of the twins or our other people pop up, but for now what it looks like to me is that they must all have been detained – possibly taken off-station. There are mentions of Gwinnet, but nothing specific yet. We'll let you know when and if we have more-definite information, but for now we think it best to bypass the station and contact Whit Fiske, the Federation board chairman, and some of Marmie's other friends, as soon as possible. If we can free her, she can help us locate the kids.'

'Thanks for trying, then,' Sean said, attempting not to sound as glum as he felt.

Pet Chan's visage vanished from the screen, to be replaced briefly by Rick O'Shay's.

'Good luck to you all,' Sean told him.

'And to you,' Rick said.

$$\star \quad \star \quad \star$$

The sleds and snocles arrived in ones, twos, and threes, first the Chugliaks from Kilgalen, then a delegation from Harrison Fjord, and another led by the Flood-Fitzhughs of Perfect Fjord.

Teams and machines were given maintenance and their drivers were fed and rested before the longhouse was opened, and two and three at a time the soldiers, warmly dressed, were given warm soup to drink and smoked salmon to chew before being bound hand and foot and strapped into the sleds or inside the snocles.

When the last of them were gone and Kilcoole's guests had been dispatched with other sleds and snocles to one of the distant communion caves not in common use by the villagers, Sean returned to their own cave and the newcomers.

He was surprised when Ke-ola, looking massive in furry snow pants and parka, greeted him outside the cave.

'What's the matter, Ke-ola lad?' Sean asked, seeing yet more trouble clearly etched on the boy's round features.

'It's the Honus, Papa Sean,' he said. He'd gone from the formal 'Governor Shongili' to 'Doctor' to 'Papa,' then decided that that was too informal and settled on 'Papa Sean.' Most older people were uncles and aunts to the Kanaka kids, but since the twins and Ke-ola had somewhat adopted each other, Ke-ola considered Sean a closer relative than most.

'What about them?' Sean asked. 'Has something happened to them?'

'No, not really, but they're restless, and they swam under the ice all the way here and since then have been swimming in circles in the water.'

'Have they told you what's bothering them?'

'No. They aren't talking to me, or any of the rest of us. But they're real agitated about something. So I was thinking, maybe if you turn into a seal again they'd tell you what's the matter.'

Sean thought about putting the lad off, since he had quite a few things to organize, but as he and his family had learned before, Honus *knew* things, and he knew very well that what they might know and not be telling was exactly what concerned Ke-ola.

He and Ke-ola were alone outside the cave, so he stripped off and dived into the hot springs, changing at once and surfacing in the midst of the circling turtles. *Now then, my hard-shelled friends, what's this game you're playing and why are you not talking to young Ke-ola? He's beside himself with worry.*

Our people need us, but they are there and we are here, the largest Honu said.

And one of them serves our enemy, the smallest Honu, the original one who came with Ke-ola, added.

Enemy? That would be that woman scientist? The one we arrested for poaching Petaybean otters and who later gave my kids such a hard time on the space station?

Enemy of Honus! the Honu replied. *Enemy of seal people and otter people also.*

Sean saw that the Honu had his priorities in order as far as he was concerned. *One of your people is serving her, then? So do you mean she's captured another Honu?*

A two-legged, the Honu answered. *They damage a third person.*

Two-legged or four?

The Honus consulted one another, closing their ring to touch noses, their shells forming a flower on the surface of the pool. *No legs,* was the consensus. *Flipper tail and grabbers.*

Sean didn't like the sound of that. Not at all. But he tried to stay calm and project calm as he clarified his suspicions. *Grabbers?*

Two-leggeds have them on top. On bottom, legs, on top, grabbers.

Arms and hands perhaps? Sean thought, but mostly to himself. To the Honus, clearly everything was best described as 'grabbers.' Instead of waiting for them to change their terminology, he asked a more pressing question. *Have you any idea where the enemy and the two-legged person of the Honus is – damaging – the person with the tail and grabbers?*

They consulted again and finally the original Honu said, *We do not know, but the seas are empty, and on the land, others of our people are caged.*

Hmm, Sean said. *I believe I know of the place. Thank you, Honus. Don't you be worryin' your shells about this a minute longer. The two-leggeds can take it from here.*

Somehow he had the feeling they were not reassured.

He swam to the pool's edge and found Ke-ola waiting with his clothing. After flipping himself dry, he related the turtles' message to Ke-ola while he pulled on his dry suit, parka, and mukluks.

'Why wouldn't they tell me?' the boy asked, clearly wounded by the reticence of the animals he loved.

'They spoke about their people doing wrong, so perhaps they meant one of your relatives,' Sean said. 'They might have extended their displeasure with that individual to your whole family.'

Ke-ola thought it over. 'Yeah, I think I remember hearing about that sort of thing happening in olden times. I think we're supposed to make an offering to appease them or something, but I'm not sure what. Not too many people still know much about the old ways.'

'You might want to talk it over with Clodagh. I've always found her very helpful where interspecies relations are concerned. I'd stay and help you myself, but I have to try to reach Johnny and his merry band of pirates and tell them plans have changed. Someone has to get my kids out of that old wagon's clutches.'

'Wagon?'

'A hateful female. Does one come to mind?'

'Dr Mabo?'

'The very one,' Sean said, but he called it over his shoulder. He was already striding back toward the com station, hoping he could still get a message to the hijacked ship.

Marmie and Adrienne kept busy while waiting for Christian's return. They each slept briefly while the other kept watch, but afterward, and when they'd eaten, they both felt the need to do something. Following Christian's description of how the records were generally organized, they covered their faces and went to work hauling the dusty files from their tombs out into the office. It was hard, heavy work even with the use of the little wheeled cart that could carry a stack of six boxes at once, but they had cleared most of one set of shelves and were halfway through another one when Marmion sat down, heavily and without her usual grace. 'Madame!' Adrienne said. 'Are you unwell?'

But Marmie was staring at one of the file boxes. After a few deep breaths, she reached for it, opened it, and began flipping through the files. Selecting one, she pulled it out, spread it on the table, and began reading. 'Aha!' she said at last, pointing. 'There it is. Read this, Adrienne.' She pointed with the wreck of a formerly well-manicured forefinger, and Adrienne did as directed, but at first did not understand.

Then Madame enlightened her. With renewed vigor, the two of them returned to the files, piling up more and more of the boxes until, once more, Madame chose a particular file from a particular box, and found another of the items that interested her. After another break for food and rest, they continued. They were still at it when they heard the scrape of a key in the door.

'We're very busy here,' Adrienne barked toward the door. 'Why are you interrupting us?'

A timid female voice replied, clearly having no idea what she was saying or why. 'I come with news from General Bonaparte regarding the retreat. You're to come with me right away.'

Captain Terry was glad to see the heads of the seal and otter surface beside his boat just before he crossed the squid hole and headed back to shore.

'Maybe we ought to stop and load them back aboard before we land,' Lloyd suggested. 'That way we won't lose track of them,'

'Nah,' Terry replied, 'They can hide easier in the water. The cat can hide aboard ship without too much trouble, but the girl isn't likely to be anything but an escaped prisoner, and these yahoos would probably shoot the otter, thinking it was a really big rat.'

'Well, yeah, but once we load the cargo aboard, there'll be two female escaped prisoners here anyway . . .'

'And once we have them safely away from port, the seal girl can come back aboard any time, and the otter too. But we don't want to attract any more attention to ourselves than we're already likely to.'

A strong wind blew up, ruffling the water and rocking the boat. The men looked up for a moment. There were no clouds, though there was a definite disturbance in the air. They could feel and almost see the air currents swirling past them. Terry and Lloyd pulled their hats down more firmly on their heads and watched the shore intently, praying that if a storm was coming it would not blow up until the transfer had been made.

Two soldiers hefted a body bag between them and heaved it onto the dock where Terry's boat routinely made its pickups of squid fodder. Shutting down the motor, Terry guided his boat in through the wind-driven waves. Then he and Lloyd hauled the heavy bag on board, unzipped it, and rolled the two bodies it contained onto the deck. The empty bag was tossed back onto the dock for reuse with the next lot. It'd never do to pollute the ocean or choke the squid with those nonbiodegradable bags, and the bags were reusable. The stiffs normally didn't mind.

One of them winked at him, which was kind of eerie, as was the warmth of the bodies under the uniforms they wore. Bodies ordinarily went out of the world the same way they came into it. Clothes, even the rags most of the longtime prisoners sported, were also thought to be damaging to the delicate ecology of the ocean and its only large denizens.

The cat sniffed the two bodies. One reached up as if to stroke the cat, but the feline gave a snort and turned its curly tail on them. The younger of the two rolled her eyes comically but refrained from saying anything. Lloyd stepped over them to start the engine again.

'Stay down until we're out of visual contact with the shore,' Terry told his newest set of passengers. They were silent as the dead while the boat chugged out to sea, until it reached the place where Terry and Lloyd would usually offload their cargo.

Then the younger woman asked, 'How did Zuzu get aboard?'

'She swam,' he told her. 'It's getting downright crowded out here lately, if you want to know the truth.'

He was watching the stern from his binoculars and saw the heads of the seal and the otter pop up again. He expected them to swim toward the boat, but instead they were looking skyward. He followed their gaze but saw nothing. Then something dropped down to the surface of the water, obscuring his view of the two sleek heads. He thought for a second that his eyes had played a trick on him, that the seal and the otter had dived, but then the water began to bubble and churn as a hole opened in the surface to admit – something.

18

Ronan thought Mabo would never stop prodding, poking, shocking, and cutting him. She was far worse than the giant squid, who had only been trying to feed themselves when they attacked. They probably didn't know the food had feelings. But Mabo did, and while she didn't seem to actually take pleasure from hurting him, she didn't exhibit any sign of pity either. At first he'd thought she was getting revenge for the time he and Murel had thwarted her attempts to experiment on the Honu and eventually caused her to flee the space station in disgrace, but she never mentioned it or actually gloated over him. Her attitude was more impersonal. She didn't care if he screamed or winced unless it spoiled her aim when she was trying to snip off another piece of him. He was one big specimen to her, not even a living creature.

Kai, after her intial expressions of dominance over him, seemed to get bored with the process, maybe even annoyed with Mabo's brisk orders, and didn't go out of her way to so much as sneer at him. It was little enough, but he was grateful that when Mabo decided it was time to sleep and left Kai with the collar control and instructions to guard him, the girl looped the strap of the control around her heavy wrist, gave him a meaningful look as if to say, 'You know what will happen if you cross me,' and walked around behind him. She probably thought he wouldn't know what she was doing if he couldn't see her, but her snores gave her away.

If she hadn't had the collar control, he could have tipped the tank over and escaped that way. But he had to do it without waking her.

The other problem was that with his bottom half in seal form, he had no leverage to raise himself out of the tank except his arms and hands. His tail was heavy, heavier than just his legs and rear. According to physics, that wasn't supposed to be possible, but physics didn't need blubber to keep its butt warm in arctic waters. Futhermore, he would stay seal-tailed as long as that part of him remained in water, which it would in the tank. He didn't see how he could dry out enough to get his legs back without flipping water onto Kai and waking her. And there was no way to climb down the ladder with a seal tail. He'd just have to figure out the water-flipping issue when he got to it. Maybe if he flipped away from her . . .

Placing his hands on the rim of the tank, he pushed with all his might, trying to raise himself. He slid up out of the water but was still too wet to change into human form. He raised himself and suspended all but his flippered tail above the water, but his arms began to shake and he felt himself caving. In order to keep from losing the gains he'd made, he twisted to one side and bent his torso over the rim. He felt the tank shift slightly beneath him, but it seemed anchored to its platform well enough to prevent it from tipping under his weight.

After a rest, during which he tried to suppress his panting so it wouldn't wake Kai, he started sliding his hands and middle along the edge of the tank's side, working his way back toward the ladder.

He had one hand on the back edge and was ready to shift when he heard footsteps outside, coming toward the doorway. He let out a sigh and dropped back down into the tank.

'Kai?' It was a young girl's voice. 'Hey, Kai, it's me, Pele. You hungry, sistah?'

Ronan groaned as he heard his guard stirring, then rising from the chair.

''Course I'm hungry. Isn't everybody?'

'We got special treats tonight and I snuck one for you,' Pele said. 'Didn't want you to miss out just because you were helping the old woman.'

'Good of you, since you hate my guts for joining up.'

'Naah, you are my sistah. Besides, you're just smarter than we were. Joining up is the only way to get out of this place. It's the only reason they keep us around. They say our folks are dead, even the ones back on the new home. We don't join up, maybe soon they stop feeding us anything.'

Kai grunted with satisfaction and tore off a big bite of doughnut, chewing it noisily.

Ronan was turned sideways to the girls and pretended not to watch. Pele and the others had certainly changed sides quickly enough, he thought bitterly. Petaybee was right about Ke-ola, but Ke-ola seemed to have far from the usual temperament in his tricky family. Exhausted, sore, and scared about what was going to happen next, Ronan wished they had just left the rest of them behind for the meteors to finish off. Then Marmie would never have been arrested, and he and Murel would never have come to this horrible place where Mabo could pounce on them.

He fully expected that soldiers would soon be dragging Murel in, to be subjected to the same treatment he'd been getting.

While Kai was munching, Pele caught him watching them. Without changing the rest of her facial expression, she gave him a one-eyed squint. A wink? Why?

She said a friendly good-bye to Kai, with a promise that she too would soon be in uniform, and departed. Kai finished her treat and settled back down beside the door. What tatters of hope and courage he'd still had deserted him. She could see everything he did before he could tell if her eyes were open or not, and even if he escaped from the tank, he'd never make it past her to the door. She'd had her nap and a snack. She'd no doubt stay awake just to push her wretched button once in a while to watch him writhe in pain.

But he was wrong. No sooner had the bully girl sat down than her snores filled the hut. That was heartening, but it didn't solve the problem of how he was to escape.

Then he heard the door open, and he feared Mabo had returned. Kai grunted and stirred but didn't wake.

Ronan waited tensely until the person who

had entered walked in far enough to see. It was Rory, in uniform, holding the collar control.

Almost silently, Rory climbed the ladder and deftly undid the collar around his neck. Ronan held his hands up, and Rory cut his bonds. A wave of anger and disgust emanated from him. Silently, he tried to help Ronan out of the tank, but it was slow going. Ronan was surprised Kai didn't wake up. 'Put that around her neck so she won't call out if she wakes up,' he whispered.

'No worries on that score, mate,' Rory told him. 'There was poppy dust on that sweet. She'll do for now. I'm saving this jewelry as a gift for my dear old gran, if you must know.'

'It will suit her,' Ronan said. He couldn't have spoken louder even if it were prudent. The collar had affected his throat, and he could barely whisper. The whisper was a raspy one, at that. 'But I've no idea how to get out of this tank, even with your help.'

'We could bail, but there's nothing to bail with,' Rory said. 'It's an awkward arrangement altogether, even for them, I'd think. I can see having it up in the air like that to make it hard for you to get out, but she wouldn't have had time to have it built especially for you, would she?'

'No,' Ronan said. 'This looks like the smaller

tanks she kept in her lab on *Versailles Station* when I was her lab assistant – not the tanks the Honu was kept in, but some others with different sorts of fish. But those had levers for raising and lowering to clean and—'

'Where were they?' Rory asked.

'Under the lower right-hand corner of the tank.'

'Found it!' Rory said, and Ronan, battered, hungry, and exhausted as he was, felt lightheaded for a moment as the room seemed to rise around him, though in reality he was going down.

So was Mabo. He intended to see to it.

'What are you doing?' Marmion cried as Captain Terry pushed the throttle of the little boat so it spat forward so fast she doubted the hull touched the water. 'I saw Murel and Sky. You did too! What game are you playing?'

In the time it took her to say that, the boat had covered the better part of a mile, and still the water swelled around it and tried to drag it backward and sideways.

'Did you see that thing plunge into the water? Look!' He pointed sternward, where the water coiled in snakelike swells, increasingly dark as they spilled into the center. With surprising velocity, the boat fought the waves, spurting away from the danger behind them.

Adrienne said, 'Even sea creatures can't survive that.'

'I think perhaps Murel and Sky will be able to,' Marmion said, pursing her lips thoughtfully. 'Something of this sort happened on Petaybee before the *Piaf* was seized. If this is the same force, it is something Murel can manage.'

Zuzu appeared at Adrienne's feet, winding herself around her ankles.

'The cat's cool, so they must be okay,' Captain Terry said thoughtfully. 'They talk, you know. The cat, the otter, and the girl. I guess her brother too. So I'd expect the cat to be upset if the others were drowned. But then, you never can tell about cats.'

Murel and Sky saw nothing when the vessel entered the water, but Murel's sonar told her exactly what it was, and she and Sky dived into the center of the vortex as the waters whirled around them.

What are they *doing here?* she wondered, as if the otter might have an answer.

Tikka missed us! Sky replied. *With no otter friends, she had to slide alone.*

It seems a long way to come for a sliding companion, Murel said. According to Sky, most issues had otters at the center.

The vortex pulled them in deeper than Murel ever remembered diving. They were in the middle of the trough containing the squid, and in the coils of water rising above them she spotted several of the creatures, or the parts of them not obscured by the turbulence of the spinning water.

The vortex was calm, a straight shot down the center, and there was air sucked from the surface. Multicolored lights blinked and beckoned from the towers inside the invisible dome. Murel feared that the alien Petaybeans, as she rhymed them in her mind, would not see her and Sky seeking entrance. Having just landed, the creatures would not have the benefit of their sursurvu equipment to show them what was going on beyond their city.

The spinning stopped as the city settled, and the pressures of the deep crushed the air from her. Above her, the squids recovered from their spins and set their courses straight for her. Then, as she touched the invisible barrier, it opened and she tumbled in, followed by Sky.

But Kushtaka and two of their other allies were there at the top of the dome, waiting for them. Tikka swam up and straight to Sky, who floated listlessly in the dense waterlike atmosphere of the dome. Murel recovered enough to realize that if the waters had felt crushing to her, they must have all but flattened her little friend.

Tikka took hold of Sky's paw in her larger one. To Murel's relief the otter turned over twice, shook himself, and said, *That slide was very big!*

Are you okay? Murel asked. But Sky wasn't listening. He pulled Tikka down toward the slide that curled around the top of one spire all the way to the streets of the city.

Looking down, she saw that the street was unusually dark. On Petaybee, Kushtaka's people had settled it over volcanic vents, which gave it a brilliant glow from the sea floor.

Did you come for us, Kushtaka? she asked.

We did not know you were here, the large otter replied. *We thought we were returning to our old homeworld again, but we must have miscalculated. Our people did not respond to our hails, and nothing looks familiar.*

Kushtaka, those beings seek entrance to the city, Mraka said, pointing up at a garden of waving squid arms and feeder tentacles within which the huge eyes of the creatures gleamed like high-tech holographic flowers, with light reflected from the city dancing across their lenses.

No, don't! Murel said. *Those things almost ate us.*

It is strange, a squid replied, and Murel knew it referred to her. *Our kind are curious. We feed seldom and it looked tasty. We wished only to try one.*

If it thinks I look strangely tasty, it is going to think the same of you, Murel told Kushtaka. She had continued staring at the squid, which seemed to be trying to hypnotize her. When Kushtaka did not reply, Murel looked at her instead. Where the deep sea otter had been, another squid, albeit a somewhat smaller one, faced the ones staring in through the dome. The other deep sea otters were changing too. *Maybe not,* she amended. The alien Petaybeans were shape shifters like Ronan and her, but had the advantage of being able to assume a wider repertoire of shapes. Mraka and Puk were in the process of changing into squid as she watched. She hoped the squid's dietary preferences didn't come with the shape.

How did you come to look this way? Kushtaka asked the squids. *And where are the others?*

Some have changed to shapes that can burrow beneath the sea floor, others live near the vents, but without our cities. Those were destroyed when the invaders first arrived, and most of our people were killed.

No word of a great war reached our adopted world, nor even tales of a genocide.

There was no war. Nor do we believe they intended genocide. Our eradication came as a by-product of them making this world suitable for themselves. Only the hardiest of us survived, and then only because of the return of spacefarers like yourselves who helped us heal and adapt.

They wiped you out accidentally? Murel asked, disgusted. *Oh, man, that's what offworlders are always trying to do to things on Petaybee. No wonder you tried to eat us!*

Not only delicious-looking, but compassionate, the squid said. *What manner of creature are you?*

I'm a Petaybean shepherd seal and a shifter like yourself. I can also look like the people who ruined your world, she replied, putting the best possible spin on her dual nature. *It comes in handy,* she added, thinking that that made her sound more like a sea creature who spied on humans instead of a human who was occasionally a sea creature.

To Kushtaka, she said, *Maybe I should go find Sky and Tikka and let you all talk among yourselves, catch up on old times, that sort of thing.*

While she found it interesting that the aliens had come home to the same prison world where Marmie was being held, she didn't see how that would make squid any less hungry, so maybe it was a good idea if she didn't hang around looking quite as yummy as they seemed to think she was. Since they were all apparently the same species, she was fairly certain Kushtaka would let the outside squid in sooner or later, and she still didn't relish being around when that happened.

Mraka and Puk followed her. *You are troubled, Murel? Perhaps you are hungry? Shall we fish?*

I could eat, but it's not my hunger that's worrying me, it's that of your long-lost relatives, she told them. *Would it be too much to ask you to turn back into otters again? You'll note these scars on my neck and back? Ronan has similar ones. Your friends nearly ate us.*

The two changed their shapes and tactfully refrained from mentioning that one of the sharks, at the time considered friends of the Shongilis, had eaten a member of Kushtaka's family.

Where is your brother? Mraka asked.

He's being held captive by a wicked old woman who wants to know how we change shape. I was trying to get help to rescue him from a boat up on the surface when you arrived. I'm afraid we can't stay long. I need to help Ronan.

Why does she care how you change shapes? Does

she wish to assume one of your shapes herself? Why does she not simply do so?

She isn't a shifter, Murel replied.

Static? But she wishes to be able to shift shapes? How sad she must be to be stuck in the one guise for life.

I'm not sure that's how she looks at it, Murel said. *I think she just likes to hurt things and make them do what she wants, but I suppose I could be – partly mistaken. Maybe she has a reason. Perhaps you should ask her.*

Then Kushtaka joined them, as an otter again, and seemed more disturbed than Murel had seen her since the death of her son. *Come. Prepare to move. We cannot remain here.*

I have to return to the surface if you're leaving, Murel told her. *Ronan is in another fix and I have to get him out. Then we've still to get Marmie and her crew and the Kanakas free, and I suppose quite a few other people.*

Are you undertaking this task alone?

There's Sky, and Captain Terry . . . she began. *But otherwise, yes, pretty much alone.*

We may be able to assist you in some way, but first we must refuel, and there are no open vents here.

I know where they are, Murel told her. *The water's a bit shallower there too, and squidless, so it would be easier for me to come and go. No offense about the squid . . .*

They are all that is left of our race, Kushtaka said. *Once this world was so overpopulated with our kind that they would not allow us to remain when we returned from an exploratory journey to the new home. And those who are left have changed. They seem to have de-evolved.*

I certainly thought so, Murel said. *I'm glad to know it wasn't just me.*

The city began to spin again, or rather, the water around it churned into another whirlpool and then a waterspout that lifted the craft above the surface.

You know, Murel said, *there are easier and less disturbing ways to do this.*

According to our equipment, much of this ocean is too shallow to permit us to travel underwater. We need to recharge before we can fly unsupported. This is the only way.

There's pontoons, Murel said. She realized it was ungrateful of her to criticize how they chose to help, but the waterspout was every bit as alarming as the whirlpool. It didn't take much imagination to picture what would happen to the displaced water in its wake. Natural waterspouts, she had read – since Petaybee didn't have any that she knew of – were formed when cyclonic winds touched the sea's surface and picked up droplets. The wake from these was said to be little more than

282

bubbles and ripples. But the domed city's fish-ing device alone generated a force that twirled tons of water around it. The force that first sank and now propelled the city through the air using seawater ultimately violently displaced the entire ocean for miles around. *Motors, paddles even. These whirly things you do are very hard on the sea life. I ought to know.*

The dense atmosphere inside the dome kept the changes in pressure from adversely affecting anyone inside, but there was still the force of the spin pressing in on the inhabitants. Murel wasn't sure when Sky and Tikka joined her, but by the time the city-ship ceased spinning, Sky had nestled between Murel's flippers and Tikka was holding on to her mother's paw.

Balanced atop the waterspout, they could look down through the sides of the dome to the sea below.

Murel was horrified by the view. If this was a rescue, it was worse than the original peril. The whirlpool pulled water into its radius for miles around. At one point, perhaps halfway to the island, she saw Captain Terry's boat. It was riding the swell produced by their passage and seemed to be doing a good job of outrunning the worst of the disturbance from the water-spout. She was mesmerized by the bizarre view from the elevated city, by the coils of water spiraling away from the waterspout's base. She couldn't imagine what effect all of this would have on the people onshore, in the prison or on the island.

At least four times as quickly as it would have taken her to swim the distance, the waterspout carried them within sight of the island. In the distance, tiny figures on the beach dashed about, pointing in their direction. The beach was much broader than she remembered it, stretching almost to the rocks where she and Ronan had sheltered. It looked surreal, and she knew it was *wrong*. Alarm bells clanged in her head, warning of danger. But the only danger she saw immediately was the pointing people. *Can they see us?* she asked Kushtaka.

No, the shields mask us. All they can see is the waterspout.

Some of the people were jumping up and down as they pointed agitatedly. They had to know this was no natural phenomenon. Why didn't they evacuate the beach while there was still time? Someone must have the sense to realize the inevitability of disaster. *Stupid, stupid, stupid,* she thought helplessly. *The eejits find this entertaining.*

Entertaining? Kushtaka tried to form an image around the word but failed.

Fun! Sky translated.

Like fish juggling? Mraka asked.

No! I mean, yes, fish juggling is entertaining. But what's going to happen onshore when we whirl underwater will be a catastrophe. Murel stopped. Her body, against her will, had been trying to go to sleep, but she kept jerking herself alert, moving her gaze so it didn't become fixed on anything long enough to allow her to drift off. Seals, unlike people, tended to sleep when they needed to, not when they had nothing better to do.

A large familiar object lay stranded, beached in the waterless expanse of sea floor that had been exposed when its waters were sucked into the waterspout.

It's the boat! Captain Terry's boat! We grounded it! she told the others.

But that was the moment the water began a downward spiral, the city sinking with it.

We have to do something! Stop it! We can't go down now! she cried. *Our backwash will drown everyone.*

She hadn't finished the thought before Mraka and Puk, experts with the vortex mechanism that provided so many services for the city, disappeared.

We will do what we can, they promised.

Their device could capture enough fish from the sea to feed the entire city. But it was also capable of ensnaring bigger prey – seals, people, whales, or even boats – by catching them up in its vortex. The same mechanism could also propel the city-vessel into space, sink it into the ocean, or, as it was doing now, drive it across the surface of the water. The problem was, the device also caused what Mum called collateral damage. The alien otters didn't mean to cause harm, but the water displacement caused by their propulsion device was disastrous to other creatures. Now it seemed about to cause the deaths of friends and enemies alike.

19

Ronan's lower parts were human before he and Rory reached the door, stepping over the sleeping Kai. Mabo had torn off Ronan's harness with his dry suit and thrown it in a corner, and he snatched it up and pulled the harness over his shoulders but didn't bother to dress. As soon as they hit the beach, he'd be back in the water again.

He hadn't counted on Pele meeting them behind the lab hut, but though she couldn't help noticing that he was naked, she paid it no more mind than if he'd still been a seal. Instead she hissed with alarm, looking at the sore places Mabo's specimen-collecting had left on his body, and said, 'You're really hurt.'

'Sun and salt water should do them wonders,' he told her.

The direct sunlight seared his skin, but

thanks to his Inuit ancestors on his father's side and the Navajo ones on his mother's, his skin bore a permanent tan that protected it, even the bits not often exposed, in human form, to the light of day.

They dodged from one building to another, and he recalled the times he and Murel had done as much, playing at being soldiers or adventurers from some story or another. Even as seals they'd played tag and hide and seek, but this game was in earnest and he would have preferred to just run for the beach and dive into the water. He was stiff and sore and rapidly becoming so hot he felt sick and dizzy.

The huts were set in ten neat rows of sixteen per row, eight huts back to back, each row like a spoke leading from the mountain to the beach, and one inward-facing row of eight at each side. Fortunately, the lab hut was in the last row to the right of the compound, so no doorways looked onto the backs of the huts. Ronan and his friends could creep, slink, and dodge behind them without being spotted from within the compound. However, Rory touched his arm and pointed up into the trees. Sturdy guard towers were perched among the fronds and leaves, an armed sentry in each tower.

The beach beckoned brightly just ahead. Ronan was anticipating the hot sand on his bare soles when Pele held up her hand for them to stop. Craning his neck, he saw a large group of kids trooping down the beach from the children's camp, herded by the matron and the doctor.

'Keep together, no talking, and try to march in step,' the matron told them. 'If you can behave like good soldiers, they're more likely to choose you to join.'

'Uh-oh,' Rory whispered. 'It's later than I thought. I'm supposed to be there to meet them. Can you wait here until the beach is clear, then make it to the sea by yourself?'

'Easy,' Ronan said.

'Look out for the net,' Pele whispered. 'I think they put it back up again, hoping to catch your sistah. I gotta go too.'

But instead of heading back into the compound, as Rory had, she took off into the jungle, staying close to the trees and out of sight of the guard towers. He was pretty sure he was the only one who saw her run out of the jungle and onto the beach behind the other children. The matron and the doctor were not very vigilant today. If the field trip was a further attempt to recruit the kids to the ranks of the Corps, as it appeared, then they wouldn't be too concerned with who came and who didn't, or with security for that matter. They wanted

289

the kids mingling around, seeing the advantages in housing and food the soldiers enjoyed, hoping those amenities would entice new recruits.

He watched the kids scrunch past, farther down the beach, where they were greeted by a friendly adult bellow. 'Good evening, ladies and gentlemen. Welcome to Camp Kindling. How many of you already know how to shoot? How many would like to learn?'

Enthusiastic shouts of 'Me! Me!' in several different languages issued from the crowd. Ronan knew he probably should wait for dark to try to make it to the water, but he didn't think he could stand to wait that long. The longer he stood there, the more likely it was that he would be seen. And the recruiting rally was the best diversion he would have for a while. Waiting for some of his fellow prisoners to be armed and begin target practice didn't seem like a smart idea. He remembered some of the kids calling him a freak and laughing when he was in trouble. Besides, he was vaguely sand-colored, so about as camouflaged in the daylight as he was likely to get.

He bent low, preparing to streak toward the water.

But just as he set foot onto the sand, his eye fixed firmly on his watery goal, the sea seemed to inhale and sucked the water away from him, so that instead of fifty feet of sand to cross, he was looking at fifty feet of sand plus three or four times that distance of rock, debris, and stranded fish and crustaceans. The seabed was exposed all the way out to the sunning rocks. The net trap was draped over other large rocks and pieces of driftwood. They had reset it, hoping to catch Murel, no doubt, after hauling him in.

All of this he noticed only briefly, his attention grabbed by a perpendicular whirling waterfall approaching from the direction of the mainland. The closer it came, the more the water on his beach was sucked away.

The roar of the waterspout was deafening, drowning out the soldiers, the children, and the motor of a small boat that had been approaching but was now utterly beached when the water slid out from under its keel, leaving it apparently still running but tipped onto its side.

Maybe they had waterspouts on this planet all the time, but to him it looked like something the so-called deep sea otters might manifest, them and their cloaked city and manufactured maelstroms and whirlpools. Murel had something to do with this; he just knew it. She was probably coming to rescue him, but she and their mutual friends had certainly complicated his own escape plans.

He should have been prepared for the wave that began rolling toward him in a huge diagonal wall even before the waterspout started to sink, but the waterspout and its implications had hypnotized him.

Down the beach the children had been pointing, but now the guards and the other two adults began running inland, some dragging smaller forms behind them, others running unimpeded as quickly as they could.

Ronan didn't see who got away and who didn't because suddenly a strong dark arm clamped across his neck and Dr Mabo said, 'Got you!'

Later he realized she probably saved his life. She began dragging him back up toward the top of the camp, away from the beach, while at that moment the water flooded toward them in a great towering wall at least fifteen feet high, bearing boulders and debris with it. He thought he heard screams, but they were like the fish churning in the flood, their noise overcome by the massive roar.

Dr Mabo lost her grip on him as he backed over her, trying to get away from the watery wall. The water knocked her down, and he grabbed for her, but his hand turned into a flipper as the water hit it.

* ★ ★

'What the frag was that anyway?' Captain Terry asked, his voice shaking as he picked himself off of the rail of his boat, where he'd been flung when the water went away. 'That was no waterspout. It sucked the ocean out from under us.'

Marmion pulled a slimy fishnet away from her face and Adrienne's. The net, tangling around various protrusions on the boat, had saved the women from being inhaled by the waterspout. 'I told you, *mon capitaine*, that I encountered something of the sort before. It is far more powerful than ordinary inclement weather.'

'You can say that again,' Terry murmured, gazing with awe at the emptiness in front of them and the thick finger of water pointing at the clouds on their starboard side. Ordinary waterspouts, even very large ones, were transparent, mostly wind with a little surface water carried with them. This one had slurped the ocean up into it like a soda through a straw and whirled it in a dense shining column far above their heads.

A pitiful meow came from inside the cabin.

'Zuzu!' Adrienne cried, and reached for the hatch.

Terry shook his head once, sharply, and tried

to yell over the roar, a sound like houses collapsing: 'Take a deep breath. Here comes the water.'

That's what he tried to say, at least. He was preparing to drown, wondering if he could choose which portions of his life would flash before his eyes. There were many he had no wish to relive.

Then a powerful force hit the boat, soaking them all. He expected to be engulfed at any moment. Expected to feel the water enter his mouth and nose and force the breath out of him. Expected his fragile grip on the rail to be torn away, maybe taking his arm with it. Instead, he felt the deck come up under his feet while the cat continued yowling from the cabin. Madame Marmion was no longer staring behind them but ahead, where the beach, the huts, and the volcano in the middle of the island were rushing to meet them.

Water wasn't supposed to behave this way. Storms weren't supposed to behave this way. Why, this one didn't even seem to have wind associated with it, except to drive it in certain directions. It was as if some intelligent force had created it and—

The boat was lifted up over the rooftops of the military huts on the island, carried beyond them, and then dropped among the trees. The sound of the wave that had propelled them, a shrill whistling roar, abruptly stopped.

He took a breath, because he could, and looked back. What he saw was what he had expected, and also something he would never have predicted in a thousand years.

The great cliff of water broke the back of the camp while engulfing it and the people who, for an instant, Terry had seen running across the grass beneath the wave's cresting overhang. But as the flood claimed the village, dark shapes moved within it.

In moments heads and bodies lifted above the floodwater. Human heads and other kinds as well, those belonging to a species unlike any Terry had seen before.

Then a somewhat more familiar form flopped out of the water, a small dark female form clutching it around the neck.

The seal barked.

Marmion called to it. 'Ronan? Murel?'

'Is that you, little girl?' Terry called, but before he finished his question Marmion and her first mate were climbing over the rail, jumping from the deck to the jungle floor, and sprinting to the wet area left in the wake of the retreating wave.

The two women struggled to extricate the seal from the grasp of the person it had saved.

Meanwhile, above the flood line, other human bodies were thrust from the water by the other, stranger species. Some were uniformed and most were children. Lloyd jumped off the boat and sprinted over to relieve Marmie and Adrienne of the small black woman. The seal waited, then was joined by the other seal and the little otter.

One of the large creatures, the kind that did not loosely resemble squid, had reminded him of something, and now he realized it was otters. They didn't look like the sleek little brown fellow that accompanied the gray seals. They looked like oversized sea otters, as big as men. A few of them climbed out of the water to examine the wave victims more closely, and he could see them clearly. Of the others, all he saw were the ends of tentacles as they released their burdens onto the beach.

'Hey, wait!' he called after Lloyd and the women. 'Wait for me! I'm the captain! I'm in charge!' But nobody waited. Lloyd started to lift the body of the little black woman, but Marmie said, in an uncharacteristically hard voice, 'Leave her. That is Maria Mabo, and though I know not how, I can assure you she is behind much of the trouble here.'

If Madame Marmie thought the woman wasn't worth saving, that was good enough for

Terry. He sprinted to the next unattended body and began resuscitating a black-haired little girl, fish-belly pale and limp as washed-up seaweed until he cleaned muck out of her mouth and she spit up a geyser of water and started breathing. She was followed by the next and the next and the next.

He saw the seal twins shove the last of their rescuees to shore, then emerge from the water. The next time he looked up from sharing breath with a drowning victim, there were two black-haired kids, naked, as was almost everyone else, working over the other bodies above the flood line.

The water carried the big otters with it back into its basin, leaving behind destruction and debris.

As more people were resuscitated, Madame Marmion and Adrienne began showing those who did not know resuscitation techniques how to employ them to help still-unmoving victims.

Terry directed the newly trained to the untreated victims, using his bullhorn of a voice to good effect, but the next time he searched the crowd for the seal twins, he didn't see them.

20

That was brilliant, Mraka, Puk, Murel told the two alien engineers. *Your fishing jet pushed Captain Terry's boat ahead of the flood. They're fine, Marmie, Adrienne, the captain, Lloyd, and I heard Zuzu meowing from the hold. And as you can see, Ronan is fine as well.*

What there is left of me, Ronan said. But he wasn't grumbling. He was immensely relieved to be away from Mabo and the island, but he was hurt and exhausted, and longed for home as he had not since this mission began.

We need your help again though, Murel told their friends. *I don't know what range your fishing jet has, but if you could give us a wee boost back toward the mainland, we'd appreciate it.*

We just came from there, Mraka said, sounding puzzled.

I know, and there's no need for you to go back.

In fact, it would compound the disaster. But since you've a power source now, we could use a lift if you can provide one. Your wake will have had the same sort of effect on the mainland and the prison that it did here. If there's flooding, the prisoners, including our friends, will be trapped.

You must not go alone, Mraka said. *There are wicked humans in that place, the sort who destroyed our world.*

I think they'll be busy saving their own skins.

Hah! Sky said. *The seal children will not be alone. I will be with them.*

Me too, Tikka said.

Not without me, Kushtaka told her daughter.

Look, that's great. But we have to go now, Murel told them. *Our friends may be drowning.*

The fishing jet was crowded. Two seals, a sky otter, and several deep sea otters and squid-forms traveled inside it. Mraka and Puk gave it as much power as they dared without causing further tidal catastrophes. The new volcanic vent provided sufficient power to propel them almost to the squid trough, across which the twins and Sky swam with great alacrity, leaving their alien allies to deal with any of their tent-acled kinfolk who might rise far enough from their deep sea home to endanger the swimmers.

The waves were not as great as they had been, but the agitation from the waterspout and its sinking had caused a secondary oceanic agitation that was compounding the damage from the first. The twins were swimming under their own power, halfway across the squid trough, when a giant wave picked them up and carried them up over the prison wall and into the moat pool the waves had made of the prison yard.

Sky washed in beside them. Behind him were Tikka, Kushtaka, and three of their people. Like Kushtaka, these three had assumed their squidlike form, but Tikka maintained the giant deep sea otter guise the twins were more accustomed to seeing.

The main entrance to the prison had been blown open by the force of earlier waves and they were able to swim inside. The floors were covered with water that would have been waist high on a human, but no humans were in sight until the rescue party reached the cells. The electronic controls on the barred doors blocking the corridors had been shorted out by the flood, but the bare overhead bulbs flickered fitfully, casting long shadows on the water.

Women's voices issued from the cells ahead of them, calling to each other, asking what was going on, some mocking, some bitter, some solicitous, and many in languages the twins did not understand. Some of the words were familiar, though, and pronounced in the melodious accents of the Kanakas.

Catching sight of them, one of the women said, 'Seals! And an otter? They're turning this place into an aquarium!'

'And me without my mermaid tail! Any of you girls got a comb and a mirror?'

'No, but I can sing. Mermaids do that.' This was a familiar voice too, but from a distance the emaciated, dirty, ragged, and very wet woman speaking was all but unrecognizable as Marmie's housekeeper, Mrs Fogarty.

'Ah, yes, dearie, let's have a rousing chorus of "Row, Row, Row Your Boat," ' another woman suggested. 'Or any selections you may have that include swimming instructions.'

'I used to like wet and wild, but this was never what I had in mind,' yet another woman said.

'What's the water level like up there?' someone called from the end of the row. 'Is it rising?'

'Doesn't seem to be,' someone called back from behind the twins, and then let out a shrill scream.

This was followed by others. The twins flipped over to see what was causing the screams. The women behind them were pointing at Kushtaka and her companions.

'Monsters! They feed the bodies of the dead

to those things and now they've turned them loose on us!'

Stay back, Kushtaka, Tikka. They're frightened of you.

So we can hear by the noises they make, Kushtaka replied.

By now the twins were near the cell of four Kanaka women. At first these women also seemed frightened of the aliens pointed out by the others, but now one asked, *Seal sistah, seal brutha? Friends of Ke-ola?*

Ronan barked and Murel flapped her flippers together and walked backward on her tail as comically as possible to allay the fears of the prisoners. Once the Kanaka women recognized the twins, however, so did Mrs Fogarty and other incarcerated crew members among the female prisoners. Then Kushtaka and her people were able to come forward and gain acceptance by association.

'It's very good of you children to try to free us,' Mrs Fogarty told them. 'But unless you happen to have a spacecraft handy, I'm not sure it will do us much good to be out of our cells.'

'At least we won't drown in here if we go with them,' someone else told her sensibly.

'I can't swim,' another woman said in a worried tone.

'Ronan and – I mean, the seals, won't let you

drown,' Mrs Fogarty told her firmly. 'Nor will I.'

First we have to unlock the cells, Murel said, eyeing the locks.

Otters know all about locks, Sky said, surfacing between her front flippers. *The cat showed me.* He carried a ring of keys in one paw.

Otters will have to unlock the doors, then, Ronan said. *I wish when our grandfather designed us to be seals he had designed seals with fingers and opposable thumbs.*

The prisoners grew quite excited seeing the little otter with the paw full of freedom and exclaimed about how cute and clever he was. Sky, who understood human speech pretty well by now, preened.

'Here, little fellow, give those to me,' Mrs Fogarty coaxed.

It's okay, Sky. She's a friend, Murel told him.

Sky otters have many friends, Sky replied smugly. *But there should be a game. I will drop the keys, then you dive?*

No time for that, Sky, Ronan told him, struggling to keep his patience with their friend. *But there is a huge game of hide and seek to be played here. Why don't you swim around the prison, keeping out of sight, and see how many friends you can recognize from the ship and Ke-ola's planet? Find the keys to all the cells, if you can, especially on this floor.*

We could just free everybody, Murel said.

I don't think we want to do that. There are probably a lot of real criminals mixed up with the people who've been falsely accused like our friends. If we release the wrong people, it could do us more harm than good.

I don't think we've time to be that picky, Murel argued.

Sky somersaulted through the water and proffered the keys to Mrs Fogarty, who unlocked her cell and waded out.

Ready or not, otters are coming! Sky's thought declared while he verbalized a lot of chitters and squeaks and swam a brown streak back through the water.

'They took Madame and her first officer to the dungeons,' Mrs Fogarty said. The twins knew she was actually addressing them but trying not to give away their secret. 'It's said that is where the worst things happen to people. They go down there and don't come back.'

'Sorry, love,' said the woman whose cell she was unlocking. 'Your friends will be goners by now.'

I wish we could tell her not to worry about them, Murel said.

Yeah, but there may be other people down there who need help, Ronan replied.

You think they'd have survived this long?

Maybe, maybe not, but there's the male crew members from the Piaf and the station to free yet. I'll lead Mrs Fogarty and the key ring over there, sis. You go help Sky. He won't be strong enough to drag anybody out of danger if necessary.

I'll go too, Tikka volunteered.

Sky, have you found the dungeons yet? Murel asked.

Yes! This way. It is a good slide.

Murel was afraid of what she might see, but at least she knew it wouldn't be Marmion and Adrienne drowned. She dived down the triple flight of stairs, Tikka right behind her. The water had forced the door open so it hung twisted to one side of the frame.

Using her sonar, Murel swam around the floating uniformed bodies. She could see fairly well. There were high windows around the top of the walls and these had also been forced open when the water flooded the floor.

There is air! Sky told her. *At the top, there is air. Up high.*

She followed him through the rooms, searching as she went, then heard the otter exclaim, *Here are humans! Live ones! They are hanging from the ceiling.*

Puzzled, she sought Sky out and found him swimming circles around three people hanging limply from their wrists, their chins barely clearing the flood. Two young men and a female. Oddly, they wore the tattered remnants of guard uniforms.

Tikka swam closer and examined what held them up. Then she dived toward the floor and came up again, clutching something in one forepaw. *I will cut them down.*

I'm not sure that's a good idea, Murel said. *They can breathe where they are now, and if we take them with us, we'll have to carry them back up the stairs, and there's no air in the stairwell. We might kill them instead of saving them.*

But I found them! Sky protested, as if they were fish he was being denied the chance to eat.

I know. But I don't know how to free them without doing more harm than good. And we don't know who they are. They could have been hung here for brutality to prisoners, for all we know. She didn't think that was true, but it could be.

This one, Sky said, circling one of the men. *The cat and I saw him through the holes. He came for Marmie and Adrienne. They did not smell afraid with him.* The little otter paused and studied the man's face for a moment before adding, *Yes, I think it is him. He was dry when I saw him before.*

Once the water drained away and the people on the roof realized it wasn't going to rise any higher, Murel knew they'd climb back down into the prison and resume business as usual. Then these people, who were evidently being punished or tortured, would wish they hadn't survived. If she didn't move swiftly, she, Ronan, Kushtaka's people, and everyone else they were trying to rescue would all be captured as well.

Sky patted the man's face with his paw. *Wake up. Time to go!*

The young man's eyes opened, then he groaned and closed them again. He looked to be in terrible pain. Tikka swam up to him and looked questioningly at Murel.

Go ahead, Murel told her. *If he's conscious, he can swim. Pat him again, Sky, and see if you can rouse the others.*

The man opened his eyes again and stared at Murel curiously, then at Sky. He tried to flinch away from Tikka, but he had no room and no strength. The alien otter cut the restraints binding him to the ceiling, and he sank like a stone, his eyes wide open. Murel dived and caught his shirt in her teeth, but it tore away. However, he was awake and surfaced again.

'So you're not here to eat us after all?' he asked aloud. She wished she could answer him.

Sky splashed him. 'Silly! Otters do not eat humans. Seals sometimes eat otters, but not river seals. Humans sometimes eat otters and seals, but not the other way around. Otters like delicious food like fish and clams. Humans do not smell delicious.'

Still, Murel could tell that in spite of his attempts to reassure the man, he was pleased to be mistaken for a ferocious man-eating otter. She, on the other hand, was appalled at being mistaken for a ferocious man-eating seal.

The man helped Tikka free the other two people, holding each of them up until they awakened enough to swim on their own. Now it was time to leave the safety of the air pocket and lead these people up to the ground level.

There was no way to tell the humans what they wanted to do, though Murel tried sending calming thoughts to them. Finally she swam up between the first man's legs, inviting him to ride her back, and he turned to the others.

'They want to give us a lift through the flood. Hang on however you can. They can swim out of this faster than we can alone. Deep breath now and—'

He ducked his head down and clasped his arms around Murel just above her flippers. She shot back through the water and spiraled up the stairs as quickly as she could, keeping her movements fluid and yet stable enough not to throw her passenger.

Have you got them? she asked Tikka.

Yes. Hurry! These creatures are fragile, Tikka replied, her thoughts full of anxiety.

They reached the surface in time to see some of the prison walls shaking. Ronan, bare as the day he was born, his skin full of terrible bruises and sores, was running down the stairs toward them. 'Our people are loose on the lower level and I just released Marmie's crew whom I found on the upper one. Did you feel that? There's a quake starting.'

He jumped back into the water, resuming his seal form. The prisoners Murel and the others had rescued were too busy breathing to notice his change.

The newly rescued prisoners began swimming toward the entrance to the prison. Up the corridors and coming down the stairs were others, also fleeing. Murel hoped they knew where they were going and what they were going to do, because she had no idea.

Kushtaka told her, *We will swim out and return to the ship now. Will you come, too?*

We can't just leave them, can we? she asked Ronan.

I don't see what more we can do to help, he replied. *And there's Marmie to think of. If we can manage saving her, she can help everyone else.*

They could see the flooded prison yard through the doors when they heard the shots ring out and shouting. They dived under and swam out into the moat, twisting to look up.

The guards are firing from the roof! Ronan exclaimed. *The prisoners will be shot like ducks in a barrel.*

Murel had reached the door by then. The prisoners were under the water, swimming for the entrance. Suddenly, the prison shook as vigorously as the twins when drying off to become human. People fell off the roof into the water.

The light was strange. Beyond the crowded roof and tumbling figures, beyond the firing guns, the sky blistered and boiled with brilliant hot color.

The twins knew what that meant. They had seen it on Petaybee a lot recently.

The volcano in the middle of the island . . . Murel said.

Maybe the alien Petaybeans upset the seismic balance or the core magma levels or something . . . Ronan said, making a wild guess.

Or maybe this planet is waking up too, Murel suggested. As they swam out to sea, she filled him in on what she had learned about the squid and about this being the original homeworld of the alien Petaybeans.

But if that's so, they invaded and overran existing sentient life-forms to make this prison colony,

Ronan said. *That's impossible! It goes against the foundations of Federation law.*

So does quite a bit of what we've seen here, Murel said. *It doesn't seem to bother anyone much.* They swam farther out, over the squid trough. The lifeless bodies of several more squid bobbed on the water's surface, their tentacles limp as seaweed.

When they were almost across the trough, the sea in front of them opened like the mouth of a giant whale. Kushtaka, Tikka, and the other three aliens swam into it and were sucked in so quickly that they seemed to vanish. Sky cut through the water past the twins and with a gleeful and slightly startled 'Hah!' also disappeared.

The twins followed and, after several breathless moments, whooshed once more into the control room of the underwater city-vessel.

Mraka and Puk looked as alarmed as giant deep sea otters could look. *We have the power we need now. But it has made danger for the land-dwellers.*

Whoops, Ronan said.

21

'We're trapped between a lava rock and a wet place,' Captain Terry told the twins when they had gone ashore and found him with the group of survivors from the waterspout's wake. It was a large group. The only people still lying down were a female sergeant whose leg had been broken by a boulder, carried inside one of the powerful waves, and a boy of about five whose collarbone was broken by some other piece of debris. Otherwise, the survivors huddled or milled aimlessly about on the beach. Most of the children had survived, since they were the lightest and easiest for the aliens to rescue. Only a few of the soldiers remained, but apparently many of them had recently returned to the mainland to be deployed offplanet, so only a core group had been on the island when the tsunami struck.

Among the survivors, Ronan and Murel thankfully counted most of the people they knew. All of Ke-ola's family, including a sullen-looking Kai, the matron, doctor, captain, Lloyd, Marmie, Adrienne, and Zuzu the cat, who had appointed herself guardian of Dr Mabo and sat on top of the woman's head, kneading her scalp vigorously with both front paws. Mabo was bound and gagged and, for good measure, was wearing the collar she had put on Ronan. Rory handed Ronan the control, but Ronan pitched it out into the water as far as it would go.

'Not even a little zap?' Rory asked, disappointed. 'I mean, *I* can't. She *is* my grandmother.'

'I don't want to disturb the cat, and if I zapped Mabo, the shock would probably kill Zuzu. She looks like she's having fun.'

'Besides,' Murel added, 'your gran is seriously twisted. *She* uses that kind of stuff. We're better than that.'

'I guess so. I don't want to do anything like she does. It might make her think there was a family resemblance.'

The ground trembled beneath their damp feet as the mountain beyond sent up plumes of smoke, ash, and sparks. The trees whipped fitfully in a strong hot wind. At least everyone had dried out quickly, Murel thought, and there was no danger of hypothermia here, as there would have been on Petaybee, though sunburn was always a hazard.

'We've been here too long,' Ronan said aloud. 'This place is starting to look like home. Or bits of it.'

'The warm bits,' Murel agreed, with a nod to the volcano. 'So now what? The boat's wrecked, the alien craft can't help as long as we're on land instead of in the water, the mainland is full of armed soldiers, and these people can't survive at sea very long.'

'You didn't mention the volcano about to blow,' Pele reminded her helpfully.

'That too.' Murel regarded the waving tree fronds and the swaying trunks, then said, 'There is one thing you might do that could help. Though this planet isn't as receptive as Petaybee, it might listen. Ke-ola had us do a birthing hula for the new volcano at home. Do the rest of you know it?'

'Not really. Ke-ola paid more attention to that stuff than the rest of us.'

'I know it,' someone muttered. It was Kai, looking defensive. When the others turned to her, the big girl shrugged. 'I helped Mama with you younger ones.'

'You know the birthing oli?' Pele asked in surprise.

314

'I ought to. She was in labor with you almost three days.'

'Ke-ola showed us the dance, but we don't know the words,' Murel said. 'And it was a while ago. Do you still remember the steps?' she asked her brother.

'I think so,' he said. 'When I see it again it should come back to me.'

There was another great tremble and another plume of smoke, ash – and flame. Glowing hot veins of red bled down the side of the mountain.

'Has anyone called for help?' the injured sergeant asked. She was a small, wiry woman who reminded Murel a bit of Pet Chan. 'We need to be evacuated. If that lava reaches this beach, there'll be no safe place for any of us. I've seen it before.'

'Most of our equipment was destroyed, Sarge,' another soldier told her. 'The mobiles aren't working.'

'That's because the same thing happened on the mainland,' Ronan told them. 'You can't expect any help from that quarter. We're on our own. I know this may look daft to you, but it's worked before, back where we come from.'

Murel had grave doubts about whether the hula would speak to the core of this planet. They'd had no indication that this thoroughly tamed world with its moribund sea and prison-populated landmasses was at all self-aware. And even if it was, it might not be reasonable. But trying to soothe it with the birthing hula would keep people busy, at least.

Let's leave them to it and go back to the city, she suggested. *Kushtaka's people know more about how this world functions than anyone around here. Maybe they have some more ideas.*

We can't abandon Marmie and Adrienne, or the others for that matter.

We're not abandoning them. But we need to come up with some other alternatives. I get the feeling that a sentient planet that's been used as a prison for so long might not be enough of an art and culture lover to appreciate the dance.

They dived in and changed, and when they surfaced, began swimming toward the city. The volcano's rumble was as fierce as the growl of some wild beast – the kind that ate seals. The water was still turbulent and full of chop from the city-ship's agitation of it. It made for slow and rough going.

They kept surfacing and turning to look at the volcano. During one such break, they saw ships descending from the sky.

Looks like someone will get evacuated anyway, Ronan said.

Probably the brass. The rest of us can become lava statues, for all they care.

As they drew closer to the underwater volcanic vent where the city had settled, they met teams of their alien friends, some of them in squid form, some still appearing to be giant otters, swimming away from the city.

Where are you going? Ronan asked.

Setting up the sursurvu – strictly routine, one of the pair, in squid form, replied. The sursurvu was a network of surveillance devices the aliens deployed in the vicinity of their city to keep an eye on the neighborhood.

You may have to move again quickly, Murel said. *It looks like the volcano is about to blow.*

Yes, it is providing the most magnificent power surges, the squid replied cheerfully as the pair swam away.

At least somebody is pleased about it, Murel said grumpily.

They entered the city through the transparent dome. The entire metropolis was brightly lit from its own lights and from the glow of the vent throbbing up through the floor. It was a wonder the place wasn't too hot for any life-form, but this race had somehow overcome that problem. Other creatures lived outside the dome and thrived on the heat and the acidic gases that Ronan and Murel had to avoid. As at the city's preferred docking vent on Petaybee, the scent of sulfur was almost

317

overpowering to the seals' sensitive noses.

Kushtaka seemed to be busy elsewhere, but the twins located Mraka and Puk, who were tinkering with the fishing ray mechanisms. All around them lay dead fish, which were less than fresh.

What happened here? Ronan asked.

The fish are arriving dead. Something's wrong with the calibration, Mraka said.

It has calibration? Murel asked, trying to peer over his front leg to see the bit he held in his otter paw.

Yes, but it is incorrect now. Too powerful, I think. As you can see, the fish do not survive being caught.

Could it be that they were killed by the force of the waterspout and you're catching dead ones because that's all there are? Ronan asked.

Oh, do you think that could be it?

Yes. You really do have to find a mode of travel that's easier on the things around you. Speaking of which, the people who didn't drown on the island are about to be incinerated by the volcano. I know you can't take them in here, but your people were native to this planet. Do you have any suggestions for something they can do to protect themselves? Anything at all?

No, Puk said, looking at her blankly. *Now about these dead fish—*

318

Just no? Murel demanded indignantly. *They're going to die—*

We wouldn't, Mraka told her. *So it has never been considered a problem for us. Perhaps, given enough time, we could find a way to build a bubble like this one over them, but it is held in place and sustained by our atmosphere, and humans unadapted for the sea cannot live in that either. So I don't think we can help you with this one.*

The fish, however— Puk continued, picking one up with a worried frown.

Throw them out, Ronan said sharply. *Isn't there any sort of lifeboat or anything we could use to help our friends?*

What is a lifeboat? the alien engineers asked in unison.

Within a few hours, shortly after the alien city-ship whirled into the waters of Gwinnet's dead sea, several ships apparently friendly to one another and belonging to the Intergal Company and the Federation entered Gwinnet's outer atmosphere. Some of them prepared to orbit. One, the *George Armstrong Custer,* landed and docked, only to be swept from its moorings by the waves generated by the alien ship's water-spout-borne departure to shallower waters.

The hijacked troop ship from Petaybee was

the third vessel to approach the planet to land. Initially, the crew was anxious to arrive before the *Custer,* but had orders from its official escort to wait.

'The port authorities aren't responding, Johnny,' Pet Chan told the captain.

'You think they've made us?' Raj Norman asked.

'Do you mean do they realize we are not the authorized crew?' Rick O'Shay asked. 'The *Custer* can't know that we're anybody but who our registration number says we are. As we've had no unsolicited contact since *Versailles Station,* unless there's been a leak in very high places, I don't see how anybody could know we are other than what we appear to be. As of our last com from Petaybee, the original crew is still enjoying its arctic holiday, dogsledding, snocling, possibly even skiing and ice skating, admiring the aurora, and no doubt holding marathon poker tournaments.'

Pet ignored his attempt at humor. She could be very single-minded when she was concerned about something. 'We're not even getting an autoresponse,' she said. Her mouth had a grim set to it. 'We're about to enter atmo, however. Your call, Captain.'

Johnny shrugged. 'I'd say silence confers consent. Can you get a visual? It would be good

320

to know if they were launching missiles or gunships our way.'

At first all they saw was a partially obscured pattern of swirling staticky snow filling the screen, but then that receded and revealed a sea and landscape quite different from the one their charts had led them to expect. Huge waves broke over the octopus-shaped, flat-roofed prison building. Loops and curls of water tangled the remains of the docking bay gantries. The *Custer* listed half out of its bay while the crew trickled out from a hatch near the nose. Shuttle craft bobbed upside down on the swells. As Pet watched, one was dashed to pieces against the prison wall. The wall appeared to be holding, but the water breaking over it had made a moat of the prison yard. People were pouring onto the roof. Pet saw a lot of uniforms and no prison fatigues among those taking the high ground.

'That does not look promising,' Johnny agreed. 'No missiles, but also no place to land. Back into orbit, then, and any rescuing that gets done will have to be done by shuttle.'

Ascending, they caught sight of the island in the distance, along with the waterspout and the waves.

They were in orbit, and in conference, when the volcano began to grumble.

This hula was not going well. Pele and Kai did their best, but there were simply too many factions represented among the survivors to be unified in their purpose. As geysers of lava sprayed upward from the cone and rivers of lava flowed down its sides and burned through the jungle, many fled to the sea. The Kanaka kids stood – or rather, danced – their ground, and Rory, Marmie, and Adrienne joined in, but Zuzu sat at the edge of the water and kept glancing back and forth between it and the shore, while Sky chittered at her in what was meant to be a reassuring tone.

Ronan and Murel did not join in the dance but swam offshore, watching, waiting. Those who had already entered the water were still fresh, but soon they would begin to tire. They had made rafts of debris left behind by the waves, and the water was warm, but when the lava boiled into the water, it would heat up even more.

This could be it, you know, Murel said. *The end. We could all die.*

Well, you and I could take refuge in the city, of course.

I'm not doing that! I'm going to stay out here and help the swimmers as long as I can.

Me too, of course, Ronan replied. *And Kushtaka's people promised to help as long as they could. But the water may get too hot for us, Mur. And there's still maybe sixty people left – we can't keep juggling them indefinitely. The volcano could blow and keep blowing for weeks, even months.*

We can probably keep most people alive with the help of the aliens, until rescue arrives anyway.

You saw what that mess was like on the mainland, Ronan scoffed. *How long do you think it's going to take them to notice what's happening over here and divert some attention to us? And when they do, we'll be right back where we started – worse even. They'll round everyone up and take the kids to prison too, and they'll know then that we're selkies and—*

Stop it, laddie. You're borrowing trouble. Let's just do what we can do when it needs doing and keep going till we can't anymore. Then, if we can, we'll figure out what else to do. Deal?

All of that goes without saying. Just trying to think ahead, he said.

Well, don't. It's depressing.

On shore, Kai ignored everyone else while she danced and sang with more energy than she had shown since the twins first met her. Pele and the other kids were sweating as they danced. The adults looked exhausted, quivering with the effort of maintaining the beat set by

Kai's chant. Kai was growing hoarse. Finally, Pele shook her head, then changed her dance and began another chant, at first in harmony with her sister's, then when Kai noticed what she was doing and stopped chanting and changed her dance, Pele led.

Ronan and Murel couldn't hear what she said above the roaring of the waters and the rumble and crash of the mountain, but the gestures she used were repeated by Rory and the others trying to help. These gestures had lots of calming motions, and the sort that a guard would use to say 'Stop.' Her hands flowed around her. She covered her face, then seemed to cover her head and cower, and then made beseeching gestures, hands out, palms up and cupped.

Through the jungle a wave of lava flowed toward them, far more daunting than the walls of water they had faced before.

Everyone except Pele and three of her sisters broke ranks and ran for the water. The four girls continued dancing.

Ronan flopped ashore on his front flippers and shook himself hard to dry.

What are you doing, Ro? You're going to be seal steaks in another two seconds.

I'm going to drag them out here, is what. Wait.

But Murel didn't wait. There was only one of

him and four girls, so she too flopped ashore and dried off and then ran forward into the searing heat, grabbing at arms. The girls, as if entranced by the flames, jerked away and kept dancing.

'Are you nuts? This volcano doesn't know you. It won't—' She started to tell them that it wouldn't listen.

But then, suddenly, the lava wave sank and drained into two channels that flowed away down either side of the compound and off into the sea, leaving char and cooling red-black lava behind.

Ronan and Murel turned back to the sea to help those trying to stay afloat, but as they were changing, Pele and her sisters dashed past them and jumped in. *I guess they figured there was no sense in trying the volcano's patience for too long,* Murel said.

Yeah, especially since 'patient' is not usually a word used to describe volcanoes.

The twins swam back out to help support the swimmers. Some of the first to hit the water were flagging now. Zuzu perched with her back paws on Adrienne's shoulders, her front paws on top of her mistress's head. The *Piaf*'s first mate dog-paddled beyond the rocks, which was about as far as any of them had gone in their efforts to evade the lava.

Already the bath-warm water was growing

uncomfortably hot, just from the lava flowing into it on the side of the ocean. If a more direct stream came at them, this would not be far enough to avoid being boiled alive. Ronan and Murel, with Sky's help, began herding the swimmers farther out to sea. They didn't want them to be in range of the volcanic area where the city-ship was moored, but if the refugees from the land were in sight of the sursurvu, Kushtaka's people could find them and help keep them afloat more easily. Unfortunately, what had seemed not terribly far to the seal twins was impossible for full-time humans.

People kept sinking beneath the waves, and Ronan and Murel kept diving to push them back to the surface again.

After doing this several times, they stayed underwater and waited for people to sink, then pushed them up in assembly-line fashion. Soon they grew tired. *If Kushtaka's people are helping, they're keeping a low profile,* Ronan observed sourly.

Maybe they're waiting until people have nearly drowned so many times they'll think they're imagining being saved by otters again. I think I sense a myth budding here.

Providing anyone survives to spread it, Ronan said, turning toward the surface again while scanning for bodies on their way down. He saw none. He noticed some swimmer's feet, but no one sinking, and as he watched, two pairs of feet vanished. *Maybe they have arrived, after all. Maybe they're just doing it differently than before. Look, sis!*

They surfaced together and saw flitters skimming the water, human crew members leaning out of hatches to scoop up grasping swimmers.

They must have another installation near here, maybe a moon, and sent ships from there, Ronan said. *The rescuers are wearing Corps uniforms.*

Not all of them, Murel said, as three flitters lifted off and three more bearing Federation insignia hovered over the water. *Those are Federation. Maybe they were coming to investigate Marmie's disappearance* . . .

Or maybe they were coming to try her for her supposed crimes. Look, there she is, he said, pointing at a figure whose dark curls were sleeked to her head like Sky's fur, while in the water nearby bobbed the apparently two-headed creature that was Adrienne and Zuzu.

With the rest of them gone, we can concentrate on helping Marmie and Adrienne remain free, Murel said grimly. As relays of flitters picked up swimmers and disappeared into the red- and fuchsia-fired clouds with them, the twins dived beneath the waves and swam for the legs and feet they had pinpointed as belonging to Adrienne and Marmie.

Sky streaked past them. *Hah! Otters are good cat savers. I will save Zuzu. She is used to it now.*

But just as they were within nudging distance of the women and the cat, the legs were pulled to the surface.

Ronan and Murel rose and popped their heads out of the water in time to see the women disappear through the hatch of a Company Corps flitter. Nearby, Sky had an ungrateful Zuzu by the scruff of her neck while she churned her sopping paws and snarled at him. *Oaf! Buffoon! Untooth me!*

Sky, bewildered and hurt at this display of feline ingratitude, dropped her into the water. Murel dived to catch the cat on her back and suffered scratches for her efforts. The cat surfaced under her own power and cat-paddled with perfect aplomb.

They've spotted us! Ronan said when the flitter continued hovering and a uniformed body reappeared at the hatch.

'There you are, you scamps,' said Rick O'Shay, grinning down at them. 'I don't know how we're to lift you great lunks of sea life up from there now, but I suppose you'll do grand on your own. Follow us to the mainland. We've a few things to sort out there.'

22

The twins desperately wanted to sleep through-out the tedious legal proceedings but didn't dare.

'I feel as though I've been awake for weeks,' Murel said. They sat on concrete benches inside the thoroughly dank common room in the main prison. The alien waterspout had thrown the bureaucracy of the prison into such disarray that they were ill prepared for the inspections of the illustrious Federation Council members and Marmion's influential friends in the company. Since Colonel Cally and his superiors and allies had arrived just before the deluge to bring final charges and sentencing down upon Marmie and the others arrested in her name, everyone involved except those back on Petaybee was represented. The twins had the considerable responsibility of representing their planet and people in the proceedings.

They were, of course, in human form, wearing prison tunics over their dry suits. They listened to the Kanaka witnesses testify to the state of their planet before Marmie and the twins had come to rescue them. Sky came out the hero as the Kanakas said that Marmie's 'aumakua, the ship's otter' had located them in the underground passages and revealed their hiding places to the rescuers. They told of their callous abandonment by the *Custer* and its crew and begged to be allowed to resettle to Petaybee, where they had gone of their own free will. Some Federation officials had tried to tell other officials that the Kanakas were actually under contract to the Federation and *had* no free will, but Marmie's very unhappy and very powerful allies, rounded up by Johnny Green and the other hijackers, were having none of that.

Cally's crew recounted its side of the story, and then Cally and his own Federation allies told of their 'arrest' of Marmion and her employees and passengers and the seizure of her assets. The *Piaf*'s crew and the crew of the space station gave evidence that cast a completely different light on what Marmion's top legal representative, who had first heard of her arrest when the hijacked ship contacted him at his home, termed 'piracy.' He declared he would file countercharges of kidnapping and false arrest, as well as assault and battery charges for the beatings, starving, and even the head shaving of the prisoners.

It hurt to see them lower their eyes and wince when their children ran questing hands over their ears and bare scalps. Newly reunited with them, the children hardly believed that their parents were still alive, after the lies they'd been told. Except for Rory and his parents, who laughed when they saw each other and embraced gratefully.

When the court recessed, Murel and Ronan sought a word with Johnny. After that, on the second day of the trial, Marmie, Adrienne, Johnny, Pet, Rick, and everyone but the highest Federation and company officials on their side arrived in the common room with hairless heads.

Marmion still looked like a queen, but a queen of ancient Egypt perhaps, her finely shaped head balanced like a delicate egg on her slender neck, her chin raised, her eyes forward. '*Alors,* this is so much cooler!' she remarked. 'And makes bathing much more facile, *n'est-ce pas?*'

Only Zuzu and Sky kept their fur on, and

they were sensibly curled up together on the bench between the twins and Johnny. None of Marmie's people had been returned to cells, but by the end of the second day, it looked as if that was about to change.

The prosecution called Marmie's allies to the stand, one by one, and asked them how they had learned of her 'detainment.' They all said they had been contacted by her captain, Johnny Green. The prosecution asked how, if Marmion was being persecuted, they supposed Johnny got a ship and crew, and they said their understanding was that the governors of Petaybee and some local villagers had found one they loaned to their guests for the purpose. They said it with a straight face.

Then they called Johnny to the stand and acted like they were tricking him into 'admitting' that he and the others, with the 'criminal complicity of the rogue world's denizens,' had hijacked a Federation ship and no doubt murdered the crew.

'They wouldn't do that!' Ronan yelled, jumping up from his seat. Murel agreed, but pulled Ronan down beside her again.

Not the murdering part, at least, she said to him.

Instead of trying to shut her brother up, the prosecutor, a handsome blond man with a lineless face and eyes as hard and cold as an ice floe in winter, dismissed Johnny and called Ronan to the stand.

'State your name.'

'Ronan Born-for-Water Maddock-Shongili.'

The prosecutor's eyes narrowed a bit at Ronan's middle name but he said nothing. Murel grinned to herself. He was going to go slitty-eyed if she told him her middle name was Monster Slayer.

'How did you come to be here, Ronan?' the prosecutor asked, using his first name in a condescending tone so everybody was sure he knew he was talking to a child.

'My sister and I went to *Versailles Station* looking for people to help Marmie – Madame de Revers Algemeine – after she and the *Piaf* were captured by Cally and his buddies.'

'How did you get there?'

'We hitched a ride.'

'On the hijacked ship?'

'No.'

'How then?'

'With friendly aliens,' Ronan said.

You shouldn't have told them that, Murel said.

They won't believe me anyway. Besides, it's going to come out sooner or later. The Federation is about space exploration. They have to realize there are nonhuman cultures out there.

They probably do. They just don't think they're in here, as well as out there.

'The witness will please answer the question seriously, out of respect for the court,' the prosecutor said sternly.

'I did,' Ronan said, widening his eyes and trying to look innocent.

'Council is sidetracking this proceeding. How the witness believes he arrived at the station is immaterial to this case,' Marmie's lawyer told the tribunal. 'What does matter is how he and his twin sister were forcibly removed from *Versailles Station* along with the other personnel in Madame Algemeine's employ or under her protection.'

'We were discussing the hijacking of an Intergal Company Corps vessel,' the prosecutor argued.

'I don't know anything about that,' Ronan said. 'I think we were already gone. But my folks and the people in Kilcoole wouldn't murder anyone, and neither would Johnny. They just borrowed the ship, like they told you.'

'Your unbiased faith is touching, Ronan,' the prosecutor said sarcastically. 'You're excused.'

'Ladies and gentlemen,' Marmie's lawyer said to the tribunal, 'council spoke somewhat dismissively of Ronan's faith in the innocence of his friends and relatives, but so far, most of what we have seen and heard of this situation hinges on what people believe happened during these incidents. How the Corps vessel came into the possession of its present crew, or how the Maddock-Shongili twins arrived at *Versailles Station,* has little to do with our inquiries concerning the kidnapping of Madame Algemeine and her staff and guests, and the piracy of her ship. We have seen that the crimes she is alleged to have committed were acts of mercy, and her arrest was an act of petty vengeance on the part of some, avarice on the part of others. I move for immediate dismissal, after which some of these other matters may be pursued.'

The prosecution was listening to the Federation official who had been whispering to Cally off and on during the trial. Now he said, 'Ladies and gentlemen, please do not dismiss the accused yet. We can bring witnesses to show that this woman and her accomplices have committed other unspeakable illegal acts and—'

'I'm sure the prosecution can bring witnesses, but that does not mean they would be truthful ones. Many vested interests are represented in this room, before this tribunal.'

'Prison officials have observed certain acts—' the prosecution began.

335

'And Madame Algemeine and her first mate have gathered certain evidence that casts doubt on any allegations made by those same officials. Evidence of corruption, sadistic cruelty, unlawful detention, and even murder of prisoners in custody.'

He pulled a tiny object from the pocket of his ship suit and handed it to the head of the tribunal. 'Perhaps the tribunal would care to view this, which has little bearing on the present case but offers many answers to past disappearances, deaths, and power plays among company and Federation officials. Madame Algemeine and her officer copied these records while hiding in the archival vault in the lower level of this structure.'

'She was never down there!' the prison warden objected, although he wasn't supposed to speak without permission. Murel enjoyed shushing him with a finger to her lips.

'Oh, but she was. But again, that is another matter.'

In the end, after unsnarling the tangle of accusations, counter-accusations, crimes, alleged crimes, lies, and misdirections, the tribunal found Marmion and her people blameless of wrongdoing, though they didn't say as much for her accusers.

The twins cheered and hugged each other

and every bald person they could lay their hands on.

Maybe we can get some sleep now! Murel said, yawning.

Or go catch a meal without worrying about Mabo, Ronan said. *Where is Mabo, anyway?*

I think she saw which way the wind was blowing and decided it was time to disappear. Come to think of it, I haven't seen her since we tried to get the aliens to help us evacuate people.

We should let them know I, er, mentioned them. I wonder if they'll want to stay here or come back to Petaybee?

Murel snorted. *That's a no-brainer. There's nothing here for anybody. I even feel sorry for the squid getting stuck here. It's hot all the time, Ronan. Who would want to live like that?*

Apparently people do, he said.

They snuck away from the proceedings, thinking they were leaving Sky still nestled next to Zuzu, and slipped into the water, swimming out to the squid trough, where they very carefully remained close to the surface. *Mraka? Puk? Don't suppose we could get a lift in the fishing beam, could we?*

Halfway across the trough they heard a ripple behind them, as of something coming at them very fast through the water, and Sky said, *Hah! Where river seals go, otters go too.*

We thought you were napping with the cat, Murel said.

The cat does not need help napping, Sky replied. *So I followed you instead.*

Before they could say anything else, the telltale bump of surface water that hid the projecting whirling ray beneath it shot out like a frog's tongue and snapped them into it.

They were so used to it now, they had come to regard it as Sky did, a wild ride and rather fun.

Mraka and Puk were in the control room, but Kushtaka, Tikka, Kisha, and some of the others they had met were there too.

Why do I get the feeling this is good-bye? Murel asked. *You want to stay here, on your original home planet, don't you?*

Kushtaka said, *Stay for now. There are no sharks here to eat my children.*

The humans who've been in charge here are just as nasty as the sharks on Petaybee, Ronan said. *Fortunately they haven't found your city yet.*

One did, Kushtaka said. *We're sorry.*

Sorry why?

We didn't mean for it to happen, Mraka said. *She came after you left. We let her in. We thought she might be like you. But – well, you can see. Bring the human, she said, and four of her people left, to return a short time later bearing* the stiff uniformed body of the small dark scientist. *She did not survive our atmosphere. We tried to push her back out into the sea when she began dying, but she was gone. Do you want her back?*

Murel and Ronan exchanged looks. *What do you usually do with your dead?*

We give them as fuel to the vent.

The twins consulted each other briefly. Would Rory want her back? Would his mother? They thought not.

Seems like as good a place as any for her to me, Ronan said.

They watched while the package that had contained their enemy was shoved into the glow below. Just a brightness enveloping darkness, a feeling of heat, a dip of the power, and nothing was left of Mabo.

That was the end of it then. They said their good-byes.

Mraka and Puk waited for them to jump into the ray again, but after a quick glance they declined. *We've a lot to think about. We want to catch fish and have a leisurely swim and hope everything will be sorted by the time we return to the mainland.*

Good, Tikka said. *I will swim with you. Sky and I will fish and play along the way.*

Sky and Tikka popped out through the

dome's membrane. *Aw*, Murel said. *I think the little guy likes her.*

It's about time he got interested in other otters, Ronan said. *But trust Sky to go in for long-distance romance when it comes to choosing a mate.*

Maybe Kushtaka will change her mind. Or maybe Tikka will bring some of them back with her and start her own colony. Oh, Ronan, I do want Sky to be happy.

He could stay, Ronan said. *Surely he knows that.*

I don't want him to do that! I'd miss him terribly.

Me too, but you know, when we get home, I think we should make some other friends as well. Boy friends, girl friends, not all of them completely other species from us, you know?

What are you saying?

Well, take Pele, for instance. She's really young, but kind of cute, don't you think?

I hadn't noticed. But she's noticed you. She looks at you like you're Petaybee's gift to little girls.

He dived, splashing her hard with a flip of his tail.

23

The tribunal was not entirely over by the time the twins returned, but many of the issues had been settled. Marmion's property had been reinstated and she was to be compensated for the expenses and business losses she had suffered during her incarceration. Additional ships, including the pilfered *Piaf*, arrived to transport the former prisoners back to their homes and duty stations. The twins were glad to see that Rory was no longer in uniform. Of all of the kids who had enlisted, only Kai chose to remain in the Corps. No one had said anything about the others, and all were allowed to leave with their parents.

The cases of many of the prisoners who had been at Gwinnet when Marmie arrived were being reviewed, in light of the evidence of false arrests Marmie had uncovered in the vaults.

The prison's management was summarily fired, and some of them were sentenced to join the inmates.

The tribunal itself had been adjourned until it could reconvene on Petaybee, to investigate the forcible relocation of the Corps troop ship commandeered by Marmie's allies and the disappearance of the crew and landing party.

It seemed strange to be back aboard the *Piaf* with the giant tanks removed and no turtles or sharks to consider, as they had on their previous trip. Everybody slept and ate a great deal, even though there was nothing stocked onboard except Corps rations until they reached *Versailles Station,* where Marmie's chefs from other holdings had gathered to prepare a feast for her homecoming. Once the station personnel aboard the *Piaf* had disembarked to return to their duties, Marmie threw a pool party for her guests at her station-top mansion.

Pet interrupted the party with a few quick words in Marmie's ear. Marmie signaled to the twins to follow her into the house. 'We have a com link to Petaybee. Would you like to say hello to your parents? We have spoken officially already of the tribunal that has been held and the one that is to come.'

It was a splendid link. They even had good visuals, with Mum and Da looking at the twins oddly. Then Murel realized their parents hadn't seen them with their heads shaven before. 'It's very hot there and there are bugs,' she told them simply.

'Ah,' their mother said. 'Bugs.'

They exchanged a few more words, and the twins could tell that their parents would have liked to talk them all the way home to Petaybee, but finally Mother said, 'While the link is clear, we have a few more coms to send so – see you soon. Slainté, my darlings.'

'Slainté, Mum, Da.'

Father smiled, gulped, and nodded, then waved. The twins realized with both shock and amusement that their handsome, important da was trying not to cry.

'We love you,' they said.

'We love you too,' their parents said in unison before the com went blank, 'be safe.'

'A bit late for that,' Murel said aloud, but she smiled tenderly. It would be good to be home again.

After the party, everyone who needed to return to Petaybee, either because they wanted to or because the tribunal needed them there when it reconvened, piled back aboard the *Piaf*. Without the personnel from *Versailles Station*, including Rory and his folks, the ship seemed empty.

The twins slept much of the rest of the journey, but the closer the ship came to Petaybee, the more alert they became, and soon it was impossible to sleep. Shortly before they arrived, crew members passed through, distributing long johns, parkas, and snow pants. The twins had retrieved their dry suits and substituted those for the long johns everyone else wore. The *Piaf*'s thermostat was lowered to keep people comfortable in the extra clothing.

They docked just before three other ships, including the purloined troop ship, an official Federation Council liner, and a very sleek ship that bore Corps insignia and registration but looked more like a pleasure vessel.

At the time, though, the twins had eyes only for the ground, where Mother, Father, Clodagh, the villagers, and a lot of extra people made a big welcoming crowd below. Coaxtl and Nanook prowled back and forth between people and ships. It was still very cold, so instead of the horses, there were dog teams and a few snocles. People also carried skis and snowshoes. Beyond the crowd, downriver, they could see the buildings of Kilcoole, smoke feathering up from the chimneys, white on white against the winter sky.

It's an improvement on when we left, with every-one hiding in the communion caves, Ronan noted.

Murel just nodded.

A path had been cleared from the docking bay to the river, and the twins half slid, half ran down it to fling themselves at their parents.

They didn't learn what was happening on the other ships for some time.

Next Clodagh enveloped them in a big hug. Coaxtl and Nanook almost knocked them down, saucer-sized paws on their shoulders and muzzles inspecting their faces before the rough cat tongues came out to lick their faces.

Clodagh said, 'Come, there is a latchkay ready for everyone.'

'Everyone?' Murel asked in a worried voice. 'The tribunal came too.'

'Everyone,' Clodagh repeated.

'For the feast and the dance,' Mum said.

Murel could have sworn every soul on Petaybee was already at the docking bay, though she didn't see Ke-ola or Keoki when she looked for them, but delicious smells came from the longhouse, and noise, laughter, and music were pouring out of it into the snowdrifts.

When Da opened the door, she heard a scurrying, then saw people, both familiar and strange, lined up on either side of the firepit.

Though it was customary for Petaybean

fancy dress to include at least one item of winter clothing, it seemed to Murel that the people before them were bundled up, their heads almost obscured by bunches of bright, knitted scarves.

'Slainté!' everyone called to the newcomers.

Then Ke-ola stepped up, kissed Murel on the cheek, took one of the scarves from his neck and put it over her head. 'Aloha,' he said.

Murel and Ronan, who had been similarly treated by Leilani, Ke-ola's older sister, said, 'What?'

'No flowers,' Clodagh said.

Aunty Aisling elaborated as she put a scarf around Pet Chan's neck. 'Everybody liked the idea of meeting you with leis, but it's winter. So we had some real fast knitting lessons. I hope Marmie brought that store-bought yarn I asked her for. We cleaned out every knitting bag on Petaybee.'

The party gave a friendly start to the tribunal. This was made even friendlier by the presence of the military prisoners who had been guests in Petaybean homes across the northern continent, where they had chopped wood, hauled water, fed animals, hunted, ice-fished, and were actually much too busy enjoying themselves doing basic survival tasks with their hosts to worry about escaping. There was no ship anyway. Where were they going to go?

During the dance, Murel noticed that some of the soldiers and some of the villagers had become very friendly indeed. The rather nice sergeant was introducing his Petaybean friend, Darla Oogliuk from Harrison Fjord, to his parents.

The fancy troop ship had been loaned as a conciliatory favor to Marmie, who acquired the roster of the hijacked ship and contacted the families of the soldiers involved, offering them free passage to Petaybee to meet with their sons, daughters, fathers, mothers, husbands, or wives for a reunion, as her treat. 'In thanks to our brave Corpsmen and -women for guarding our Petaybean friends and allies during another trying transitional period,' the politically astute Marmie had phrased it.

Ronan's eyes widened in admiration when he saw the engraved invitation carried proudly by the cute younger sister of one of the women military 'guests.' *For a pretty honest lady, that Marmie can bead a moose turd with the best of them,* he told Murel.

The tribunal was convened and dismissed the same day. No one would testify that any crime or even coercion had taken place.

Colonel Maddock-Shongili and the others had come aboard the troop ship to warn the crew that their hull was icing over. The others stayed aboard while she went outside with the crew to supervise deicing procedures with which she, as a longtime Petaybean resident, was familiar. While her friends were still aboard the ship, it accidentally took off due to some sort of mechanical failure. By the time they corrected the failure, they had been informed by Federation officials of the situation on Gwinnet and were asked to accompany them to investigate.

Talk about beading a moose turd! Ronan said when the tribunal reached its conclusion that it was all just a big mistake and everyone involved in this incident was innocent of any wrong-doing or even ill will.

And adding a fringe as well, Murel agreed. *That was a tall tale worthy of an entire latchkay worth of songs.*

When all of the military, company, and Federation officials had returned to their ships and into space along with the soldiers – some of them promising tearful friends that they would return soon – and with their families, Marmie and her crew also boarded the *Piaf.* 'I have much to do to restore my properties to the condition they were in before seizure, and my people will want to settle back into their jobs and see their other friends and family members, you understand?'

They did. They boarded with her long enough to pet Zuzu good-bye. Sky was nowhere to be found and had, indeed, been a bit subdued since the *Piaf* left Gwinnet. Zuzu, who was napping on the back of the chair at Adrienne's duty station, opened one eye, stretched, yawned, and went back to sleep.

Returning to the village, they prepared for the real latchkay, the night chants at the communion cave.

As Kilcoole and its guests made the procession to the communion cave, the bright new scarves and hats worn by the returnees did indeed look like flowers against the snowy background. The setting sun cast a rosy glow on the white drifts, reflected from the magenta sky that was a sign the volcano was still busy building a home for the Kanakas.

As soon as the villagers reached the hot spring, they noticed that the water teemed with life – Honus and otters swam and dived to greet the celebrants.

Sky was among his hundreds of relatives until he climbed onto the bank to greet his friends. *I have the biggest rock pile of any otter!* he told them. *Hundreds of rocks. Hundreds and hundreds. Females all want me to catch food for them – and other things. Males wish to hear my songs.*

Of course they do, Murel said.

The whole planet wishes to hear our songs, Ronan told the otter. *Let's not keep it waiting.*

THE END

Powers That Be

Anne McCaffrey and Elizabeth Ann Scarborough

The first collaboration between two of science fiction's mightiest names.

It was a world of ice and snow – a planet that just supported life and that had been terraformed from frozen uninhabitable rock. The people of Petaybee were hardy, self-reliant, friendly – and also very secretive.

Major Yana Maddock, medically discharged from the service, was shipped to Petaybee in the hope that her burnt-out lungs might just recover in the icy air. And at the last moment, she was given a special commission. Unauthorized life-forms had been seen on the planet and, more seriously, geologic survey teams had vanished into nowhere, the odd survivor being discovered abandoned and insane. It was Yana's task to infiltrate Petaybee society and find out who – or what – was causing the eerie events on the planet.

She discovered a primitive ice-bound community of extraordinary people – people who possessed some mysterious quality of surviving – and people who Yana discovered she both liked and revered as she found herself becoming one of them.

9780552140980

Dragon Harper

Anne and Todd McCaffrey

All Kindan ever wanted to do was become a Harper, singing and teaching the ballads of Pern, and he is thrilled when he becomes an Apprentice at the Harper Hall. But then he is offered the chance to attend a hatching and succeeds in Impressing the magnificent bronze fire-lizard, Valla.

There he meets Koriana, daughter of Lord Holder Bemin of Fort Hold. She also Impresses, in her case a gold fire-lizard, and there is an instant attraction between her and Kindan. Unfortunately an Apprentice Harper is not considered a suitable consort for a Fort Holder's daughter and they are quickly separated. Things go from bad to worse for Kindan when he is accused of starting a fire which destroys ancient and extremely precious Records. He is banished to Fort Hold in shame and dishonour but his own worries soon pale into insignificance when a terrible plague starts to spread across Pern, killing nearly everyone infected. As it reaches Fort Hold, Kindan and the rest of Pern's inhabitants know their very survival is in doubt.

9780552153492